Unbreakable Heroes

UNDER FIRE

ZOE NORMANDIE

Under Fire
ISBN # 978-1-83943-795-3
©Copyright Zoe Normandie 2022
Cover Art by Erin Dameron-Hill ©Copyright May 2022
Interior text design by Claire Siemaszkiewicz
Totally Bound Publishing

UNDER FIRE

Dedication

To Claire, for your patience.

Chapter One

Alisa

"No, I am already cleaning three houses." Alisa Kelly ran her golden-brown fingers around the edges of the note that had been handed to her by her manager. Analyzing the property details, she shook her head upon hearing the woman's challenge.

"You don't want an extra hundred bucks a month, then?" Maria asked. "This will be a regular client."

"I don't have time for more work."

"This client is rarely home. He's usually away for work, so you won't have to deal with people."

Maria, a middle-aged lady with dyed eggplant-colored hair, leaned back in her white office chair, something twinkling in her eye. She waited for Alisa's next move.

Alisa frowned, tossing her long black hair behind her shoulder.

Maybe it wasn't so bad. *Three-bedroom home in a gated community. No kids. No pets.* She grazed her teeth over her bottom lip, thinking. She *did* need the money, but she needed time for her studies as well. Skipping out wasn't an option, even for a few hours, not if she wanted to get licensed the following month.

"Look… Try it out once, and if you can't manage, I'll give the job to someone else, okay?" Maria said as she shuffled papers on her desk. It was her typical signal that the meeting was concluded.

Alisa arched her eyebrow. The cost of her exams flashed before her eyes. Those things weren't cheap, and the last thing she wanted to do was put her hand out to beg for money. She was almost at the finish line.

"Fine." Alisa pushed herself up and out of her chair, stuffing Maria's note with the address into her purse.

She'd have to find a way to make it work, which was what she'd been doing for the past four years anyway. Buried in a textbook most of the time, all she'd done was study, work and study some more.

Maria shot her a self-satisfied smile, grinning like the cat that had eaten the canary. It was the look she gave when she was up to something. Running a property management company, Maria was the sharp-as-hell businesswoman and motherly figure—always watching out for Alisa like she was her daughter. Damn right, Alisa had endless respect for Maria's business acumen and, frankly, her sheer nerve—the type that Alisa hoped to grow over the years.

"One last thing"—Maria reached behind her desk and pulled up a used shopping bag—"the client is expecting our services this morning."

"This morning? Like, right *now*?"

"Like, *right* now. I promised him."

"No"—Alisa waved her hands, unwilling to bend—"I didn't wear clothes to clean in. This was supposed to be my study day."

"We work around the clients' schedules, my dear. You know that." Maria tossed the bag at her, a devilish glare in her eyes.

Catching the squishy bag, which clearly had clothing inside, Alisa knew without a doubt that Maria had a game plan. And when Maria was conniving, it wasn't good. The matron stiffened her spine, shooting Alisa the 'don't defy me' expression.

"*God*, fine. You owe me," Alisa said.

It sure as hell wasn't how she'd wanted the day to go—but jobs were scarce, let alone ones that were flexible enough to work around her demanding schedule. So, Alisa did what she had to do. Tucking the bag under her arm, she spun and strode toward the office door.

"Enjoy," Maria said.

The matron's self-satisfied chuckle forced Alisa to turn back, perplexed. Maria then offered a wink, validating all Alisa's concerns.

"Let's get this over with," Alisa grumbled to herself as she exited.

She took a deep breath and pushed out of the small building toward the parking lot. She had to get the job done fast if she had any designs on studying how voxel pixels were made to be proportional to the sum of the attenuation coefficients.

The drive across the city toward the Bixby Hill gated golf community could have been a lot faster if Alisa hadn't been slowed down by at least ten car accidents on the way. It was unbelievable how slow LA traffic could be, even considering it was just past morning rush hour. Signing in at the golf community's security post as the house cleaner, Alisa silently huffed that she didn't have time to change at a coffee shop along the way. Side-eyeing the lumpy bag of clothes provided by

Maria as she drove into the beautifully manicured neighborhood, Alisa regretfully accepted that she was going to have to change at the house.

That wasn't something she liked to do. God only knew the type of people who lived there.

Her clunky silver economy car — too old to be nice, too new to be vintage — brought her to the address provided, making a strange new noise that drove an embarrassed flush up Alisa's cheeks. The car was beginning to whine like a dying rhinoceros. She groaned quietly to herself, wishing her entrance could sound a little less conspicuous — a little less helpless. She shouldn't have ignored that check engine light for so long.

She parked in the driveway next to an expensive-looking navy-blue pickup truck, turning her car's engine off as quick as possible before the damn thing blew. She grew a little more anxious as she drank in the beautiful stonework and natural wood finishes on the outside of the sizable home she was approaching. *Who the hell is the client?*

With her bag of mystery clothes in one hand and her black purse in the other, she walked up the three stone steps toward the front door. That was always the hardest moment — meeting the client for the first time.

Her hand trembling, she outstretched it to ring the doorbell, but oddly, the door flung open before she got there. She shuffled back, drinking in the mouth-watering physique filling the frame of the wide doorway — the type of male specimen she'd only seen in movies.

"You the cleaner?" The man smoothed back his vibrant auburn hair, leaning into the frame.

Tall and intimidating, he was adorned by rippling muscle, broad shoulders and a big chest. Clearly impatient, he narrowed his gorgeous crystal-blue eyes on her, waiting for her reply.

She stuttered out nothing, shifting foot to foot, eventually choking out real words.

"Uh, uh…yes."

He opened the door fully, beckoning her inside with exposed tattooed arms, which appeared tanned and weathered. As she fumbled behind him, she inhaled that noticeable smell of a new home alongside distinct traces of leather and pine. His house smelled…*amazing*. The man paced into the hall, shooting her a quick side glance.

"I'm Warren," he said, crossing his arms and looking her up and down from his great height… assessing, judging. His face was stone cold, if not strong and perfectly aligned.

"A-Alisa."

She tried to smile but felt stiff. That was par for the course for her.

Wasting no time, he nodded to a closet on the side of the hall. "Everything you need should be in there."

"Oh, okay," Alisa murmured. Holding the bag of clothes so tight, like a safety blanket, she warily eyed the most perfect-looking man she'd ever seen.

He peaked his eyebrow, clearly trying to draw a conclusion, like was she human or was she an alien? *Alien, for sure.*

Alisa cast her eyes down, the only way she could return to the task at hand. *The job.* She needed to get at it and change her clothes. She refused to clean in the only jeans she owned that actually were decent enough to wear in public. She bit her lip, flashing her gaze back up at him. Should she ask to use the washroom?

"Need anything else?" he asked, as if sensing her unease. The way he studied her was sharp and quick.

Under his gaze, she felt a tension coiling inside her, a pressure — but was sure it was one-sided.

"C-could I use the washroom?" Alisa squeaked, following up with a mumbled "Please."

"Of course."

Warren shot her a sly grin, widening his mouth, showcasing a row of white teeth. He motioned to another door in the hallway beside him. Relieved, she started heading in that direction, moving a little closer to him as she did.

"Help yourself. I'll try to stay out of your hair…"

She halted, just a foot in front of him.

His gaze drifted from her long black hair, falling loosely over her shoulders, to her waist — kept trim from being overworked and underpaid. The unexpected twist in their interaction — from awkward to heated — nearly sent Alisa backward. She felt dazed.

But she composed herself, thankfully, and scurried into the washroom.

Only once the door was shut behind her did she let out a breath, that apparently, she'd been holding for far too long. *This guy… He isn't the type I'd anticipated running into*, she thought as she yanked the lumpy clothing out of the bag. She tore off her jeans and tried to figure out what exactly Maria had sent her with. There was something that looked like a white T-shirt, but then she realized it wasn't. It was a pair of bright white shorts. *Shorts?*

Looking in the long bathroom mirror, Alisa held them against her semi-nude golden-brown body. Sure, it was a hot LA summer, but the stretchy shorts looked like they'd barely cover anything. Panic seared up her throat. *Holy hell. What is Maria up to?* Alisa again dug into the bag and found that there was also a stringy white tank top. It looked like someone's hot yoga outfit — not an outfit that lent itself to modesty.

Immediately, Alisa flipped out her cell and texted Maria, sending her a pic of the outfit.

Are you setting me up?

Shit — I gave you the wrong bag. That's my yoga bag!

Maria… OMG.

I'm so sorry, girl. I've got the other bag here. I'll drive it to you.

That will take an hour. I can't just wait here for that long!

He's not going to bite…really.

Please. How well do you know this guy?

Well enough… Give him a chance.

"You okay in there?" Warren grunted from the hall.

"*Fuck, fuck, fuck.*" Alisa chewed to herself, widening her dark eyes into the mirror.

"Hello?"

"Yes, sir. I'm good," she called back and realized her fate was sealed.

It's too late to run.

So, she did the only thing she could do. She sucked it up and buckled in. *This is what life has come to*, she grumbled to herself silently as she threw on the ridiculously skimpy hot yoga shorts and matching tank top and stuffed her jeans and shirt into the shopping bag. She looked like she should be serving drinks at one of LA's hottest bars, much to the appreciation of a sea of men — something totally foreign to her. She'd killed off that sexy, fun side of herself long ago, her intense ambition driving her to focus on only one thing — her growing collection of textbooks.

With the words *no, no, no* running wild through her mind, she tried to breathe, pulling back her hair into a high ponytail that kissed her back and browned shoulders. Alisa shook her head, contemplating herself in the mirror. She nervously toyed with the long, thin gold chain around her neck — falling low, down the line of her cleavage. The ring on the end of the chain seared into her breasts.

I shouldn't be doing this.

Hoisting the bag over her shoulder, she put on a fake confident smile and pushed her way back out into the hallway, only to release it when she realized that Mr. Perfect wasn't waiting there for her. *Thank God.* She let her mouth drop into a neutral hyphen, absently flinging the bag holding her jeans onto her purse and went searching for that damn cleaning closet.

It was time to get to work and pretend that no part of her was secretly enjoying sharing air with that terrifyingly perfect man.

Chapter Two

Alisa

Silent as a mouse, starting from the second floor and working her way down, Alisa knuckled into the cleaning. She observed that the master bedroom seemed to be only occupied by *one. Interesting*—Mr. Perfect lived alone. And there were no women's clothes or items to be found. Wiping the baseboards in the second and third bedrooms, what was even more interesting was that Alisa could see that these bedrooms weren't even being used. They were almost empty, except for a few boxes of unpacked things.

What's his deal? Has he just moved in?

In the upstairs hallway, she rubbed down a dusty mirror, catching her reflection. Softly brushing her eyebrows flat and swiping at her lip balm, she took in a deep breath. The way her genes were expressed, her appearance had always been unique. An Indian mother, a Caucasian father—truly, no one really ever could guess what her ethnic origin was. Most men she'd met in LA just called her *exotic*.

She didn't really like that.

Suddenly, she wondered what Mr. Perfect saw when he looked at her.

As she wandered down the hardwood staircase, polishing as she went, she overheard his booming voice on the phone in the living room. Demanding and dominant, his was the type of voice that hit her in her core, awakening her senses. Cresting into the open area, she saw his muscular frame seated on the edge of the couch, and he was having an animated discussion—and he didn't seem happy about it.

"No, I'm not fucking going," Warren roared into the phone. There was a pause, then he continued, "Because I'm not. I don't care if the entire goddamn platoon is."

Platoon.

The word hit Alisa, and she stopped in her tracks on the first floor. There it was—a big piece to the puzzle. Warren glared upward before waving her into the room but continued drilling into his phone, barking at whomever he was speaking to. Like she was walking in on something she wasn't supposed to be, she anxiously looked for something to work on and get busy. The wooden coffee table was the closest thing that needed attention, so she made a snap decision and marched toward it.

So, Warren was in the military, she mulled, covertly glancing up at him. *He certainly fits the bill*, she thought, watching his tattooed arms flex with his growl. She could hear muffled words shooting back at him on the phone. Whoever he was talking to, it was clearly a full-blown disagreement.

"That's just fucking offside," he said, chucking a magazine from the coffee table to the couch, giving

Alisa room to clean in front of him. "Why the hell is this rookie trying so damn hard to get me there?"

Warren settled his gaze on her as she knelt in front of him, polishing the table. Alisa kept her eyes down, working hard, but couldn't ignore the intensity of Mr. Perfect's burning glare. It was almost like he couldn't look away, and he didn't seem happy about it.

Once again, she let her gaze trace upward from her kneeling position, locking eyes with the crystal-blue ones staring back at her. Something about his demeanor changed in that split second, and she noticed him shift his heavy body.

"Fuck, whatever—I've got work to do. And so do you," Warren grunted, ending the call.

As he threw his cell phone across the couch, a sudden silence flushed over the room. It felt like all the air got sucked out, and they were in a private vacuum. And here she was—kneeling right in front of him in her little white shorts.

Why in God's name didn't I let Maria bring me a new outfit?

Quite the difference from when he'd met her at the door—his stone-cold face had turned fervent...fiery. *A hot-headed man.* It wasn't hard to see it—between the color rising in his cheeks and looking at his gleaming auburn locks. He exuded intensity.

And he was *watching* her...with something growing in his eyes. Something flooded the air in between them. She could taste it.

It was too much for her.

He was too much for her.

Uneasy, Alisa quickly jumped up, spinning around. She found her way to his entertainment center, removing what little dust was there and shining the dark wood. She bent lower, polishing harder, working tirelessly—the only thing she'd come to know. She folded her legs underneath her and shifted to reach to the back of the furniture piece. She was usually pretty damn motivated to do an impeccable job, but that morning she felt an extra vigor that she couldn't explain.

Trying to keep her eye on him, she could just barely see him through the reflection of his massive TV. Mr. Perfect was making her think of something she hadn't thought of for a really long time. He was really throwing her off.

Through the reflection, she observed him leaning back on his couch, crossing his arms and watching her. She couldn't tell if he was absently sitting there, stewing in anger, or actively studying her ass in those skimpy yoga shorts. What type of service did he need?

As she worked, she adjusted the seam of her shorts to cover more of her ass cheeks from his view. That proved to be a mistake—slowly running her finger along the back of her shorts gave him more of a show than she'd meant and was met by a low groan from the couch.

Then she heard him shifting again.

That fucking *groan.*

Masculine, heady, aroused.

Oh God.

He was making her dizzy.

Immediately, she felt a gush of wetness in her panties. There was something so damn erotic about him sitting there, watching her. *I can make this man — this hulking, beastly man — squirm?* Her attraction to him hit harder, and she found her provoked body taking her places her brain wasn't sure she wanted to go. She was fully off plan, navigating blindly in uncharted territory.

Pleading with herself to stop, her libido refused to listen, like a man hadn't so much as looked at her in four years. Polishing the wood harder, she bent over in front of him, her white shorts likely showcasing everything—every crease, every crevasse. She really needed to get out more.

Warren's breathing intensified, and through the reflection, she observed that his eyes weren't leaving her. Whatever she was doing, she had proven that it was clearly intentional—and a tease.

Through the corner of her eye, she caught him adjusting the waistband of his pants. *It must be getting a little tight in there.* A sly grin spanned her lips, which she subdued. She just needed to hear him groan one more time.

She'd never thought herself to get off on exhibition, but something about his reaction was so damn validating. She felt fucking *hot* for the very first time in...forever? And maybe that was what she needed in that exact moment, after what had been four insane years.

She rolled herself back up, as gracefully as possible, and reached for the upper cabinets. The way she moved had ridden her shorts up, and she felt like she was wearing nothing more than a wide white thong in front of him, her ass cheeks having fallen out for his viewing pleasure. As much as she wanted to adjust her shorts again, she didn't. She kept cleaning, letting them stay ridden up—torturing and teasing the man.

And it was paying off in boatloads. He let out another lungful that sounded less restrained than the first. The sheer idea of a dominant man so turned on that he would claim her was a fantasy that had lingered for too long in the back of her mind and was only visited in the quiet dark of night when she was alone.

Maybe Maria had just wanted to remind her that she was still alive. It was no mystery that the matron didn't approve of Alisa's life choices.

Turning to fold a stray blanket, Alisa flickered her eyes back to Mr. Perfect, putting on her most innocent expression. His gaze locked with hers, his unquestionably furious, just shaking his head at her. That flush in his cheeks, the flex in his jaw, the hardening in his shoulders? It was clear what was happening. She was playing with fire.

"It's been a while since you've had a cleaner," she said.

"Or just one that works as hard as *you*," he retorted. Calling her out.

Frozen, trying to think of something clever to say back, she didn't miss how his teeth grazed his bottom lip, as he studied her up and down. He looked hungry as hell, and ready for *dinnertime*. That was when Alisa knew she had to back off. She was antagonizing the wolf, and she was going to get bitten.

"I should get to the basement." She bit her lip, a little too giddy. Laying the folded blanket on the chair, she tried to get her head screwed back on.

"The basement's not finished," he countered in a low voice, his frozen eyes never leaving her.

"You paid for a full house."

"You don't need to go down there," he said — like he was issuing orders.

Alisa could tell there was a lot more that Warren wanted to say — but at the same time, he didn't want to talk. And she was out of words.

So, she spun, striding to the other side of the first floor, wiping accent tables and chairs as she went, like she was doing what she was *supposed* to be doing. Regaining some semblance of herself, she recognized that it was harder to breathe properly in front of him. It was harder to be *Alisa* in front of him. He wasn't the type of man she was used to. He clearly drew something out of her.

She walked through Warren's kitchen and around the wide hallway. Her pile of used washcloths in her hand, she knew she had a few more things to get done before she could run out and get paid. Usually, Maria asked cleaners to put all dirty washcloths in the client's laundry room and even get it started, minimizing their impact. But Alisa had finished cleaning the two upper floors and hadn't seen the laundry room yet.

Could the laundry be in the basement?

She slowly opened a door leading to the unfinished staircase of the basement. Curiosity was killing her, but she paused. *He said no.*

Just before she could close the door, something caught her eye at the bottom of the stairs—a large black trunk that looked like a pelican case, armored and heavy duty. She knew that type of case. She'd spent enough time with a Marine once. Typically used for transporting guns, especially used by military folk, those cases were built for deployment. Through the dim light in the basement stairwell, she could barely make out a few more things laid out on the concrete below—body armor, boots and something black. Only when she focused a little harder did she realize that it was a rifle, leaning against the pelican case. And not the type of rifle used for hunting animals.

"Jesus—" she breathed out, stumbling back.

Who is this guy?

A growling voice arrived behind her. "I said…don't fucking go down there."

He dropped his heavy hand on the door, slamming it shut with more vigor than needed. She felt her mouth open as she spun to witness his dead-serious face.

I shouldn't be here.

Chapter Three

Warren

Leading Chief Petty Officer Warren Cameron stared down at the stunning woman before him in that stupidly hot outfit, creeping on his shit. *What the fuck is she up to?*

"I'm—I'm sorry," Alisa said, pushing her way back from him. Her back hit the wall on the opposite side of the hall.

He pivoted, turning toward her, suspicious as all hell. A few feet between them in the hallway, he narrowed his eyes on her. He was getting answers.

"This—" Warren eyed her up and down, growling— her overly exposed body, wrapped in glowing tanned skin, egging him on. "I've never seen a cleaner show up like she's ready to hit the stage."

"I didn't— I'm not—"

He cut her off. "Why don't you just tell me what your game is here? I saw your little tease. I see what you are doing. What the hell are you after?"

His challenge was clear.

She opened her eyes wide, her plump lips forming words that didn't come out. She was good, real good. He'd give her that.

"Warren, I swear—"

"Swear, what? Swear you aren't trying to drive me insane?" Again, he dropped his gaze to her long legs in those super-hot shorts.

"*Please*, believe me."

"This isn't how I expected my goddamn house cleaner to behave," he growled, determined to get the truth. "Don't act like you are innocent."

"You're right. I'm not," she acknowledged. "I—"

Alisa's gaze dropped, her feet twisting underneath her childishly. Then, Warren saw something he didn't expect—true shame. He'd been highly trained in interrogation techniques…and spotting truth.

"I'm not after anything," Alisa whispered with downcast eyes, something sweet drifting to his nose. "I just want to do my job."

"And what else?"

"And…nothing else. Please, just let me go."

When she mustered up the courage to glance back, her dark eyes told him what he needed to know.

She was being genuine.

The realization immediately tempered him.

Oh, fuck.

He rubbed his chin with his rough hand, feeling where he needed to shave. He'd been working too hard. Pre-deployment was never easy. Maybe he was in a mood, being too hard on her. Maybe he had overreacted.

"Look—" he started.

"I'm sorry," she offered again, authentic as hell. "I know what I did, and I shouldn't have."

Second apology. He nodded, recognizing that. *Authentic, too.* She hadn't stopped surprising him. So, he stood back, giving her space to continue.

"I'm really not after anything," she carried on. "I know what it looks like, but things just got away from me. I'm engaged — and I did not plan on wearing this."

Engaged? Christ.

"I don't see a ring." His tone remained low, suspicious. He didn't want to believe it.

"Here."

She intertwined her fingers in the gold chain around her neck, pulling it up and out of her mouth-watering cleavage. That's when he saw it — a gold ring with a massive diamond at the end of the necklace.

"So, maybe you are telling the truth," he said.

"Does that change anything?"

Under his gaze, she shifted, biting her lip, waiting for his response as she eyed her escape route. He chose to say nothing, enjoying how she fidgeted like a little schoolgirl in front of him. The way she pulled at the tight fabric of her top made her trim hourglass shape bob in all the right places. God, her nervousness... It was the type of thing Warren loved to sink his teeth into, rip apart. The more anxious she grew under him, the more focused he became, turned on beyond fucking comprehension — ready to snap.

The depraved thoughts running wild through his mind drew him to stifle yet another groan and tighten his hands across his chest. She was off limits. She wanted to leave. But, damn, he wouldn't forget how easy she'd given him a hard-on with her little show. All he wanted to do was reach across and teach her what a man like him wanted.

But what the fuck was he supposed to do — pin her down and have his way? No, he wasn't the type of guy to gnaw after women unless he was sure they wanted it. He didn't falter. Never did.

So, he backed up a little more.

"I should get going," she said quickly.

"Fine—what do you have left to do here?" Warren asked.

Alisa shook her head. "I can't."

"Why?" he challenged, a little confused.

She shifted, clearly trying to put words together.

Finally, she replied, nodding at the basement door, "I don't like guns—or weapons of any kind—and I don't..."

But she let herself trail off.

He wasn't dumb. The implication was there. *I don't trust you.* He cocked his head in laughter. How the tables had turned.

"I'm not a fucking psycho," he grinned, assuring her. "I have stuff for work. I'm in the military. Don't worry. You can finish up, then leave."

"I know guys in the military, and they never had that...*stuff* sitting around," she pointed out.

"It's just a rifle."

"I'm sorry it's been weird, but I'll send someone else to finish." A snappy confidence grew in her voice that matched the woman who'd teased him so hard.

She's back.

Then Warren realized that his kitchen wasn't going to get cleaned, and she wasn't going to come again...because he'd pushed her too hard. He didn't know which was more unacceptable to him. He just knew he wasn't going to let her get away so easy.

"Look... I don't usually tell people this, but I'm in the special forces. A lot of us buy our own gear," Warren said. "None of it will be here the next time you come. I'll take it with me when I ship out."

"Special forces?" She raised her eyebrow at him.

He flexed his jaw, studying her. "Military. Special forces. Heard of it?"

"Well, you're pretty special, all right," Alisa smirked.

She wrapped her long fingers around her waist, staring back up at him defiantly. That goddamn defiance drove him over the edge, his cock twitching in response. He had to double-down.

"I'm a SEAL," he said with broadening shoulders, waiting for the usual female response.

But she didn't do it.

An awkward pause hit.

She just stood there, eyeing him like he didn't just tell her that he was a fucking Navy SEAL. Where was the swooning? The smiling? The oozing?

"Oh, okay—cool," she replied, deadpan. "Good talk."

Good talk? His jaw dropped, and he was a little speechless. *What the fuck?* Taken aback, he felt a wall of frost emanating from her.

"I'm going now." She twirled toward the front door, showcasing that lithe body that he'd grown fucking hungry for.

Warren watched her step away, stunned to find his fists shaking. She'd shut him out. While studying her tight ass march down his hallway toward the front foyer, her black ponytail bobbing on her shoulders, he yet again stifled a groan, only half succeeding. *Damn*—he had to stop her. He had to grab her shoulders, heave her up to his mouth and show her exactly why she had to come back.

Guys like him didn't watch women walk away.

But she was fucking *walking*.

He could have sworn she heard his grumble, because her body twitched in a certain type of way. Unable to not, he followed her to the front door as she grabbed her purse and bag of clothes. Throwing on her shoes, she grasped the handle, briefly glaring back at him. He wasn't crazy. There was something there in her eyes, something that matched what was stirring inside him, too. She didn't let her gaze linger, though, immediately ripping it away.

Opening the door, she said, "Maria will be in touch."

"You don't have to go."

"Yeah, I do."

Pouring his intensity into her, demanding her cooperation, he growled, "Next time—"

She cut him off. "There won't be a next time— I won't be coming back, Warren."

Hearing his name roll off her lips broke the last straw, and he consciously flexed his fists to keep them still by his side. But it didn't matter. Alisa was already out of the door, out of his life. Unfortunately so, because he just then realized that she was the type of enigma that he enjoyed solving.

A peculiar emptiness grew in his chest as he became, once again, the sole occupant of his house. The words 'missed opportunity' ran roughshod across his mind, taunting him, and he snarled at himself to sit the fuck down. She was just a chick. He had other shit to do. It was time to forget it and move on.

Work was heating up, and deployment was coming around again. He had made his choice, years ago promoting to Chief. He'd become the leader of the pack. He lived, breathed and would die as a SEAL. Planning and preparation were his focus. There was no time for new distractions. The next deployment was going to be a long one, he understood.

And the rule always was—no relationship would last the length of the deployment unless it had pre-existed for at least the same amount of time back home. It was a fact. People thought life was unpredictable, but Warren knew better. He predicted everything. He was never wrong about people.

But then something he didn't predict happened.

The sound of a car backfiring in his driveway echoed into his front hall—the distinct sound of a car unable to get going.

Alisa.

Chapter Four

Alisa

"Come on. Come *on!*" Alisa pleaded with her hunk of junk, trying to get the engine to turn over. "For the love of God, don't do this to me."

Nervously pushing loose strands of hair behind her ears, she glared back at the house, hoping to hell Mr. Perfect wouldn't come out. That morning had already been all shades of weird, and she was nothing short of mortified...mostly at her own behavior. She needed it to all go away so she could pretend she'd never tried to tease a Navy SEAL while cleaning his house, all for some misdirected gratification.

But the car's whines were too loud to be discreet, and she groaned. Sure enough, within moments, her hulking savior sauntered outside, locking eyes with her—the midday LA sun scorching above and his auburn hair glittering red like Hades himself.

Damn, she snapped to herself, shaking in pure agony.

"Need a hand?" Warren opened the driver's-side door, casual and confident like nothing had just happened between them.

"No," she replied too fast. "I'm good."

"You don't seem good."

"I said I'm fine, but thanks." She shot him a stiff sneer, trying to slam the door on him.

He pushed the door open. "Try turning it over again."

"Please, just go."

Ignoring her, he focused on the car's dashboard, investigating.

It was either him or a tow truck, she grasped, which would be way out of her budget. So, she reluctantly obeyed, letting him lean in over her to assess the angry flickering lights on the dash and the corresponding dying noise that the car was making.

"Ah, this looks familiar," he confirmed, leaning back. "Get out, champ."

From her seated position, she gazed up to where he stood, realizing she was stuck between a rock and a hard place—or his rock-solid body and that hard-on she'd clearly given him earlier. The warm and intoxicating scent drifting off his body made her woozy.

"Come on. Let's go."

"I don't have time for this." Alisa then let out an exasperated sigh, beating her head against the steering wheel.

The last thing she needed was to miss out on studying and show up the next day unprepared. That would really be the icing on the proverbial shit cake.

"Time or not, this is happening." Warren's deep voice permeated the space between them.

Reaching down, he unbuckled her seat belt and offered his hand. *Chivalrous*. Her mouth watered just a little bit, but she shook her head. It was peculiar how she continued to feel both extremely sloppy and very captivated.

"Fine," she relented, stumbling out of the car.

Falling into him, he grinned down on her, unwilling to budge and clearly as entertained as fuck.

"Ah, a sadist—" she griped as she pushed off him.

He roughly grabbed her shoulder, moving her away from the car to give himself space, making her quiver.

"Kill me now," she whispered to herself, mostly sure he didn't hear it as he dove into the driver's seat.

"How old is this puppy?" he called up to her while investigating the cause of her car problems.

"We've had it for fifteen years," she admitted. "It was nice when we got it. My mother drove it for years before…"

Then she stopped. That wasn't something she wanted to get into.

She hoped he hadn't noticed. Maybe he was as bad at reading people as she was.

A silence growing between them, the rugged, tall man ejected out of her small economy car, moving over to pop the hood. Through his thin gray T-shirt, she could see the definition rippling up and down his core. He was solid and athletic, and she bit her lip as she found herself unable to look away, kind of in disbelief. That only intensified when he shot her that icy blue gaze, amplified by his outdoorsy tan.

"Before? Before what?" he cross-examined, reaching into the car's engine, yanking at something.

Alisa felt her throat constrict. He didn't miss a beat, did he?

"You going to finish that sentence?" Warren followed up, standing straight.

"It used to be my mother's *before* she passed away," Alisa let it out finally. "I guess that's been just about four years now."

Warren's body stilled as he was watching her. "I'm sorry."

She let herself breathe in slowly. Cancer was a bitch. Everyone was sorry. That was something they all said when they heard, but it just felt different coming from him. It felt more intense. More real. Like he meant it, truly meant it.

Like he'd lost someone as well.

"Thanks." Alisa nodded slowly, observing him turn back to the engine.

But then a weird laugh escaped her lips as she blurted out, "I'm just wondering who's going to be next...me?"

Warren's blue eyes caught her once more, throwing her balance off. Then he turned back to his work, not replying to her offbeat remark. She sucked in a breath, feeling ten times more self-conscious than before. Now *she* looked like the psycho.

She wasn't a fucking people-person.

As he worked wordlessly, she relocated into the shade by his house, still just feet away from him. Then, he stood up, striding to look for something in his garage. As he walked by, she couldn't help but blurt out what was on her mind.

"So, you're a SEAL—" she started, but he shot her a glare, telling her to stop.

"Keep that quiet."

"Why'd you tell me, then?"

He shrugged, reaching for a wrench on his workbench before turning back to the car.

"I just had to trust you," he replied, giving her a warm and fuzzy feeling all over her body.

As he bent back over the engine, he fired her an expression that screamed 'don't fuck with my trust'.

His muscular arms deep in the block, she couldn't help but admire. That same wetness in her pussy tingled. *Damn, special forces, huh?*

It didn't take Warren much longer before he stood, wiping sweat off his brow while leaving a dash of engine grease on the side of his face.

He nodded at the car. "This should be enough to get you going for now, but you're going to need to get this car to a shop — or a junkyard."

Alisa let out a breath. The shop meant more expenses, more money she needed to beg for. And she couldn't go without a car. Her body language certainly didn't disguise her distress.

He watched her, assessing.

"Look... I could do the work. It's fixable. I just have to get a part."

"Really?" She parted her lips, apparently trying to understand his offer.

"Sure."

"But, why? What's in it for you?"

"Well" —his grin widened, and he nodded back to his house—"come back and finish the job. I think you left a few spots."

He trailed his gaze up and down her body again, and she stiffened. *That's* what he wanted.

"You in?" he asked.

"I don't know. I wouldn't wear this again."

"Thank fucking God."

Alisa narrowed her eyes on him, issuing a warning.

He grinned back, like he couldn't give a fuck less.

Dogged, his gaze tracked her as she strode to the driver's door, opening it. Everything in her body screamed 'get the fuck out as quickly as possible'. She'd learned her lesson against inexplicable generosity. She'd learned what happened when you got sucked down a rabbit hole, indebted.

"Thanks for your help," she concluded, a little pinched. "If I don't see you, best of luck."

"No problem. You, too."

Her heart racing, she plopped into her driver's seat. Thankfully, the engine turned, and it actually sounded better than it had before. He crossed his arms, watching her reverse out of his driveway, and offered her a curt nod as she drove off.

Her heart thumping out of her chest, she couldn't keep her eyes off the rear-view mirror, watching the striking man standing there, his gaze never drawing away. It was only once she got out of view that she felt the tension in her body release. When she yanked her hair elastic out and let her locks cascade over her shoulders, there was something curious that endured in her heart.

Again, she found herself asking, but meaning something different from before — *who is this guy?*

Chapter Five

Alisa

Alisa draped her pink stethoscope around her neck as she took the patient summary being handed to her. It was time for morning rounds in the wards of the hospital, and among the circle of final-year med students, she was trying to wrap her head around what the hell was wrong with their young patient.

"Callum presented to the ER with severe abdominal pain," the lead student explained at his mobile laptop stand, reading the electronic chart. "He's been admitted for three days and so far, we've done scopes, scans and biopsies to determine the cause of his pain."

"Tumor?" one of the students asked.

"Doesn't look like it, but we are waiting on biopsy results," the lead answered before continuing, updating the group on the details of the procedure that had taken place the day prior.

Alisa observed Dr. Zucker, a pediatrician, in the background scribbling notes into his journal, ostensibly grading student participation. This was what the end of med school had been like—real-life experience on the cusp of final exams next month. They'd all write their exams, hopefully get licensed as medical doctors and proceed to residency, where they'd finally be earning salaries. Meager salaries, but at least that meant Alisa wouldn't be begging for help and eating ramen noodles twice a day.

Before the group moved on to the next patient, Dr. Zucker pulled her aside. The other students shot her the side-eye, and she knew what they were thinking. Everyone was getting nervous about residency and getting a good spot. In fact, things had grown quite competitive between the students as the doctors graded their aptitudes.

"Alisa, I want you to check in on Callum with me this morning," Dr. Zucker said, closing his journal.

She took in a deep breath, knowing that it was going to be another critical moment in her assessment. More and more, the doctors were requesting that med students get more hands-on with patients. By that point, it was like an on-the-job interview for residency. That only made her all the more nervous.

"Okay." She nodded, following the lean, mature man into the patient room.

Don't fuck it up. Don't fuck it up—caution and self-doubt bounced through her mind. She chewed her lip, trying to dig deep into those books she'd read on how to become a people-person, how to improve her bedside manner—that little thing that she'd never thought mattered…until it had started proving to be the difference between a job offer and bust.

Dr. Zucker pulled out his journal again, ushering Alisa forward to the sick boy's bedside. She greeted him stiffly, trying not to show her nerves. Reviewing his vitals, she began robotically asking him how he was feeling.

"It hurts…a lot," Callum groaned, grabbing at his gut, his thirteen-year-old eyes blinking in agony.

"He's in a lot of pain," the teen's mother restated, clutching at his blanket. "Isn't there anything you can do?"

Alisa checked his pain medication record, shaking her head. He'd been receiving lots of narcotics—too many. She shot Dr. Zucker a look. Who signed off on that? The hospital typically sought to administer narcotics sparingly on teens, given the addiction rates.

Dr. Zucker widened his eyes—telling her to answer the mother.

"I'm sorry, Callum," she reluctantly spoke after an awkward break in the conversation. The air felt stale. "All we can offer you at this point is more Tylenol, because you've already had the maximum of these other drugs."

"I don't want Tylenol!" Callum cried out, coiling and sobbing. "I want more of that!"

He pointed at the IV drip, and she knew he was angling for more narcotics.

Alisa stepped forward, taking his pulse, checking his oxygen. Was he faking it? Was he trying to squeeze her for drugs? That was unfortunately something they saw from time to time, especially when there was no clear answer as to what ailed the patient.

"Callum, we'll get to the bottom of this *one way or another*," she said, too much suspicion in her tone. "For now, you just have to muscle through."

"What does that mean?" his mother demanded, picking up on her subtle message. "How can you say that?"

"Alisa." Dr. Zucker's tone was challenging, urging her to explain herself.

She fumbled, her eyes darting back and forth.

"We see a lot of cases," Alisa started, trying to find the right words. "And in your case, I think you can get through the pain as best as you can. I think you'll just have to deal with it until we have answers."

"Alisa" — Dr. Zucker stepped forward, pointing at the door — "a word."

The boy's sobbing behind her escalated as the pediatrician escorted her out of the room, taking her aside in the hallway to have a conversation. His face didn't read happy.

"You can't talk to patients like that, especially children!"

"He's thirteen," Alisa offered, as if that would save her.

"Exactly, Alisa — he's *only* thirteen. You can't make a child feel like they are making up stories about their pain, and you certainly can't make them feel like you aren't willing to help them," Dr. Zucker said. "You are one of my brightest students, but your head needs to get out of textbooks and into reality. This isn't how we deal with people."

"I'm — I'm sorry," she said, but was cut off by the lead med student, who'd suddenly appeared.

Dr. Zucker turned to him, receiving an update from the biopsy.

"The results are in, doctor — Callum has an atypical bacterial infection at the base of his stomach. We should be able to resolve this quickly with antibiotics," the med student explained, trying to keep his eyes averted from Alisa. He definitely knew she was getting in shit.

"That explains the pain." Dr. Zucker flashed back at Alisa, sending her a clear look.

She'd failed the test. A little part of her dropped to its death inside her. *I'm hopeless.*

Dr. Zucker turned to head back into the patient room to deliver the news. Alisa moved to follow him, but he stopped her.

"I think I should do this alone," he said, his expression disappointed. "You know, Alisa, you are at the top of the heap in academics, but you won't get far if you can't find a way to round yourself out."

"And how do you suggest I do that?"

He flipped his journal, shrugging slightly. "Spend more time with people."

Then he marched into the patient room.

Chagrined, Alisa lumbered behind the nurse's counter to grab her bag. It was time for a break. She needed some air. She needed to think.

Time and time again, her bedside manner was proving to be problematic. She just wasn't good at it, she grumbled silently to herself, walking out of the ward's locked doors. Her dream of becoming an effective physician was threatened by the fact that with others, she was too cool, too unfeeling—not nearly friendly and sympathetic enough.

Pacing down one of the quieter hospital corridors, she tugged her cell phone out of her bag for needed distraction. There was nothing more depressing than working so damn hard and still feeling like a failure. She sifted through app notifications, none of them social, but she wasn't able to analyze much because a call from a blocked number came through.

"Hello," she answered.

Warren's deep voice came through the line. "What are you doing later? I've got the part for your car."

A little smile spanned Alisa's lips.

"I can't," she replied slowly, wondering how he'd gotten her number. *Maybe Maria gave it to him.*

"Tomorrow morning?"

She bit her lip, wondering what the hell to do. What was his endgame?

"You in?" he probed. "This kitchen sure as hell needs a cleaning."

"Okay, fine. Tomorrow," she squeaked, resolving to finish what she'd started.

Immediately, manic butterflies unsettled her stomach. The unbelievable reality dawned on her. She'd just made plans to return to him.

"One more thing," he said, smooth as silk, "what do you like in your coffee?"

The question drew a curious laugh out of her, throwing her off guard. She subdued it, trying to correct herself.

"Cream—and lots of it," she grinned, reaching a little too hard for her answer.

He offered her a chuckle in return as he ended the call, but it didn't help. As she stared at the screen of her cell phone, she found herself shuddering. *Cream—and lots of it?* Why the hell did she say that? That wasn't funny or cool. Grumbling to herself for being so weird, she anxiously flipped back to her notifications for a diversion. It hadn't turned out to be a great morning for interpersonal skills.

Her fingers hovered over her recent calls, and she grasped the fact that she didn't actually have Warren's cell number—but he had hers. He'd called her from a blocked ID. A sense of surrender settled between her shoulder blades as she accepted that Warren was the type of man who liked being in charge — and their recent exchange had absolutely illustrated that. He liked holding all the power.

She chewed her lip, knowing full well that *she* liked that, too. And that was the problem, she thought, toying with the gold necklace holding her engagement ring. Something about Warren was simultaneously a little dangerous and unquestionably safe.

Grinning, Alisa turned to glance at the staff milling about in the hospital corridor. There was something so awakening about her dynamic with Warren. He was the type of hunter that she'd only dreamed about at night, when it was safe to fantasize. Something about their interactions made her feel like he'd been hunting her. Her thighs trembled at the thought of him on top of her, wondering what it would be like to stare back into those icy blue eyes while he —

Dr. Zucker poked his head out of the patient room, beckoning Alisa back inside, cutting through her thoughts. And that was a damn good thing, Alisa realized, as she sucked in a shallow breath. She'd have to be very careful with Warren.

She may not be a warm and squishy woman, bound for domestic bliss with three kids, but she wasn't dead. And cleaning Warren's house, enjoying how she aroused him, reminded her that she could feel... impossible, throbbing desire.

* * * *

Alisa arrived home a little later than usual. It was well and truly time to crash, she thought, chucking her keys and purse on the tiny apartment table. Shedding her blazer and slowly peeling off her clothes, she found herself flipping on the hot water tap in her out-of-date shower stall.

Standing in front of the cracked mirror that was slowly getting foggy, she pulled her long gold chain up and over her head, running her finger over the gaudy diamond on her engagement ring. She'd gotten away with keeping it on a necklace during med school because of all the latex gloves she had to haul on and off, but one day she'd have to reckon with the fact that it belonged on a finger. The size of the jewel and the style of the ring were so unlike her that they threatened to expose the truth.

She sighed as she placed the chain in the bowl on the counter and turned to hop into her sickly-pink tiled shower, a relic from the 1950s, to be sure.

Letting her long hair soak, steam wrapping her body in the glass stall, she started soaping her body with a luxurious shower gel that had once been given to her as a gift from Dean, her fiancé. The gift itself had been some sort of appeasement, a non-verbal apology for something he'd done...or hadn't. She'd lost count over the years.

Grabbing the cheap plastic loofa, she grazed her skin. Sometimes it felt good just to feel something. She scrubbed harder and harder. A little pain sometimes felt right. To hell with anyone who called her unfeeling.

She wanted to take the moment to savor something that had been bubbling at the back of her mind like a small, delicious dark chocolate. In her hot shower, she immersed herself in a hotter fantasy. Fantasies were the only things that kept her sane throughout the long, lonely years of med school. And the thought of Warren leaning over her engine under the scorching sun was etched in her mind—him with a full body of muscle, shooting her sly looks. Those eyes. Those shoulders. That smile.

She chewed her lip, knowing it was all pure fantasy. Knowing it could never happen, she allowed the daydreams of Warren to erupt from sexual to emotional, distributing an intoxicating mix of chemicals throughout her brain. Maybe it was infatuation, maybe it was addiction—but those chemicals felt so damn good sometimes. And what happened between her two ears was her business and no one else's.

She ran her hands up and down her body, soaping and awakening. She found her breasts, her nipples— and imagined Warren touching her. Pinching her. Gripping her. A soft moan escaped her lips as her arousal grew when she trailed one of her hands down her abdomen. She replayed the sound of him groaning, watching her from his couch, again and again in her mind. It was sending her over the edge. He'd wanted her.

She toyed with her hairless mound, teasing herself open, pretending it wasn't her own hand. What would his hands feel like? *Rough, calloused, strong, warm.* She bit her lip, her eyes closed, circling her throbbing bud. Moaning, she kept the image of Warren working on her car front and center. God, he was too damn hot. The fantasy so real, so tangible—she knew it wouldn't take long for her to climax.

He'd be a savage in bed. He'd be so dominant. She just knew it. She could push him over the edge—and he'd claim her without mercy. He'd claim her and teach her how to love and steal her away—

She knew he was the type of man that wouldn't take *no* for an answer.

Alisa let out a load groan, panting. She really liked how he seemed to like her. It was refreshing, really. As she found herself cresting the peak, she palmed the slippery shower tile for balance, feeling the rush. *Damn.*

Hot water flushing down her back, she straightened herself, then turned off the water and grabbed a towel. The excitement of having a plan to see Warren the next morning simmered to the surface. Drying off her skin and dark hair, she reminded herself that it never hurt to fantasize.

Chapter Six

Warren

At the end of a quiet road in Wrightwood, California, Warren prepared his platoon for the next deployment, one that was promised to be long and hard.

"Boys, there are three types of people in the world." Warren gripped his M4 carbine rifle, the infra-red laser pointer steady on a cardboard cut-out.

"Wolves," he barked as he shot at the target.

Spinning, he stared at the Navy SEALs under his command, all hand-picked. He nodded past the gate as he began pacing around the team.

"Sheep."

Halting, he growled. "And sheepdogs."

The men stirred, holding onto their rifles and eyeing the simulated targets in the distance.

"We're sheepdogs," Warren continued. "Wolves are bad guys, trying to eat the sheep. We protect the sheep. We kill the wolves."

He spun, aiming his rifle again, and decimated the target. Standing back, he watched each man carefully as he adjusted his suppressor. He was the leader who allowed no mistakes, exemplifying perfection. At his rank, he wasn't always so hands-on, but this time, he had to get into the weeds. It wasn't the platoon's first rodeo, but the conditions for the next op would lead to tricky circumstances. They'd gone over the mission a hundred times, but given the tight timeframe and the rapidly approaching deployment, he had no choice but to keep drilling until everything was perfect. They only had one shot at it, figuratively and literally.

After they ran through the plan yet again, Warren glanced out over concrete walls and realized that the horizon was waking. The sun would rise soon over the training facility, purpose-built to Warren's specifications. It was a replica compound, based on aerial shots of the enemy's base just outside of Erbil, Iraq. Soon, they'd see it in real life.

Maybe Iraq wasn't in the news as much as it once had been, but the fire raged on there — threatening all the hard work of allied troops over the years. There were some assets that the government wasn't prepared to let slide and some enemies that would be hunted for the rest of their natural lives. A lion among men, Warren was more than happy to hunt them, tour after tour, for the rest of his natural life. He'd lost count how many times he'd been there, but he sure as hell knew Iraq had felt more like home in the past five years than his house in California.

After another half-hour of intense training, Warren's crew circled around him, catching their collective breaths. He worked his men hard — harder than any other SEAL team. That was the expectation for being in this crew — for being the best of the best.

"Nice work, lads, but the party ain't over," Warren called out, stern and sharp. "Don't expect to get any sleep tonight. We'll meet back at o-dark-thirty for another long one."

The rookie stepped forward, removing his helmet and sweeping back his sweaty brown hair. Warren shot him a look, wondering what the hell it was all about.

"Chief, um — Crash's got his thing tomorrow," Gaudet nodded to the guy beside him. "We're all supposed to be there."

Warren gritted his teeth as he sized up Crash, not mistaking how the other junior sailor inched backward. Sure, Warren knew all about the engagement party the next day. He knew because the bride wouldn't stop fucking texting and calling. She'd been trying fucking hard to get him to go. Suspiciously so.

"So?" Warren barked. "Who gives a shit?"

Gaudet looked at Crash then back at the chief.

"So, if we don't get any sleep tonight —" Gaudet coughed out but stopped.

Warren narrowed his eyes, his cold silence threatening.

Shifting in his stance, Gaudet slowly added, "He's getting married — or at least trying to before we deploy."

Warren let out an unamused, short laugh, shooting directly at Crash.

"Getting married? That's an excuse to stop training? What the fuck do you think you signed up for?"

"We'll be pretty fucking sapped," Gaudet pointed out. "If we've got to go all night then go do that tomorrow."

"So, ya'll want a break to go play dress-up?"

Warren remained still and stiff, sensing the uneasiness he was driving in his men. *Good.*

For fuck's sake.

He continued, "Don't give me this wedding planner bullshit. I didn't raise you to be bitches. We don't stop. We *never* stop."

He stared around at the silent SEALs before him, glowering. He was nearly at a loss for words. As much as he wanted to chew into the crew even more, he let his silence do the talking. That seemed to be the most effective way to communicate his displeasure.

Heaving his rifle over his shoulder, he shot one last disappointed look, like the type of disappointed look that Daddy would give and marched off to his truck. They'd fucking train hard when he told them to, and if they were fucking lucky, he'd cut it short so they could show up to the goddamn ridiculous engagement party. It wouldn't be the first night of sleep deprivation for the fucking prima donnas.

Boots drumming the ground behind him told him that he was being shadowed. Warren ignored the sound, opening the back of his truck to begin peeling off sweaty body armor. He had places to be that morning.

"Chief." Crash's unmistakable voice found its way behind him.

"What's up?" Warren fired back, still undressing and unholstering his pistol.

"Name your price," Crash offered, strong and serious. His tenacity was inspiring.

"Price?" Warren spun, eyeing the junior SEAL, who was several years younger than him.

"Listen… I'll do anything. I've just got to get this done." Crash explained and referred to his fiancée. "I gave her my word."

Crash grew silent, stoically holding his weapon.

Warren shot the man a questioning look, but the junior SEAL didn't budge. He held strong. *That level of commitment is admirable, at least.* It would bode well for the many challenges he would face. And, really, Crash was a decent guy. Hard worker. An important part of the team.

Maybe he was being too hard on his guys.

A recurring pattern.

Crossing his arms, Warren assessed his unmoving subordinate, flexing his jaw as he did, acknowledging how important morale was for the platoon. Operational tempo wasn't fucking easy, and burnout was real. The ugly truth was that Warren had lost more friends on home soil, by their own hand, than at war. It was a horrific reality that disproportionately affected the SEALs in particular, given all that was demanded of them and all they continued to sacrifice.

Turning, a vision of Alisa flashed before his eyes as he chucked his chest plate on the back of his truck. He didn't know why, but thoughts of her just tempered him, like she had once before.

"Chief?" Crash pressed, respectfully.

"Fine—no work tonight," Warren resolved. "But tell the boys that they better not get too drunk, because they'll make up for it, double time."

"And you?"

"What about me?"

"Are you —?" Crash then stopped himself, shaking his head.

Warren leaned back, stern and waiting.

A telltale expression spanned Crash's face, telling Warren that the junior SEAL wasn't prepared to push any harder. *Good.*

"Get going before I change my mind," Warren said.

Crash nodded and spun, breaking into a run.

Warren unloaded his rifle, preparing it for transport. The battle rhythm had been decided — and in the back of Warren's mind, he knew it wasn't the worst thing. Crash's engagement party the next day and wedding just days later would give the platoon the chance to blow off some steam before blowing up some shit in Iraq.

Plus, he was giving Crash the best wedding gift he could — a chance to be a married man before he once again risked his life for his country. Some guys needed to know they had something back home, needed the security of marriage. Not him — He'd gotten married to the SEALs a long time ago. A cruel wife but rewarding as fuck. That was all he needed.

He hoisted himself up into his pickup, saluting the crew as they hastily piled into their vehicles.

"See you tomorrow, boss," Crash called out over the arid landscape.

Warren let out a sardonic laugh as his truck rolled away. *Tomorrow?* There was no way in fucking hell he was going to be at that engagement party for a thousand reasons.

He gripped the wheel of his truck then flipped on the music. *Classic country.* Hell, he'd been born and raised an Arizonian country boy, on a ranch and all. The windows down, air blowing through his truck, he inhaled the dry air of the desert morning, just his thing. The sun just popping over the horizon, Warren had about an hour's drive back to the city. *Bliss*.

Checking his black military watch, he saw he'd make it just in time for his morning rounds. Sure would—he was never late.

* * * *

The grumbling noise of Warren's navy-blue pickup truck polluted the snug streets of a typical So-Cal neighborhood not too far from where he hailed.

He slowed his speed, watching kids preparing to leave their homes on the way to school. The morning's rays were in full effect, compelling him to draw his dark sunglasses over his tired eyes. He'd been awake for over twenty-six hours, and counting, and was starting to feel wary.

Not that he'd admit it to anyone.

Pulling up in front of a pert yellow and white bungalow, he turned off his engine and jumped out of the truck. It was time to check in on the most important lass in his life. The powerful sound of the V8 had been enough to tip off his target that he'd arrived—a young girl, kindergarten age, ran out of the front door shrieking for him.

"I was afraid you wouldn't come!" The little girl beamed, soaring into his arms.

Tucking her blonde hair behind her ears, he knelt and tightened his arms around her in a big bear hug. Holding her air-tight against his chest, he reminded her, "Katy, when I tell you that I'll be here, I'll be here."

Standing up slowly, he kept her tiny little hand in his big one, waving at her mother in the doorway with his other hand.

"We better get on our way." He shot Brooke a tired grin. "I'll be back in a few."

Brooke smiled, waving back as Warren steered Katy down the cracked sidewalk toward her school.

"So, little miss—how's your day going?" He squeezed her soft hand as he held it in his paw.

She beamed up to him. "Good! I had Chex for breakfast!"

Warren let out an honest laugh, feeling her infectious optimism. She hummed a nursery rhyme as they walked the short distance to her school, like they did every morning when he was back on home soil. Going long stretches without seeing her was so damn brutal—and they'd been in that holding pattern for almost five years.

As they got a little closer to the school yard and he knelt down to give her a hug, she whispered into his ear.

"When are you leaving again?" Katy pulled back, blinking her bright blue eyes at him.

Her innocent question and expectant expression nearly drove him to choke. His throat constricted and face tightened, but he held it together.

"Soon," he admitted.

"But, why?"

"I told you, little miss. I have to go on a big plane to another place for a little while."

"Please, stay." Tears sprang to her eyes.

He leaned in, kissing her wispy, impish hair, holding her tiny skull underneath his. He couldn't watch her cry. Not again. *For fuck's sake.*

She sputtered. "Please, please, please—"

"Katy, I'm always here for you. I'm always going to be here for you," he assured her.

Katy looked down, kicking at a small rock.

In a small voice, she whispered, "I miss Daddy."

"I miss your daddy, too," Warren's voice grew gruff, crackling.

She licked her lips and a tear fell out. Warren grabbed her little body, squeezing her against him. He guessed Katy wouldn't even remember her dad. She'd been just a baby when he'd died. But, she still talked about how much she missed him. And Warren couldn't fucking stand it. He wanted to make everything bad go away. He'd never loved someone so much as he loved that little girl.

The bell tolled in the schoolyard, and Warren let out a deep breath, adjusting the straps on Katy's tiny pink backpack.

"Will you pick me up after school?" she tried to smile.

"I absolutely will." He grinned at her. "And it's Friday, so—"

"Ice cream!"

That seemed to clear the air, enough for the little girl to give him a big kiss on the cheek.

"I love you."

Then she ran off into the yard to meet her class.

Warren watched her go, that wild hair catching in the wind, just like her dad's. He couldn't believe it had been five years already. Life could be shit, he griped as he felt his shoulders flexing in latent anger. He refused to think about it and never did—nor did he talk about it.

Turning back up the sidewalk, he checked his watch, letting the horrible memories fall out of focus, clearing his mind. He was good at compartmentalizing.

It was the only way he survived.

Approaching his truck, he heard Brooke come up behind him. He spun, seeing her pull her sweater tighter around her form and standing at the edge of her grass.

"She's growing up fast, you know." Brooke narrowed her eyes on him.

"I can see that," he replied, crossing his arms.

"Maybe you should let some of these deployments go. Stay home and spend more time with her?"

"I can't."

Brooke tilted her head, questioning.

"I made a commitment." He held strong, unmovable.

"Geoff said that, too. Now he's gone." She pulled at her sweater nervously again, a haunted look overtaking her face.

Warren felt his limbs stiffening, as he studied her.

Brooke shot him an indicting look. "She misses you."

"She misses her father."

"You're all she knows."

Warren bit his tongue, not letting himself say what he really wanted to say. *I'm not her father.*

But Brooke seemed to know it anyway, the sneer emerging on her face. "Do you want her to grow up without a father figure?"

He refused to reply.

"Whatever," she resolved, waving her hand in the air dismissively. "Just go."

He didn't miss the shaking in her voice as she turned to walk back up her lawn. He watched, standing firm on the sidewalk. He should have reached out and grabbed her. He should have said he was sorry. He should have done anything, especially when he saw the telltale signs of her shoulders heaving, sobbing silently.

But he felt numb.

So, he let her go, and he turned back to his truck.

It was almost nine. He had to make it back home to receive his guest.

Chapter Seven

Alisa

Once again, Alisa found herself pulling up to a beautiful house in the Brixby Hill gated community — Warren's place. This time, she fidgeted with her black tank top, not because she didn't know what to expect but because she knew *exactly* what to expect. For someone who could be so cool and unfeeling, she was losing herself in emotion.

Her silver car huffed and puffed as it wheezed its way into his driveway, very clearly somewhere on its last legs. She reminded herself that she just had to get through the morning — get through her side of the deal — and everything would be fine. She'd walk away with a finished job, a payday and a fixed car. She had nothing to lose.

Right?

As soon as she stepped out of the car in tight black yoga capris that were ten times more modest that those previously worn hot shorts, she felt herself tremble. Waiting for her, Mr. Perfect cascaded down his stone steps in a fitted black T-shirt and boardshorts, sipping on some drink that looked deliciously cool. Nearly as delicious as he looked—tanned, muscular, rough. *Ready*.

"Morning," he grumbled at her, his own dark shades covering his eyes under the blistering sun.

"Hi," she replied, her heart thumping already.

Unable to get a read on him under his sunglasses, she nervously reached up and twirled her black ponytail, trying to find some great icebreaker to prove she knew how to talk to other humans. But, under his gaze, even her most basic functions froze. No words came to mind, so a nice, awkward silence ensued, and she felt herself choking on her own saliva.

Seemingly amused at her plight, he turned to his open garage, grabbing tools and what looked like a car part. He came back, motioning for her to toss him the car keys.

"Right," Alisa replied, kneeling and fumbling in her black purse. "The keys."

There were too many goddamn things in this bag, she silently complained to herself, trying to make it quick. Pushing aside a stethoscope and a book on magnetic imaging, she fingered the abyss for her keychain.

"Need a hand?" His shadow loomed over her, and she didn't mistake the amusement in his voice.

"I'm fine." She frowned at him.

Then, she realized that his hand was outstretched to her.

Finally feeling the sharp edges of her keys, she put her much smaller hand in his, allowing him to hoist her up. Unfortunately, she stumbled forward, stunned by his sheer strength, and found herself pushing off his chest. His lips curled in obvious self-satisfaction at her touch, but before she could say anything, he snatched the keys from her hand and paced toward the hood of her car.

"You know where the supplies are," he called back at her, gesturing toward the house. "Get at it."

"Right, okay," she murmured and uneasily twirled on the balls of her feet, marching to his front door, trying to remember her self-talk.

She just had to finish the house cleaning. Everything was going to be fine.

Just fine.

Catching the last glimpse of him before she shut the door behind her, she sucked in air so fast that she almost grew dizzy. He was leaning his hulking body over, digging into her engine—and there she was cleaning the remainder of his place. For a second, it almost made her feel like they were playing house.

But, as the door snapped shut, she shook her head. That was a hard 'no'.

Focusing on the job at hand and pushing her tedious thoughts aside, Alisa kept her eye on the prize. And, truthfully, it wasn't that painful to do—when he wasn't looming over her. Cleaning Warren's house was one of the easiest jobs she'd had that year. He was a tidy person, and his house looked barely lived in. The worst thing she saw was a lot of dust. The best thing she saw was a framed picture of a little blonde girl with bright blue eyes, hung in a place of honor in his kitchen. She suspected that the girl was his daughter, which made it all very sweet. Seeing the photo also gave Alisa a little extra security, knowing that whatever her attraction to Warren was, it was never going to go further than that.

However terrible she was with people, she was hopeless with kids. Dr. Zucker had drilled that home.

As she scrubbed and scrubbed, she had to readjust her ponytail several times, finally just tightening it up into a very messy bun. It wasn't pretty, but she was determined to do a top-notch job and needed all distractions to go away. She was nothing if not a perfectionist and workaholic.

And truly, she was so appreciative that someone was fixing her car for free that she wasn't going to let a speck of dirt or dust linger in Warren's home. As she moved quickly through her work, the air conditioning blasting through his house wasn't enough to keep her cool, and she felt a layer of dew amassing on her face and body.

Nearly done and finishing up the kitchen, she wiped her brow. A trickle of sweat ran down the back of her neck from her pinned-up bun. Her gaze drifted to the windowsill where a small invitation leaned against the glass. It was dark and solemn, and as she leaned in to read the words, she realized it was an invitation to a funeral.

A funeral that had happened five years ago.

Geoff?

A man who looked strong and healthy smiled back from the funeral card. If she had to guess, she'd say he was military, just like Warren, based on appearances alone. She wondered how he'd died and why Warren kept the card propped up, in plain view—like a reminder.

Gazing up through the window, she noticed Warren's fit frame in his backyard. He looked like he was clocking out, and she wondered if he had been able to replace the part successfully. God, she hoped so. She needed to conclude the morning as soon as possible before she did anything...*embarrassing*.

Folding her dirty cloth, she watched him wipe sweat off his brow with a grimy hand. If she felt a little turned on seeing that, then she absolutely died when he tore off his black T-shirt, giving Alisa a clear view of his naked torso.

Like, fucking *died*.

Her thighs quivering, and she grasped the edge of the countertop for stability. If nothing else, Warren proved to her that blood still pumped in her veins, and she'd been neglected for far too long. Like, four years too long. The gold chain was searing into her neck, the sham of her so-called engagement ring burning between her breasts, and for the very first time, she regretted her deal with Dean.

Studying Warren from the shadows, she saw a gorgeous tattoo sprawled across his upper back and over his shoulder, accentuating his rippling muscles. Every aspect of his body looked like a bronze statue, even with that massive scar that ran up the side of his back toward the top of his spine. It just made him look even more dangerous, more badass, like the type of man who could actually fight Dean and win.

Alisa fumbled backward, hitting the table behind her as she watched Warren run his hand absently up his cut abdomen. How was it even possible to have so much definition, she gasped as she gripped the counter so tight that she feared she was leaving imprints.

It was at that exact moment that Alisa realized she had to calm down—but still, *holy hell*. Warren...was something else.

Mr. Goddamn Perfect.

"I didn't know they made men like this," she groaned to herself, widening her eyes as he turned back to the house.

Her pussy immediately throbbed as his gaze seemed to penetrate the glass, screwing something hot right into her chest. Shit, the man made it hard to breathe. Dirty cloth still in hand and dazed, she stepped to the patio door, staring. He shot her a curt nod, beckoning her to him. *Ordering her.* Then he leaped into the pool, popping up and whipping his gleaming auburn hair back.

Why shouldn't she? *A thousand reasons.* Grumbling to herself, her body and mind at war, she opened the door slowly, peaking out like a timid kitten.

I can't.

"Coming out?" Warren called over to her, that same self-assured grin on his lips.

She stepped out, closing the door behind her carefully and fidgeting on the step. She had to wipe the thought of Dean from her mind, reminding herself that he was on the opposite side of the country for the time being. She was safe. It was a gated community. She could breathe.

"I'm finished," she reported to Warren, biting her lip as she watched his biceps bobbing in and out of the water.

An inevitable pause struck as he thrust himself up on the side of the pool, his muscles flexing in harmony.

"You sure about that?" he countered and nodded to the poolside patio table and chairs. "Looking a little grimy, don't you think?"

His bottom half still in the water, he looked her up and down with that same hungry look she'd gotten used to — the one she craved. He looked like a hunter and a protector — and she just felt safe with him.

With that, it was game on.

That familiar tugging at her lips told her that she was well under his spell. Unable to say no, she found herself bringing the cloth over to the glass top table and giving it a good wipe down. Just like a few days ago, she felt the heat of his gaze as he watched her scrub. And just like a few days ago, she felt a similar flush up her neck and cheeks, equal parts dying and coming alive.

To the stone steps at the edge of the pool, he leisurely walked up and out, letting all that water cascade down his rock-hard body. A little part of her wanted to cry. She couldn't help but wonder if he was getting back at her by teasing her harder than she'd ever teased him. As her lips parted, powerlessly drinking him in, she couldn't look away from his soaking wet boardshorts and how they clung to his package, revealing a thick manhood that made her quiver.

As if sensing his power over her, the clearly confident man seized a chair on his stone patio, swung it to him and sat down. Leaning back, he gazed at her with intensity and gestured to the table.

"Missed a spot."

Her mouth now fully agape, she glanced back at the table she'd just cleaned. So, that was the level he was playing at. A game she desperately wanted to win — she reached over the glass top, wiping toward her, letting him enjoy a full view of her ass in her tight yoga capris. Unlike before, she didn't hear him groan or squirm, and her disappointed gaze flitted back to him.

"I've got some bad news for you," Warren started.

"What... What do you mean?" Her body stilled as she waited, a deep sense of unease rising in her stomach.

His face grew dead serious. "Your car — I did what I could but it's going to die on you sooner rather than later unless you rebuild that engine."

Her mouth dropped, her head beginning to spin. "But that would cost..."

"Thousands."

"...just as much as just buying something else." She felt her shoulders drop.

She did not want to be stuck in a situation where she was having to sit on the bus for hours in the middle of the night after a long shift at the hospital. Not a chance — not in LA. Her car was the only thing getting her through it all.

But she didn't have *thousands*.

Warren leaned forward, glancing down at the tabletop, shaking his head as if she hadn't done a good enough job. His demeanor changed in a flash, thick tension spreading through the air between them, and Alisa realized that the game was back on.

"I might be able to help you." He slowly gazed back up at her, letting his lip curl in a sly grin.

Leaning back once again, he awaited her next move.

She knew he was waiting to see if she wanted to play. His words screamed across her mind, and a warning alarm went off. She knew was he was after — *quid pro quo*. Something she couldn't give him, undoubtedly. Stretching across the table, her mind racing, she wiped the glass again, a little more stiffly than the last time.

"My, my...can't you try a little harder than that?" His voice darkened, like a disappointed daddy. "I wouldn't think this is how you audition."

Audition — the word hit her. That's exactly what it had always been. *What had Maria been up to?*

"I—" she started, trying to defend herself. "I'm—"

He shook his head, cutting her off. "No...harder."

Again Alisa's thighs trembled, and she reached across the table, trying to work a little harder to get the distant spots. He had a way of making her need to play along.

"Harder," he demanded, reminding her of the fantasy she'd had of him the night before.

Dominating her, forcing her — making her scream his name.

As she stretched as far as she could, she heard him say, "That's it."

Heating up, getting dizzy under his velvety gaze, she found herself getting after it one last time, seductively reaching, dragging her breasts across the sparkling glass. Her conscious mind unable to figure out what she was doing, her warming body stilled for a second, in a way that pleaded *'do what you want with me'*.

And the way she slowly rolled back up, she was reassured she was sending the right message when she heard his breathing shift.

"Much better," he growled, like a proud daddy. "Good job."

Bashful but eager, she straightened, holding the cloth in her hands as she waited for further instruction.

"What about down here?" he nodded downward to the leg of the table, which happened to be situated right in front of his chair. He then pointed at the leg of his own chair, "And over here?"

Alisa bit her lip, feeling him continually push her out of her comfort zone. He was good at that. But then, he made it so damn easy to obey. He was good at that, too.

She slowly started wiping down the leg of the patio table right in front of him, bending over into a fold. Her ass up and tempting fate. She waited for his hot hand to reach out and touch her, but he didn't. He just shifted in his chair, adjusting his boardshorts. She knew it was wrong…all of it. But she couldn't stop herself. It felt too good. She wanted to hear him tell her that he liked what she was doing, again and again. Maybe she just wanted Daddy's approval.

She drew herself up, flickering her eyes at him, waiting for more.

"You might be able to help me?" she repeated his words from earlier, tilting her head to understand.

"Sure." He let his teeth graze over his lip.

"In exchange for?" She breathed out, almost afraid to hear the answer.

"Services."

"Cleaning services?"

He let out a dark laugh, nodding at her capris. "It's so damn hot out. Why don't you launch those? Jump in with me."

Her mouth dropped yet again, much to his amusement. He was clearly enjoying himself too much, testing her boundaries. Yet, so was she. The one thing she loved was receiving instruction…especially from a confident leader like him.

Without even letting herself think, she slid her fingers under the waist of her yoga capris, peeling them down her hips to reveal an athletic black thong. She hadn't expected to be showing off her naked ass that morning but was damn glad of her panty choice. There were far worse options at the bottom of her panty drawer.

As she slid the fabric of her yoga capris down, inch by inch, she watched his body stiffen and flex. He had a damn good poker face, but the pulsing in his boardshorts told her what his face wouldn't.

And, respectively, there was enough blood pulsing southward in her body.

"I shouldn't be doing this." A guilty grin dashed across her mouth.

"You're a grown-ass woman. Do what you want."

His words flushed over her, making her feel like maybe, just maybe, she could let herself slip up a bit. No one was going to know or hurt her. She was safe.

As she slid off her pants, she turned back to the patio table leg, doing the exact same thing as she had before—this time, just in her thong. It felt so good to be wearing a little bit less in the insane heat. Sweat immediately dewed and slipped down her legs. As if focused only on her task, as if it were normal to clean in a thong right in front of a client, she bent over with alacrity, letting her tailbone rise high in the air, giving him a perfect view of what was between her legs. She knew he liked that.

He groaned as she found the bottom of the table leg, and she scrubbed as hard as she could at dirt that didn't exist, just wishing he'd grab her hips and bring her ass right into his face. There was nothing her throbbing pussy wanted more in that moment that to feel his hot breath against her wet slit. The thought alone was pure fire. God, he was making her so damn aroused.

But Mr. Perfect maintained control, sitting back and just watching. She rose slowly, more provoked and needy than ever, feeling dazed by the broiling sun. *Damn him.* He knew how to drive her crazy. The heat from the scorching LA summer was only outdone by the heat between their bodies, heaving as they stared at each other.

Crouching down, she felt the blood rushing from her head. Taking in a deep breath so she wouldn't faint, she proceeded to run the cloth down the arm and leg of the chair he was sitting in. Flickering her dark eyes up into his ice-blue ones, she wished he'd just make a move and put her out of her misery. He was damn near going to make her faint from anticipation alone. Pressing her breasts together, her face came closer and closer to his crotch, wanting more than anything to rip back those boardshorts and taste what was underneath.

But she wouldn't dare.

Not without his permission.

It seemed he was thinking the same thing, shooting out his rough hand and grabbing her jaw, inches from his cock.

"You're damn good at this," he growled as he gazed down on her, licking his lips. "What else are you good at?"

Alisa couldn't help but laugh, searching a little too long for a clever comeback. The heat, the scene — she had grown seriously dizzy.

"You sure have lots of questions," she breathed out the only thing she could think of, bobbing on slippery, sweaty legs before him.

"Hell yeah. Next question is — what am I going to do with this hot as fuck chick on her knees before me?"

The question burned across her mind, the provocative question unsteadying her. She stumbled back, black stars rushing over her vision. Hazy, she grasped at the table for stability, but her hand didn't quite get a good grip. Whatever gracefulness she'd pretended to have evaporated in a flash as she nearly passed out right in front of him, her body buckling and stumbling. But, with his sturdy grip, he found her, hoisting her whole body up against him with ease.

Standing toe to toe, his other hand came around the back of her neck as he held her, massaging her back to reality. His face had switched from turned on to deeply concerned.

"You okay?"

"Yeah," she grimaced, leaning into him.

Under Mr. Perfect's gaze, Alisa grew painfully embarrassed. *Smooth — real smooth.* In one fell swoop, she'd ruined the moment. She pressed her trembling hands into his still-wet chiseled chest. Guilt ran rampant over her, sobering her.

Warren drew her body a few feet past the edge of the pool toward a picturesque poolside shower that had been built into lush flora. She remained silent, obedient — wishing she could shrink away. Flipping on the cool water, he rinsed the back of her neck, kneading spasming muscles, more like medical triage than intimacy. Maybe it was the tension she'd carried for years, maybe it was nearly fainting, but he was finding knots in her neck that she didn't know existed.

"Wow, that feels good," she mumbled, between his skilled hands and the cool water.

"Good."

Exhaling deeply as he worked her neck, he ran his other hand down the side of her body, holding her wobbling body steady. The concern in his eyes never left, in fact, it only seemed to get worse.

"What— Did you almost pass out?"

"Um—yeah."

"You need water." He tilted her mouth to take in the cascading water falling on them.

She opened her mouth, closing her eyes, feeling the cool water filling her. Swallowing, she opened her eyes to see his heated gaze locked on her, totally turned on. She didn't move but kept on. That split second was pure bliss. And she just wanted to enjoy the last two seconds of whatever that was.

Finally, he pulled her close, running his rough hands over her as he assessed for lucidity.

"I think we'd better call it a day."

"You want me to go?" she squeaked.

As he held her inches from him, Warren trailed his gaze down her lips and neck.

He reluctantly let out, "It's been fun—but let's take a tactical pause."

She angled her head, questioning. She wrapped her long fingers around his, drawing his eyes back to hers.

"We both know where this is going." He plucked the gold chain out of her cleavage, running his fingers along her engagement ring, as if testing it to make sure it wasn't from a cereal box.

"You must think I'm a terrible person," she said quietly.

"Only God can judge you." Still, he held her engagement ring as if he were ready to rip it off.

"It's a complicated thing."

"I'm not asking you to explain." The way he focused on her told her everything.

That's when she knew that the ball was in her court. Once again, she recognized she shouldn't — but something about Warren was too damn addictive. Warren held her so captive that he made her almost forget she'd grown to be someone else's prisoner.

"I don't want to go," she bit her lip, not sure what was happening to her but just not wanting it to be over.

He grazed his bottom lip with his perfect teeth before dropping his head a little closer to hers.

"I've got seven days," she whispered so low that she barely heard herself through the rainfall shower, "before he's back."

Before I'd be too scared to do this.

"Seven days?" Warren growled, reaching up to grab the back of her wet head. "Hell, wouldn't that be fate."

"Fate?" She felt her lips tingling as she stared into his hungry eyes.

Warren pulled her face down to his, hovering. He waited a second then breathed onto her lips.

"I've just got seven days, too."

Before she could ask, he closed the gap, kissing her rough and heartily. Drawing her tongue out and onto his lips, tasting and toying with her, he wove his fingers into her messy bun, ripping it partially out of its place. She felt long strands of hair pouring down her back with the water as he deepened his kiss, heavy with lust and desire.

Her shower fantasy hadn't done the reality justice.

Dominant as hell, he easily had her submit to him, wordlessly expressing everything he wanted to do to her. She could tell right away that she liked how he played. Her skin tingling, she melted into his thick arms, letting him hold her soaking body and run his hands down to squeeze her ass. He was in control, moving her like a doll.

Seemingly listening to her body and hearing her responses, he ran his hands up and down her frame, teasing and testing every part of her, just to feel how she liked it. As she moaned and twisted, she felt his throbbing cock in front of her, promising her more fun. It was clear what type of lover he'd be.

Heaving up her leg so he could better cup her cheeks, his mouth never parted from hers, arousing her more and more with his delicious tongue. She could only imagine what he could do with a tongue so skilled.

Just as he toyed with the back of her thong, a loud crack hit his backyard fence — the sound of the gate being flung open. Warren snapped his gaze over, hauling Alisa's body protectively behind him, defending her against whomever was coming in. As he yanked the water of the shower off, his muscles tensing to fight, Alisa crumbled in fear, immediately fearing the worst — Dean. *He's going to kill me.*

Over Warren's shoulder, she barely could see anything — until the intruder marched farther into view. High and mighty, a fit man shorter than Warren with receding brown hair stopped six feet into the backyard, his hands on his hips.

Alisa released a tight breath.

It wasn't Dean, but she didn't know who it was. *Someone from the club?*

"Chief," the man addressed Warren, his eyes wide as he took in the scene. "Catching you at a bad time?"

Warren grew fiercely silent, and Alisa gathered two things. First, the guy was there for Warren, not her. Secondly, something was really wrong. She shrank back, feeling the tension between the two men, wishing she were anywhere else. *I shouldn't be here.*

Chapter Eight

Warren

"Gaudet—what the fuck?" Warren pushed Alisa farther back behind him, needing to shield her.

Of all the years he'd been enlisted, he'd never seen such fucking audacity.

"Chief, I didn't want to do this. Don't get me in shit," Gaudet said.

Warren's cold gaze intensified, sending a message. "Too late."

Insistent, Gaudet waved his hands in the air. "Boss, look… The engagement party is tomorrow. I'm the best man. I promised Crash I'd get you there."

"It's not my thing," Warren countered, keeping his cool. "I made that clear."

Over-trained, Warren's threatening gaze didn't leave this opponent's face as his mind worked through options for getting rid of him. Alisa didn't need to get dragged into his shit. That was all that mattered. Why was the goddamn engagement party such a big fucking deal, anyway? Who gave a shit? The more they wanted him there, the more suspicious he became.

"So, this your girlfriend?" Gaudet stepped forward with a scheming look, trying to get an angle to judge Alisa. "She can come, you know. You can bring her."

Warren held Alisa behind him, firing a cautioning look at Gaudet, then at the gate. "Get going."

"Come on, boss. You've got to live a little." Gaudet cocked his head, and Warren had no doubt unhealthy machinations swirled in the guy's mind.

Warren wouldn't have it. He shook his head dismissively and held his ground. "You want to test me, kid?"

"Look, boss. If your entire team will be there, except you" — Gaudet thought aloud — "how does that look?"

"Crash's wedding is not a team event," Warren retorted fast and hard. "It's time for you to leave."

"The guys need you. Crash needs you," Gaudet urged. "I've got to get you there. We have all been through a lot together."

Warren jutted out his jaw, biting his comeback. He had something to fucking say about that, but Gaudet was not the type he cared to get into a debate with. Gaudet didn't fucking get it, as much as he pretended he did. So, Warren left the man with his signature cold-as-fuck death stare, making it damn clear that he wasn't going to engage with terrorists. Most sane people got the message pretty damn quick.

But apparently Gaudet wasn't a sane person.

And so Gaudet kept pushing.

"Morale is low," Gaudet said. "If you keep riding us so hard, you aren't going to have many left — "

Seeming to realize he'd hit a nerve, he halted.

Warren kept his body unmoving, his face stern and he said nothing else. The silence in his backyard became deafening. And just like he'd expected, Gaudet eventually got the message. His grin wavering, he finally realized it was over and turned on his heels to leave.

Warren mulled over all sorts of sick options to punish the rookie. No one came at him like that and lived to tell the tale. It was going to be a fun weekend at work.

But in the back of his mind, Warren knew that Gaudet had hit close to the truth. Pressure rising, operational tempo was throttling forward — hard — and team morale was dropping. Recruitment wasn't as easy. Warren couldn't let that stand. He had to be part of the solution.

Hand on the gate, Gaudet stopped dead in his tracks, shooting Warren one last conspiratorial look over his shoulder. The unabashed gall was almost amusing. *Almost.*

"I'm telling everyone that you're coming and that you're bringing her. You've got to learn to take a break, Chief."

Warren let out a furious growl as Gaudet spun and marched out, slamming the gate in his wake. The rookie had no idea what was coming for him. Warren wasn't going to make it nice.

"Fucking brutal." Warren rotated to find his guest. "Who wants a goddamn break?"

Drawing Alisa in, he assessed her for damage, as if they'd just survived a brutal firefight. Finding the gorgeous creature still dripping wet, her bright brown eyes flickered at him in surprise as he touched her chin. Then, running his hands down her arms, he finally released her, like his shoulders had been flexed for too goddamn long.

"Wow." Alisa pushed herself farther back, shaking him off. "That was intense."

"We're an intense group."

"He seemed pretty concerned about you? He was being brave…"

Her voice trailed as he fired a warning look.

"He was being insubordinate," Warren said.

Warren could see the wrong kind of emotion flushing over Alisa's face and knew the fun had just been sucked out of the morning. Bullshit had a tendency to do that.

"I should go." She stepped over to pick up her discarded yoga pants.

Standing back, processing, Warren watched as she fumbled to pull the stretchy fabric on over her damp legs. Clearly frazzled and trying to get out of his sight, she was moving too fast to be graceful, once again losing her balance and grasping at the table's edge. Enjoying the much-needed diversion, a grin crossed his lips as he watched her — a bit clumsy, a bit cool — yet, so damn authentic. He could tell she hated all that about herself.

Finally dressed, she paced right past him toward the gate, trying to make a break for it. Her still-averted gaze and flushed cheeks told him everything about how embarrassed she was.

Hell, she was charming.

"Hey." He shot out his long arm, not willing to let her walk out of his life.

She trembled slightly, flashing her eyes up to him, silently pleading to let her go.

"Your car —" he began.

"I'll figure something out." She fidgeted with her hands. "I really shouldn't."

For the first time, Warren saw a little more than nerves. He saw fear just a scratch beneath the surface. *What's she scared of?*

"When I said I might be able to help you out, I meant it," he said, shifting to square himself to her.

"I don't know," she responded. "I'm maxed out on hidden strings."

Warren let out a low laugh. "I'll tell you the strings upfront. It won't be charity. It will be a transaction."

"Transaction?"

"How about—I buy you a new car," he stated, studying her reaction. "That's what you'll get out of this."

"What?" She froze. "You can't be—?"

"I'm very serious, and I can be very convincing." Warren stepped forward, reaching his hand out to touch her jaw again.

Her eyes wide as hell, the way she seemed to fall into his touch told him everything he needed to know.

"In exchange for what?" she whispered.

"Look... I've got a week. And I'm not a relationship type of guy."

"So—?"

"So, give me the girlfriend experience...for seven days."

Firming his grasp on her jaw, he angled her face up toward his, enjoying her feminine beauty. She had a look he craved—and a body he wanted to devour. He had a feeling she'd provide him that extra something he needed before his tour.

"Wait— What do I have to do?" she asked.

"Only whatever you want."

"Like?"

He shrugged. "Come with me to this damn party tomorrow. I need to get them off my back."

"I—I'm probably not the best to bring along," she said as she tried to smooth her wild hair into one manageable piece. "I'm not great at...meeting new people."

His eyebrow quirked, and a competitive grin crossed his lips. "You were great at meeting me. And you're fucking hot and cool. They'll love you."

"No, you don't understand—"

He reached out, taking her thin hand in his thick one, challenging her. "Prove me wrong."

His gaze locked with hers, issuing a reminder. If she was in for a penny, she sure as hell was in for a pound. The way she paused, searching his face, leaning into him slightly, told him that she was genuinely interested—that she wanted him just as much as he wanted her. But the way she then pursed her lips told him she was looking for an excuse to not.

He didn't blame her one bit.

"You don't feel bad faking it?" Alisa nervously licked her bottom lip, flickering her dark, seductive lashes at him.

She was testing him, and he knew it.

"That's what makes it more appealing," he growled, running his thumb across her bottom lip, his gaze falling to her engagement ring. "Because we both know that this can't happen for real."

"All the fun and none of the commitment?"

"Exactly." His eyes darkened, looking into her. "Something tells me that you need it, too."

She darted her eyes left and right across his face, considering it. It was clearly an offer she couldn't refuse. Her lips parted, but it became clear to Warren that, like him, she didn't really want to think. It could all be so simple.

She was so damn wickedly hot. He tightened his fists at his chest, barely able to contain himself. But Warren knew he had to keep his cool. Now that considerable money was involved, things were going to be different.

Alisa's gaze flashed to the gate, like she was trying to decide if she should run. But the decision was made for them both. His cell phone rang at the patio table.

"Seven days?"

"Okay," she finally whispered, a little smile curling at the side of her lip.

Deciding between kissing her again and taking the call was harder than he expected.

"Fuck," he groaned, turning to grab his work cell.

Answering, he had to stifle one last grunt as he had the pleasure of watching Alisa's sweet fucking tail disappear out of his backyard gate. And it immediately hit him. It was going to be damn hard keeping his hands to himself.

Chapter Nine

Alisa

Alisa searched desperately for an outfit that a fake girlfriend of a SEAL would wear to an engagement party with a bunch of people she didn't know. Then she melted down to the aging hardwood of her apartment and ran her hands over her face in defeat. The party... Well, there was no chance that she was going to come out unscathed. It wouldn't take long before someone asked what exactly she was doing there...with a guy like him.

"How am I going to pull this off?" she asked herself, shaking her head. "I was stupid to agree to this."

She had no idea what had gotten into her. Something about her fiancé being on the opposite coast had given her a false confidence. If he found out what she was doing, he'd lose it. That wouldn't be pretty.

Alisa talked some sense into herself. She'd have to end the deal—focus on her qualifying exams the next month, focus on getting a residency. And her car? She'd sleep at the hospital if she had to. Apparently there were beds open in the morgue.

Hell, she'd be the morgue's newest resident if her fiancé caught on.

Envisioning her cold, dead body on a stretcher, Alisa jumped as her cell rang. Checking the display, she suspected it was Warren—calling again from a blocked ID.

"Hello," she shakily answered the call, preparing to punt him off.

"I'm outside."

As Warren's baritone came through the line, she jumped as she heard a knock at the door to her second-story walk-up apartment. She hadn't heard the telltale creaking on the metal outdoor stairs, but then again—her head been stuck in her closet for a while. And, he was a fucking ninja.

"Is it unlocked?"

She let out an uncomfortable laugh. "You must be kidding. This is LA."

It didn't take her more than five seconds to glide from her closet over to the heavy white door that sealed her into her tiny one-bedroom apartment. She'd have to figure out a way to tell him she couldn't go.

After sliding the lock, she opened the door.

But she wasn't prepared for what was on the other side.

Warren stood there, tall and built as usual, dressed up in tailored black chinos and a dark green button-up shirt. With the sleeves just slightly rolled up, his expensive-looking watch was shadowed by his ornate tattoos that spilled onto the tops of his hands. His auburn hair was slicked back, and his five-o-clock shadow delivered that dangerous look. It was just the right kind of scary — enough to chase away her demons.

"You're not ready," he pointed out, eyeing her in her oversized T-shirt and shorts. "Or, are you?"

Alisa beamed, enjoying his humor. But she forced a serious expression.

"Are you going to let me in?" Warren asked.

"Listen... I'm sorry you drove all this way — "

"No, don't start with that. If I'm going, you're going."

"I can't."

"Why?" He crossed his arms, sturdy and unmoving.

She flinched as she heard a car backfire in a distant parking lot. He raised his eyebrow, analyzing her. The way he watched her, seeming to care, reinforced that same feeling she had before, like he was protective already of her. That was the only way it could work.

"What's it going to be?" he asked.

"Okay. Fine."

God help me.

She turned back into her apartment, shaking her head. She was digging herself a grave, but he stirred things in her. Inexplicable things. Some risks were worth taking — especially if it were to be her last.

Warren trailed in her wake, making his way behind her into the bedroom. She'd never heard footsteps that heavy on her crackling wood floors, and it occurred to her that Warren was officially farther into her apartment than her fiancé had ever been.

Standing in front of her bed, she exhaled slowly, pulling the loose elastic from her shiny straight black hair, letting the long locks flow down over her shoulders. She didn't miss how Warren's eyes twinkled in response, driving a tingling sensation up and down her body.

"We've got to get going soon." He checked his watch.

Even just the way his arms flexed as he tilted his thick wrist made her stir. She let out a long, hopefully relaxing, exhalation.

"I'm having trouble...figuring out what to wear," she confessed, turning to her closet.

She dreaded that moment, the first of many to come. Sooner than later, he was going to see for himself what her shortcomings were — and why making the deal with her was not his finest choice.

But Warren just laughed, sitting down on her double bed, leaning over. He seemed unfazed.

"Show me what you've got."

The anticipation in his eyes reminded her of her so-called audition. He liked it when she put on a show. He liked to watch her. Turning back to her closet, she bit her lip. She wasn't good at his game.

But she obeyed. She naturally wanted to follow him. There was security in submitting to a man like him.

Reaching in, she sifted through her top options — pants, blouses, knee-length skirts — pulling them out and showcasing them to him one by one — all the stuff she wore in med school. And, one by one, he dismissed them. Frustrated, she slammed the last one back in. No, she wasn't a fashionista, but surely things weren't that bad?

"I'm learning something about you right now," he said.

"What...? What's that?"

"That you're a big fucking nerd, aren't you?" He shot her a heart-melting grin. "Do you do *anything* outside of school and work?"

She opened her mouth to contend—but she knew it would be fruitless. She'd spent the past four years buried in textbooks. She had no social life.

"I'm sorry," she whispered.

"Don't be. I like that. I'm married to my work, too."

Her mouth dropped, and her mind spun. He couldn't have just said that.

"Don't you have a dress? Or something less...daytime." He drew his hand across his jaw, tracking the rough stubble there.

"Well, there is something." She reached to the far back, finding a black dress she'd worn to her cousin's wedding two summers before.

It was cute, kind of casual and looked like fire on her. The only problem was that it was one size smaller than she'd prefer. She flashed the hanging garment at him, seeming to draw a heated response.

"Put it on," he growled, leaning forward a little more.

Alisa's gaze darted to the washroom and back to him. *Does he want... Does he want me to strip in front of him?* She toyed with the zipper of the dress nervously, her lips pouting to make words that would never come.

"Look... We made a deal." He read her mind and nodded to the washroom. "But you don't have to do anything you don't want to do. You make your own choices."

"Okay," she said and took a step away from him, trying not to blush.

Maybe she wanted him to be a little more savage about it. Maybe she wanted to feel.

Her gaze flashing back at him, she observed him watching her. His blue eyes cut into her—reminding her who was leading. Something about him made her never want to walk away.

"That said, if you want to play a game, we could keep things interesting tonight," he concluded. "Since this party is bound to be fucking excruciating."

"A game?"

"There would be rules. I have a feeling you love rules."

Sure do.

"Like?" She turned to square herself to him, still holding the dress, waiting on his every word.

Warren leaned back, resting his hands on his thighs. His arms and shoulders flexed slightly as he assessed her, like a predator waiting to take down his prey. He had read her right, that was for sure.

"You better start thinking of your safeword." His teeth grazed his bottom lip.

Flushed, Alisa let out an anxious laugh, clutching the dress tighter to her body. *A safeword?* The way that rolled off his lips drove something wild inside her. And she realized…that was his way of having fun.

"You want to play? Safeword first."

"Magnetic."

He grinned in response. Something flickered in his eyes.

"What's rule number one?" She exhaled, focused only on him.

"Take that off"—he motioned to her T-shirt and shorts—"and put the dress on. Right here."

His movements stilled as he waited for her.

It took her all of three seconds before she dropped her loose shorts, exposing a lacy thong in a caramel color that matched her golden-brown skin. Then, she hauled her T-shirt over her head, letting it drop onto the scratched floor as her gold chain danced around her neck. Her matching bra, lacy and uplifting, gave her cleavage that she could only dream of—cleavage that absorbed the engagement ring she wanted to pretend didn't exist.

"Great—you're ready." He slapped his thighs. "Let's go."

Alisa fumbled forward, nervously giggling. "Stop. Please stop."

He grabbed her hand as she fell forward, pleading with him. Intertwining her fingers with his, he pulled her down a little more until he could breathe on her. He smelled so damn good. And, God, she could never get enough of those cold blue eyes—eyes that she was sure had seen a lot.

"The rule is…I'm the boss."

She let out a sigh as he ran his hand up her thigh, giving her the chills.

"Now, get that damn dress on," he growled at her, licking his lips as he savored her cleavage. "Before you make me fuck you."

And so she did.

Slipping into the super tight mini-dress, she pulled the thin straps up her shoulders, adjusting the fabric to cover her ass.

"It's perfect," he said definitively, nodding. "You're perfect."

"Come on."

It was someone else's style, she thought, catching a glimpse of herself in her cheap over-the-door mirror. She drew her long hair over her shoulder, shaking her head at her reflection.

He wrapped his firm grip around her waist, heaving her backward, forcing her to fall into his lap. He held her arm with one hand, her face with the other — turning her to look at him and only at him. She didn't miss the approval in his eyes.

"I can't wear this," she said.

The harder he gripped her jaw, staring down into her eyes, the more he drew a little grin across her lips. It was so wrong how much she enjoyed it when he overpowered her. All she could fantasize about was how savage she could make him.

"How about we revisit a blouse and jeans combo?" she said.

"No — the dress."

"*Warren* —"

"Are you challenging me?" he demanded.

"No," she whispered, playing into the game.

"You mean — no, *Sir*," he growled.

A pause between them, and all Alisa could feel was his steady breathing and the wetness pooling in her lacy panties. There was no denying how much she wanted to feel him over her.

"The dress," he said again. "Don't change."

She bit her lip. "Yes, Sir."

Alisa grasped that if she wanted to play the game, she just had to own it and be the hot-blooded woman that apparently still lived, if not just deep inside. There was no halfway anymore.

"I should finish getting ready." She tried to get up.

He slammed her back onto his rock-hard thighs again. Authoritative. Commanding.

"You mean — can I please finish getting ready?" He stared into her eyes, heated and intense. It was clear that she wasn't the only person getting aroused.

"Can I please finish…getting ready, Sir?" Alisa replied slowly, trying not to look like she was melting on top of him.

"Hurry the fuck up," he snarled as he pushed her up, leaving her in his wake as he headed toward the front door. "And don't forget the heels."

The glint of intensity in his eye caught her off guard—the last look he gave her before he marched through her door, ostensibly heading down to start his truck. Hearing the roaring sound in the parking lot, she validated that was the case. Everything suddenly became so surreal.

He was waiting for *her*. To take *her* to a party. To present *her* as his girlfriend.

Twenty-five years of life on the earth, and she'd never experienced anything like it. She'd never seen anyone like *him*. How was she going to pull it off for seven days?

"Well, once this blows up in my face, it will just prove what I already know. There are some things I'm great at and some things I'm not—" her voice trailed as she caught herself in the mirror again.

For the first time in forever, she saw herself, and wondered if she was meant to be something more. That's when she realized that she was about to get a lot more than she bargained for in their little deal. And hopefully—just hopefully—it wasn't going to end up shattering her.

Chapter Ten

Alisa

"I've never been up here before," Alisa said, running her finger along the passenger window in Warren's pickup truck. No dust. She wasn't surprised.

She took in the wild range around her. It was absolutely breathtaking. Higher up, into the mountains framing the LA basin, the air grew drier, more arid with every mile. And the population grew scarcer, as did the amenities. It struck Alisa as an odd setting for an engagement party.

"Wrightwood?" he asked, turning down a long, dark street. "Not much to see."

"Then, why are we here?"

He didn't reply.

She glanced at her cell. Reception was getting thin, and dead spots were becoming more frequent.

She continued, "Should I be nervous that you are carting me into the desert?"

"You're funny."

"I'm serious."

Warren grinned. "Guys on my team live up this way."

"But, you're a SEAL—"

"So?"

"*So*, SEALs train down the coast, out of the Navy base on Coronado, right? That's not really a secret." Alisa turned to him, recalling the few facts she knew about the Navy's elite special forces.

"Yeah, we are stationed there."

"This must be a little far to commute all the way to San Diego."

He just shook his head—clearly unwilling to reveal anything more.

She pursed her lips to ask, but something about his flexing arms told her to stop. She arched an eyebrow as she realized that she was getting a little too close to something she shouldn't know. She wondered if he was working up there...somewhere off the grid. Anything was possible. What did she really know about Warren?

Yucca trees peppered the gritty land. In the setting sun, she swore she saw the reflection of tiny eyes emerging from holes. But she couldn't focus as they whipped by. Turning in her seat, Alisa caught on to something unusual—a high-security gate off the side of the road, high-tech looking.

"What was that?" Twisted in the seat, she was losing sight of it already.

Warren shrugged, adjusting his watch. "Who knows."

"Who knows?" Alisa mused. "I bet you know."

His side-long glare told her to stop. So, she kept going.

"Could it be a secret military training facility?" She leaned over his way.

Sure enough, a clear threat crossed his face. "You want to start off the night like this? Just give me a reason to bend you over my knee, pull that dress up and —"

Then he raised his hand like he was ready to release the spanking of her life. She shrunk down a few inches, unable to wipe the grin off her face. *Maybe that's exactly what I want.*

"Keep smiling. You'll regret it," he said.

She bit her lip to stay silent, for the moment. She wasn't scared. He was just too damn hot right then, gripping the wheel, looking ferocious. She didn't want to interrupt and sat back to enjoy the view.

She hadn't had the chance to kill off her smile before he turned into a long driveway of a ranch-style home. A dozen cars and pickup trucks were parked alongside the driveway, leading up to the house, twinkling with lights. He parked at the end of the row and turned around to her.

"Let's get this over with," he said.

She didn't miss the unease that had crept into his eyes and his slow, methodological exhale, like he was preparing himself. It was the first time she'd ever seen him that way.

"This should be fun." Alisa gripped her tiny cross-body purse, fiddling with the strap.

"Like hell."

"Well, certainly not with that attitude."

Hand on the door, ready to jump out, Warren shot her one last sultry glare. "That's why you're here — to make it fun. Isn't that what a girlfriend would do?"

"You don't know?" Alisa asked.

"It's been a while," he said.

Before she could say anything back, the man was already out of the truck. She stepped out, walked around then stopped in front of him, adjusting her dress. He stilled, taking her appearance in once again, but that time was like the first time he ever had. It was like he absorbed every detail, trailing up and down her frame. The coolness in his eyes warmed, just a touch, and he held out his hand.

"Ready?"

"Ready as I'll ever be," she said.

Reaching out to take his hand, weathered and calloused, every overstimulated nerve in her body threatened to implode. He ushered her up the long driveway, shooting her occasional glances fueled by lust and desire. She grasped that she was starting to feel something she shouldn't.

Lock it down, Alisa.

"So, how do we know each other?" she broke through the silence.

"Narcotics Anonymous."

"*Warren.*"

"Just be cool. You'll be fine." He laughed her off.

"Famous last words."

Her heart had started beating too fast that evening, and she self-diagnosed as suffering from spontaneous tachycardia. Perhaps she would be needing a bed in the morgue sooner than expected, and she spiraled as he drew her up to the brilliantly lit front door.

She took a deep breath as he knocked, not hesitating to open it, and push her inside a loud room full of striking, energized people—people that she wouldn't have anything in common with. It felt like everyone in that space was lively and social—and *relaxed*. That was the exact moment where Alisa's body tensed into an ice cube. She just wanted to melt back into her textbooks, melt back into her apartment—where it was safe, where things wouldn't change. Everything in her mind screamed—what was she doing?

Get out.

"Sir." A young-looking man nodded at Warren as they entered.

Curt, Warren greeted him, along with many other young men who stood stiffly, respectfully acknowledging what Alisa could only guess was their superior officer. Most of them seemed partially in shock that he was even before their eyes. In fact, as Warren escorted her through the throngs toward the back of the house, it occurred to Alisa that Warren appeared to be superior in rank to…all the men.

Her gaze flitted up to him, the realization dawning on her. He was used to being in charge. And, if that wasn't going to turn her crank all the way up, she didn't know what would. Suddenly, she felt the metal of her engagement ring burning her skin, hidden underneath her dress. *Don't feel guilty. Dean has cheated on you since the day he gave you this.*

Finally, they found their way into the kitchen, and some drunken blonde woman screamed. "Warren!"

The woman raised her arms, clearly already drunk. She ruthlessly pushed her friends aside, angling to wrap her arms around him, flipping her blonde hair back as she did.

"You came! Crash isn't going to believe it," the woman said.

"Jen." He offered one sharp icy nod and promptly tugged Alisa into him.

"Oh, right." Jen stopped dead in her tracks, surprise flashing across her perfectly painted face, but corrected herself and offered a fake bright white smile.

"Gaudet mentioned that you have a girlfriend?"

"Yeah, this is Alisa," Warren said. His arm remained protectively across her.

Before Alisa could open her mouth, she was already being assaulted.

"So nice to meet you. Have you met anyone?" Jen grabbed Alisa's hand without so much as asking, foisting her into a group of women hovering around the kitchen island.

Alisa fell into the edge of the quartz, observing the disapproving faces of the women surrounding it. They all looked pretty damn similar. They all looked like So-Cal girls. She felt immediately like an outcast, despite having been born and raised in LA.

"This is Warren's new girlfriend." Jen smirked, as if feeding her to the hounds. "Have fun."

Then Jen flicked her long, bleached hair, spinning back to Warren and yanking him away as she loudly exclaimed that they would go see her fiancé. Alisa felt like a puppy being dropped off, wondering if she'd ever see him again. His gaze darted back to Alisa, mouthing that he'd be back in a minute.

Just be cool. Only a minute.

Alisa's heart rate rose even higher, and she wasn't totally sure she'd last long. Turning back to the group of women, she felt her anxiety screaming higher and higher. She danced her fingers on the quartz, looking for interesting textures.

One of the women at the island flashed pictures of her baby at the group, talking about it had just hit a milestone or something. The chatter continued, and Alisa struggled to keep track. As someone pushed a glass of white wine at her, she tried to decode the last comment made, but the women kept moving through topics — babies, mothering, daycare.

"How many do you want?" A brunette turned to Alisa, raising her eyebrow and looking in the direction where Warren had gone. "Fine stock like him, I'd think you'd want to have as many as you can."

"Have as many...what?" Alisa tilted her head, a little confused.

"Babies!" Another woman laughed, as if Alisa couldn't be serious.

The other women around the island chuckled, and Alisa found herself shaking her head. She should have just lied to them, but she didn't. She didn't fake it. And that was her first mistake.

"I don't want any," Alisa said.

Her words were met by radio silence. In fact, several of the other women's mouths dropped. Alisa cringed, hating her own reply. *They don't understand.*

"I'm just not like that," Alisa added, as if she had to defend herself.

"Does he know that?" The brunette confronted her, eyes wide open, searching between Alisa and the hallway where Warren went. "I'd disclose that upfront, if I were you."

Alisa shook her head, unsure how to respond. She chewed her lip and finally just admitted, "I'm more career focused. That's my thing."

But around the island, they did not seem to buy in. Eyes glazed over, and she could tell she was being rejected. Then the chittering started.

"Wow, I didn't expect he'd go for that. His last girlfriend was like *Miss Homemaker*," said one.

Another leaned in conspiratorially. "He's like a totally different person now."

"Well, I made a choice to give up my career and focus on supporting Travis," said a woman with dark blonde hair. She proudly beamed at the rest of the ladies. "That was the only way it would work since we wanted kids. He's a real family man, always has been."

"I knew what I was getting into when I married a SEAL," another agreed, then let out a girlish giggle, clearly a little tipsy.

"You can't have three young kids, a husband on back-to-back deployments and still make partner at the firm," the first chimed back in, cutting Alisa completely out of the conversation. "Unless you want your kids to be raised by a nanny, which I don't."

Alisa opened her mouth to say something but realized she had been forgotten. She felt her body floating backward into the empty space in the kitchen. Alisa could just barely hear that the conversation between the women went on without her at the island, and she was thankful for that. She wanted to stop being seen.

Zoning out, Alisa gulped back whatever wine was left in her glass. She winced at thoughts running wild through her mind. As much as she'd left the island, she'd promptly created her own—an island of one. Hovering by herself, hoping to disappear, she gazed around, mortified that Warren would catch her being anti-social. People were talking, drinking, laughing everywhere around her. *What are they talking about? How am I supposed to talk to them?* Her gaze darted from left to right, finding herself increasingly disconnected from the present.

She felt motionless, suspended in mid-air, observing a room she wasn't really in. She couldn't drum up the energy to paint on a fake smile. She didn't want to talk to anyone. She didn't want anyone to talk to her. She just wanted to be alone, in the middle of that loud, busy party. So, she cowered — afraid of what that meant.

"Hey." A warm, strong hand pressed onto her lower back.

She flinched and turned to find Warren's ice-blue eyes bearing into her.

"You okay?" he asked.

Her head bobbed, but her lips remained sealed. Clutching her empty wine glass for dear life, she felt the urge to run, even from him. He assessed her quickly and moved to tow her down the hallway.

"Come with me," he said.

As he dragged her, he absently addressed men along the way while they deferred to him. It was like he was a damn celebrity. Gazes drifted to her with questioning looks that told her everything.

I'm not the fake girlfriend this man needs.

In less than a minute, Warren had her outside in a dark spot on the backyard porch. He moved her body as he wished. Pushing her against the hard beam of a pagoda, Warren leaned in, concentrating. She tried to reconnect to the world, but she couldn't. She shook her head, her gaze still off in the distance, finding stars on the horizon that she never saw in the city. She felt too self-conscious to even look at him.

"What's going on?" Warren's sincerity pushed through the fog in her brain.

"Nothing."

"Liar. Tell me." He traced his familiar, rough-feeling hand up her cheek, brushing stray hair off her sensitive skin. "Is this about the wives? Did they rake you over the coals?"

"Maybe. If it was a test, I failed."

He let out an honest laugh. "You know, I like you because you're different."

"Easy for you to say. You're Mr. Perfect."

"Damn, couldn't be more wrong."

Her gaze shot up to him, confused. His hand never left her cheek, moving it down to hold her jaw in that firm, controlling way she liked. She fell into his touch as he wrapped both of his arms around her. It was the hug she needed, and she closed her eyes as she inhaled his masculine scent.

"Now, I didn't give you permission to whine, did I?" he growled into her hair. "So, you better smarten the fuck up before I show you what happens to girls who defy me…"

His threat washed over her, reminding her of the game they'd once played. She felt something brighten in her chest, but her lips remained a hyphen. Unwilling to let go, he ran his hands up and down her back, finding her ass and squeezing it hard. She flinched with the momentary pain but felt a rush of arousal. She flickered her eyelashes up to him and bit her lip, wordlessly begging for more.

"You want me to hurt you," he said, reaching up to grab her hair for leverage. He angled her lips to him. "I know you do."

A little grin crossed her lips, and she was unable to hold it in.

"Yes, Sir," she prayed, feeling his heat steep through her body.

In a second, he'd managed to flick a switch in her, reconnecting her to reality.

"You want it rough."

"I want to feel something," she admitted, biting her lip as she watched heat flush up his neck.

Loud voices spilling out onto the backyard patio interrupted them, and despite being in a dark spot, a couple of guys caught them. Warren exhaled, giving her one last, sly look. He then escorted her by her waist into the well-lit patio where drinks were starting to flow again. She felt herself ease up with him firmly by her side. It was certainly enjoyable to watch how he interacted with his team.

Unfortunately, the vibe shifted as Jen and her fiancé, Crash, joined the group on the patio, making a big show out of sloppily kissing each other in front of everyone. The resulting cheers told Alisa that almost everyone at the party was drunk — everyone except her and Warren. They'd clearly arrived a little too late, a little too sober. And she didn't intend on changing that.

Then a guy she recognized stumbled through the circle toward Warren and Alisa. It was that same fit guy with receding brown hair and a face full of mischief who had shown up in Warren's backyard.

"Chief, you made it," the guy slurred. "And Crash was just about to cancel me as the best man. I told him I'd get you here — and he didn't fucking believe me."

"Gaudet." Warren gave a curt nod. He seemed about to say something more but stopped himself.

Alisa analyzed the two men, curious what that was about. She didn't have to wonder long.

"It's a big deal for the guys that you showed up." Gaudet motioned to the party, clearly starting a drunken rant. "I kept telling them that I got you."

Alisa could practically sense Warren recoil in that same unease she'd felt earlier. She couldn't tell if it was because he was surrounded by his drunken subordinates or the aggressive guy standing before him. Whichever it was, Warren's body language was shifting.

Gaudet's rambling didn't stop. "And you being here? Makes us feel like you actually give a shit about us — as people, not just warm bodies."

The comment came across backhanded, and Alisa didn't miss how Warren's eyebrow quirked.

"Obviously, I give a shit," Warren said. He tightened his grip on her waist, drawing her closer against his body as Jen circled with a full glass of wine.

Gaudet turned to Alisa, gesturing to Warren. "You with this guy? He's a fucking beast."

"Her name's *Alicia*," Jen said in a fake Latina accent, lunging in. Wine sloshed against her expensive-looking dress, but she was too fixated to notice.

Warren shot an unimpressed look, and she felt him tensing. Alisa kept her mouth shut, scanning quickly for escape routes.

"I didn't know you were dating," Jen said.

"He doesn't tell us anything," Gaudet said.

"So, where is your family from?" Jen asked, focusing on Alisa.

"Why does that matter?" Warren started.

Alisa took a deep breath, knowing what the woman was after and hating those conversations more than anything. Warren tugged at her to turn them away, like she didn't have to answer, and they could just bolt. But something stopped Alisa. She put her hand on his bicep, stilling him, and the silent look she gave Warren only seemed to rile Jen up.

Unbalanced, Jen continued to eye Alisa up and down, pointing a finger at her. "Aren't you a Mexican?"

"No, I'm not Mexican," Alisa explained slowly. "I'm American."

"But where are your parents from?" Gaudet pointed at her golden-brown skin, demanding answers.

"That's enough." Warren waved his hand over the group.

Gaudet stepped forward. "No, really—I just am curious."

"My father had Scottish heritage, my mother was from India," Alisa relented, crossing her arms protectively.

She was used to shielding herself, and the topic of her deceased parents wasn't a happy one.

"Oh, Warren—how exotic." Jen smirked. "All the way from *India*."

Alisa felt her jaw tighten and heard Warren grumble about why he didn't go to parties. The way he pulled again at her waist told her it was time to go.

"So, wait." Gaudet laughed, his drunken mind seeming to process. "Like, you're from India?"

"My—" Alisa started to correct.

"And how'd y'all meet?"

"It's—"

Gaudet cut her off, pointing at Warren. "So, like, is he your owner?"

Everything stopped. Everyone else in the circle sucked in breath, some people gasping.

Warren took one big step forward, right into Gaudet's space. "What the fuck—?"

Laughing, Gaudet didn't get it. "Like, she's your *slave* and you're her—"

Warren drove his hard, fierce fist forward, landing square on Gaudet's smirking face, knocking the words right out of him. Standing over the top of the man as his body crashed to the ground, Warren snarled down, flexing and clearly ready for more if the body so much as flinched.

Alisa stumbled backward, gasping for air. What the hell had just happened? A familiar choking feeling swarmed up her neck.

Warren spun back to her, wrapping his arm around her, and moved her swiftly beside the house toward the long driveway. Heated voices flooded the backyard as they marched away, silent. Determined, he dragged her, until her heel got stuck in the packed desert ground. He wasted no time hauling her up into his arms. If she expected sympathetic, caring eyes, all she got was a cold expression briefly flashed at her before concentrating on the horizon. She closed her eyes, sinking into his chest. He was done. She felt that.

So am I.

Bobbing in his arms, she wiped a few fallen tears from her cheek. She couldn't think. She couldn't process. She felt cold inside. Gazing up into his face, intensity painted across it, a part of her still wished he'd connect with her once more, just like at the pagoda.

But that Warren was gone.

Chapter Eleven

Warren

He was going to kill that motherfucker. Warren snarled in silence as he drove into the parking lot of Alisa's apartment. *Gaudet* — what a fucking joke.

Warren couldn't even describe his level of anger. He had stewed silently for the entire hour's drive back to the city, with Alisa cold and broken beside him. He gritted his teeth as fury coursed steadily through his veins. He should have listened to his instincts and avoided the party — kept Alisa to himself all night to kick off their seven-day deal.

But there they were. And every second that passed since they'd left the party, he had grown more and more incensed. Though, if he were to be honest with himself, that rage had been simmering since he'd been promoted...and had been forced to train the new guys. They were a different breed than him. Half of them didn't deserve the trident. And guys like Gaudet? Well, they were fucking pieces of shit.

The Navy SEAL lifestyle brand — that's all the new guys gave a fuck about. Warren clenched his jaw as he slammed his truck into park in the empty, dark parking lot. Pussy, money, status — new recruits didn't care about the old ways. They didn't know one thing about quiet honor, serving the country for the good of it and not for a fucking tell-all book deal. Hollywood just wanted them to parachute out of helicopters onto red carpets, but that wasn't the way it used to be.

With his hands still tense on the steering wheel, Warren shot a look across the bench. Alisa remained still, curled up against the door, clearly desperate to get away. She was hurting. He could clearly see it. But, what the fuck could he say?

He was who had exposed her to that. He was sorry that a guy like Gaudet wore the trident. And he was going to beat the actual shit out of anyone supporting that mentality. Hell, he was going to beat the shit out of any guy who didn't get it — being a SEAL meant pissing excellence, personally and professionally. He'd accept nothing less.

The truck motionless and quiet, Alisa glanced across the bench at him, unclicking her seatbelt slowly, as if she'd just woken from a long, slow nightmare. He felt how distant she'd become again, but he understood why.

"I should go," she said.

He couldn't find a reply, too angry to get words out. She gazed away, resigning herself to focus anywhere else as she pushed open the door. Watching her edge out, something inside him lit on fucking fire.

"No," he snapped, seizing her backward, causing the door to slam shut in the process.

He hauled her body across the front bench, staring down into her eyes.

"Where the hell do you think you're going?"

Her lips parted, stunned. "Home."

"We have a fucking deal. Seven days."

She found words, though unsteady. "It-it wasn't supposed to be like this."

"That's true for a lot of things. Doesn't change what I want."

As he watched the lamb fold her arms, sheltering her body, a haunting thought ricocheted through his mind—the dishonor of what he was doing. She didn't want it anymore. She wanted to go home. Was he going to force her? He couldn't be that guy. He had to show restraint.

"You don't have to protect yourself when you're with me," he pivoted, giving her an assurance that he knew he should not offer. "Okay?"

She gradually released her arms, very much still tepid toward him. She bit her full lip, flickering her lashes up at him. He twitched. *Does she even know what she's doing?* He covertly adjusted the hardening length in his pants, telling himself to calm the fuck down.

"Let's talk about what happened," he said.

"I don't know."

"Talk to me."

His urging landed. He didn't know her well, but what he was coming to believe was that she was damn misunderstood—and he wanted to understand her more, engagement ring dangling around her neck or not.

She shook her head, resting her cheeks in her hands.

"I hate it... I hate it so much," she said. "I hear I'm exotic. I'm ambitious for a girl... I get questions about my damn engagement—"

Then she stopped, cutting herself off. He didn't miss how quick she stopped that train of thought, irking him. But he didn't want to ask.

"You don't have to explain yourself to anyone," he said.

"Not even you?" she asked.

"Not even me."

"What if I want to?"

Alisa rolled her tongue over her shiny bottom lip. Damn, the way she looked up at him, something inside him got ticking uncontrollably, like a live grenade. *What is she doing?* Grazing that delicious-looking lip with her teeth, she grinned. He couldn't contain it anymore. The pin was out.

With one arm, he hoisted her up and plunked her into his lap, where she fucking belonged. He knew he shouldn't, but he fucking did. He was going to be that guy, and he damn well didn't want to hear anything about it. She gasped as he held her jaw, her small face drowning in his big hands.

"You're gorgeous. You better fucking know that," he growled.

Then he kissed her. *Hard*—before he could stop himself. The one thing he knew about himself was that he was a man who didn't stop.

She opened her mouth right up to his, letting him taste her like he had beside his pool. This time, he wasn't so nice. All that built up wrath inside him, all that built up passion, emptied out in the way he kissed her, the way he gripped her face. Her skin was too damn soft. She was damn inviting.

She moaned as his tongue left her mouth, running down her throat, tasting every inch of that juicy neck. No fucks left to give, he let his hands run wild down her body, first fondling her breasts over the dress, then ripping the dress down so that her bare skin spilled out. He pushed her back against the steering wheel and took her full cleavage into his open mouth, tasting the sensitive skin of her tits.

"Warren," she moaned again, rocking her head back as he buried his face into her chest.

She entwined her hands in his hair. He knew he wasn't just hungry for her — he was ravenous. The way her body responded told him she was goddamn turned on, too. None of it made sense, but he didn't care.

Without hesitation, he yanked her bra aside, letting her breasts spill out of their prison, and ducked his head lower to tease each nipple. They were the nicest set of tits he'd ever seen. As he adored each full mound, teasing and circling, he dropped his hand lower to her thighs, pushing aside her panties to feel what he'd been aching to feel all fucking night — her hot, wet pussy.

It was just as he had imagined.

"*Warren*," she said. Her words turned to pleading as her hips bucked up to his hand.

He traced up her slick slit, feeling the throbbing bud, pleasuring her. She was so goddamn wet, and she was losing it as he touched her. He felt his own hard-on raging in his pants and plotted how to get her on it.

"You make it damn hard to keep my hands off you," he confessed. "Tell me to stop."

"What if I don't want you to…"

"Don't open that box, Alisa —"

Chest heaving, she pulled back. Fluttering her innocent brown eyes at him, that familiar flush rose in her cheeks.

"Why not?" she asked.

"You're vulnerable," he said the right thing, feeling his angry cock pulsing in his pants. "I'm taking advantage of you."

"You're not," she said, almost convincingly. "Like you said, I make my own choices —"

He adjusted his dick once again, trying to suppress his appetite as he watched her straighten her dress and that fucking gold necklace. That goddamn ring.

"Fuck." Warren cut in, barely in control. "I'm a lot of things, but I'm not that asshole. I'm not Gaudet. Hell, I shouldn't be doing this."

She grinned, warm as hell. "You are allowed to be human."

His jaw dropped as her words hit him. *Allowed to be human.* That seemed like an invitation without condition. Clearly, she did not realize the depths of what he wanted to do to her. He moved again, unable to sit still. She reached up and caressed his cheek for the first time, subduing him. Tempering him. Tempting him.

She inched forward, whispering onto his lips, "Have you ever made a mistake?"

He just stared in response, unwilling to respond. If she only knew about the mistakes he'd made.

She let her lips gently dance on his, flickering her lashes up at him. Damn, she was hot.

"Don't tempt me," he defied, trying to hold his ground.

"Let me be your mistake." She pressed her mouth delicately on his before pulling back, smiling. "And you can be mine. What's a week in the grand scheme?"

Seven days. He closed his eyes, bringing her forehead against his, and just let himself breathe with her. A weird rush ran up his body, something he never felt before, not even when he had literally escaped death.

But, what if seven days isn't enough?

"Just don't screw me over," she whispered. "Please."

He opened his eyes, studying her. She was goddamn impossible. Impossibly addictive. Her scent, lingering in the air, imprinted on him in a way he knew he'd never forget. Before he could say anything, she continued.

"If you screw me over, it might just shatter me."

"Fuck," he groaned and took her mouth once again before adding, "me, too."

Chapter Twelve

Warren

It didn't take long before Warren relocated them from the front seat of his truck into her bedroom. He needed space for what he wanted to do to her. The lights still off, her bed lit only by moonlight, he tore off her velvet dress as they crashed down together. Her body writhing underneath him, he drank in the sight of her — so goddam blazing.

Let me be your mistake, Alisa's words echoed through his mind. She wanted it. Underscoring this, she ran her hands up the front of his shirt, fumbling to unbutton it. With quivering fingers, she got underneath the fabric, feeling his abs and turning him on past the point of no return. But he grabbed her wrists — hard, authoritative. She was about to see a different side of him.

"Did you ask permission?" he asked.

Her lips parted, a little surprised. "Can I undress you, Sir?"

He growled over top of her, tightening his grip on her wrists so she winced. His already-hardened cock throbbed as he watched her response but paused as her gaze flitted to the door.

"Don't tell me your fiancé is about to walk in," he said.

"He's not, I promise. He's far, far away. I wouldn't be doing this."

"Afraid of his wrath?" He meant it as a joke, but the flicker in her eyes told him it was real. "I'll keep you safe."

"I know."

As she said it, he reached down and slid his finger over her clit, gaining the expected reaction. She jerked, then moaned, sinking into the feeling he gave as he massaged her sweet spot. He compartmentalized, drinking in the fleeting moment.

"There's something I think you like." His tone darkened as he watched her twist in agony underneath his hand.

"What?"

She groaned as he worked her clit faster.

"You like being overpowered," he said, his tone amused. "You like being forced."

And to prove his point, he pinned her legs down on either side, making her totally vulnerable to him. He brushed his fingers farther down her wet slit and up into her hungry pussy. He kept going for as long as it took to make her breathless, feeling up and down her body as he worked.

"*Fuck,*" she squeaked out as he pumped his one hand into her.

As he took control of her body, it only seemed to drive her closer to the edge, her back arching back in near euphoria. He knew how explosive that felt.

"Don't come until I tell you to," he ordered, reaching into her bedside table.

She was so distracted that she barely realized that he'd found her long, blue vibrator. *Naughty girl.*

"I'm getting so close," she gasped as he worked her pussy harder. "*You're* making me so damn close."

He ripped his fingers out and away from her, much to her surprise. He could be cruel when he wanted to. Her eyes widened with his sudden absence, searching for breath. Before she could ask him a question, he tore off his shirt and pants, leaving him in his boxers.

Back on the bed, he manhandled her, determined to make it a night they wouldn't forget. Flipping her onto her stomach, he tore off her lacy bra, sending it across the room. Fired up from the fight and too turned on to think, he pushed her face down onto the pillow, gripping her neck with one hand. With the other, he flipped on her vibrator and pushed it underneath her clit, forcing her body down onto it hard. It was time to let the vibrator do its work.

"Oh God." She panted as he held her down, rocking her pelvis back and forth on the vibrator. "It's too much."

"All you have to do is use that safeword and I'll stop right here, right now." He pushed her ass down harder, hearing her moans getting louder.

"*Please—*"

"Remember the word?"

"*Yes.*"

"Make me stop."

"Oh, God—"

He grinned as her words spilled out because he sure as hell didn't want to stop. Her own safeword— *magnetic*—never rolled off her lips. 'Magnetic' was exactly how she was right then.

Watching her twist in ecstasy on top of her vibrator, he cupped and caressed her ass, sweeping down her crack, toward the opening to her pussy. Every time her hips bucked to him, he roughly pushed them back and slapped her ass even harder. Based on her reactions, he knew she liked it when he smacked her, so he spared her no pain. She wanted it to hurt.

"Don't come until I say you can," he growled, edging her, making it rougher. "Don't disobey me."

"*Please.*" She squirmed under his hold.

"Fucking try to move again and you'll be sorry," he threatened, listening to her breathing.

He kept his hand gripped on her neck, the right amount of choking—a little painful, but very satisfying. With one hand pushing down and one hand holding her neck, he stayed firmly in control of her body. He could get used to that view. He was so fucking hard.

But he didn't care, because it wasn't about him. He just wanted to feel her orgasm. Still pinned down underneath him, he quickly pushed three thick fingers into her needy pussy, finding that spot that made her scream. He wanted to feel her hot core tightening on his hand.

He could tell by her responses that she was on the edge of an intense orgasm. He knew damn well it would only make it more intense if he kept edging her. The idea of driving so much pleasure through her was turning him on in a way he couldn't explain. And the sight of her submissive form writhing underneath him made him want to come all over her ass.

"Open your legs for me," he demanded, aggressively slapping the inside of her thighs as she opened them.

"Warren, *please*," she begged through a ragged breath, her body trembling in arousal as she approached climax. "Please, can I come?"

"*Hell no* — I swear to fucking God," he used his most intimidating voice, relishing in his power over her, his cock now hard enough to break glass.

Fuck, her wriggling ass was so damn hot, and he growled as he leaned over to bite her juicy flesh, temporarily releasing his hold on her neck. His teeth hitting her skin, grazing and drawing pain was her undoing. He gripped her tight ass and fingered her soaking pussy hard and fast. Sweat beaded at his forehead as he felt her unable to hold it any longer, falling apart underneath him, finding total ecstasy in everything he was doing to her.

She climaxed onto his hand, her orgasmic juices flowing down into his palm. It was incredible feeling her come onto his fingers, feeling her completely vulnerable and surrendered before him. Panting and groaning his name, she pressed her face into the pillow, enjoying each exquisite after-shock of her climax. Taking care of her well, he ran his hands up and down her form as she came back to reality, flipping her slowly on the bed to face him again.

"I'm in love with you." She grinned seductively, running her hands up her face.

"Oh, yeah?"

"Not *really*, I wish — but holy damn..." her voice trailed, still in another world. "Wow."

Different from before, he felt like he was in that other world with her.

Then she tracked her gaze down his long body—from his chest to his abs to his rock-hard cock, bouncing in his boxers.

"Sir, is that a lollipop?" she asked in her sweetest, most innocent voice.

He couldn't contain the guttural noise that escaped his throat, hearing the words drip off her perfect lips. Reaching up to swirl and pinch her own nipples, she arched her back, presenting her wet pussy to him.

"Please, fuck me," she pleaded.

"I can't— I mean it." He stood his ground, not even sure what he was standing on anymore. "You got yours. I'm just here to help."

Not buying it, Alisa sat up in front of him, gripping his hips and waist, worshipping his stomach. He knew he was in shape, and he knew the effect it had on women. He just didn't usually give a fuck. But Alisa? She made him feel a sense of pride.

She pawed at the edge of his boxers, sending him pouting and pleading looks. He remained still, hating how he had to do the right thing and walk away. That was his moment to prove that he wasn't that type of guy. He wasn't an asshole.

But holy fuck— It was damn impossible with those full lips kissing down his treasure trail.

"Please, *Sir*." She tugged at his boxers, asking him to let her pull them down. "I want it."

Breaking, he reached down and popped out his cock, letting the thick appendage bounce and smack her in the face. Surprised once again, she gasped as she took his length in her hands. He could tell right away she wasn't experienced, but her enthusiasm and arousal were more than enough for him.

"What do you want me to do?" She pouted her lips against the tip, gently touching her tongue against his pre-cum, clearly savoring the taste.

He groaned, holding the back of her head in place, realizing how fucking bad he needed that release. Was he really going to let this happen? What about not taking advantage of her?

Christ.

"Open your mouth."

And she did.

Her mouth widened just enough to take his cock in, and she danced her tongue around it. He didn't miss how her eyes rolled back briefly, like it was turning her on as much as it was him. God, he was going to fucking lose it.

"Use your hands," he instructed her, holding them around his base where her mouth just could not reach. Pumping them and showing her, he realized she was a good student—a quick study. "That's it—just like that."

He intertwined his hands in her long dark hair and quickened her pace, pushing and pulling her hair like a lever. He let himself get rougher and rougher with her, hearing her moan in pleasure as she sucked his cock.

"Say my name while you suck." Warren's tone grew more aggressive, achieving the intended effect.

Eager to please, Alisa mumbled words as she sucked his cock, all while choking and gasping for air. The vibration of her words as she took his length was enough to get him throbbing nearly in pain. Feeling her spit run down the base and over his balls made it all even hotter.

It probably went on for minutes, but it felt like seconds. Her imperfect blow job was the hottest damn thing he'd ever had. She was driving him wild.

Everything amateur, inexperienced, unpolished about Alisa just felt so authentic—like he was getting the raw cut—him and him alone. And that was so damn unlike any other woman that usually chased him.

Gripping her hair, pumping into her mouth, he let out a guttural grunt as he released his cum into her, feeling her drink it all down with so much goddamn enthusiasm.

"Show me your tongue," he demanded through ragged breaths, roughly angling her head just right, intently watching her as she licked any remnants off his cock.

Like an obedient sub, Alisa leaned backward, opening her mouth to prove that she'd swallowed every last drop. The way her tits knocked together threatened to make him hard all over again. He fucking loved manipulating her body the exact way he wanted it. He fucking loved being her Dom.

"Good girl." He ran his hands down her hair, affectionate and caring. "Good fucking girl."

He pulled her down onto him as they fell onto her bed together, that damn gold chain around her neck slapping against his chest.

Post-climax, they both found themselves in sated stillness. Tightly holding her against him, he kissed her hair too many times, saying what he shouldn't. High on the moment, he uttered things in the dark that he had no place saying to an engaged woman.

And as his tired eyes turned to slits and him running his hand over her silky black hair, his spent mind wondered what that tiny sparkle of light was shining from his chest. Then he realized that it was the diamond on her damn engagement ring, sparkling in the moonlight.

Sinking into sleep, Warren refused to acknowledge that they had an expiration date—and that they were nothing more than a fucking ticking time bomb.

Chapter Thirteen

Warren

Typically Warren didn't sleep over at anyone's place, and especially not to share a bed. He hadn't in over five years. There was a damn good reason for that.

But now he was passed out, in and out of REM sleep, clutching Alisa in her too-comfortable bed, in their too-intoxicating deal. REM sleep was a necessary evil — but dangerous for Warren. That's when he remembered things he didn't want to remember, especially when he was as damn fired up as he was then, and his mind ran wild with memories he couldn't stop.

Memories that he knew he talked about in his sleep.

Memories he didn't want anyone to hear.

In the early morning hours, when he was in a light sleep, a vivid dream he hated but often had started playing out in his mind. His body twitched as his dream brought him back to *that* deployment. It wasn't the last one, and he'd forgotten how many he'd had since then. *Too many.*

There he was, at the height of the war in Iraq, lying on the top of a crumbled building, well before his promotion. Midday, the sun scorched the back of his neck, covered partially by a keffiyeh. The wind had blown part of the fabric off his neck and jaw, but he didn't dare move to adjust position – his finger was flexed on the trigger of his sniper rifle, locked dead on the doorway of the building where his high-priority target was situated.

He was alone, as still as hell and hadn't moved for hours. He waited and waited…and waited. A grayish grit circulated in the air, moving all around him, getting into his nose and mouth. It was like a shit dust – and tasted the same. The unforgiving climate threatened any outsider, making it clear that he wasn't welcome.

"Whiskey Charlie, you sitting tight?" He heard the voice of his leading chief, Geoff, through his earpiece.

"Ten four," Warren muttered back, keeping his voice low, despite the blistering gusts at the top of the five-story building in the heart of the Iraqi city.

"When he comes out, you engage. Don't fucking hesitate. I'm right down here."

Before the dream could continue down its usual path, Warren felt himself coming out of it, rumbling and thrashing in Alisa's bed, causing searing pain in the scar on his back—reminding him of the moment he'd gotten it. He recalled blood gushing down his back as he writhed, and he remembered how the cold steel of the blade had felt when it had dug into his ribs.

In the dark of Alisa's bedroom, hearing her asleep beside him, curled up and facing the other way, Warren ran his calloused hands over his rough stubble, willing the phantom pain to go away. That had been a bad fucking op—and his mistake had cost the team dearly, let alone him. That nightmare was on repeat, a not-so-friendly reminder of what type of mistakes he'd made — and the consequences he'd have to fucking live with for the rest of his life.

He didn't have the option to be flawed. He didn't have the option to be imperfect. His aching scar sprawling up his back would never relent, would never fully heal. It was a painful reminder of the cost of mistakes.

Coming to his senses, waking up, drinking in Alisa's bedroom and the sheets that smelled like a mix of sex and conquest, only one question crossed his mind. *What the fuck am I doing?*

Alisa's message from the night before ran across his mind as he pushed out of the bed, careful not to wake her. *You're allowed to make mistakes.* He shook his head, rejecting the notion, disgusted by himself. He shouldn't have allowed himself to falter — but he had. Taking her to the party? Fucking around with her? What the hell was wrong with him? She needed money. He was holding that over her, taking advantage.

Like an asshole.

And now, he gazed around her room, realizing how deep he was in. He'd slipped up and slept over.

A goddamn mistake.

It was clear as day to Warren that things had gone too far. He'd *let* things get too far. He had to do better. He had to get out of there.

Thank God she was a heavy sleeper. Even better, he knew how to be stealthy, slipping through her apartment soundlessly. The sun was just threatening to rise on the horizon, giving the quiet morning an eerie dark orange glow.

Dressing quickly then drawing a blank check out of his wallet, he cut her a large enough sum that she'd be able to buy herself a new car, an amount he believed was beyond generous. He dropped it near her phone on her kitchen counter with the memo...housework services. He wasn't going to hold it over her head anymore. That was the price he had to pay for his honor.

As he twisted to push his wallet back in his pocket, he winced in agony, gripping the kitchen counter before him for stability. Hauling her body up in his arms the night prior, angrily whisking her away, passionately claiming her for his own—he shouldn't have done any of that. His old nagging injury was back with ferocity. His scar throbbed, like it had just reopened...for the first time in years. A reminder.

Warren's mind shifted, compartmentalizing. He had things to do, no matter that it was early Sunday morning.

Slipping on his shoes, mission-focused, he bent low enough that some of the book titles on her coffee table screamed out at him. But they weren't novels. They were textbooks. He read some of the titles— *Musculoskeletal Magnetic Imaging, Thoracic Imaging, Pulmonary and Cardiovascular Radiology, Nuclear Medicine...*

'Magnetic'. *Her safeword.* It hit him in the chest.

What the hell is she in school for? Radiology, imaging...nuclear medicine? *Christ.*

Gritting his teeth, he couldn't deny that he barely knew her. He'd spent more time trying to fuck her than trying to get to know who she was. His cock had an agenda of its own. That was exactly what he hadn't wanted to happen. He leaned in farther to read the name of her university program from a printed-out sheet, partially covered, but heard a soft moan from her bedroom. He stilled his movements.

But everything went silent again.

Exhaling slowly, he soundlessly exited. He found his truck in the parking lot—jumping into the driver's seat. At barely five-thirty in the morning, he wasn't prepared to have *any* conversation.

As he rolled out of the lot, keeping his V8 engine as quiet as possible, something happened that struck him as out of place. A loud blacked-out motorcycle crept down the street, a driver with a black tinted helmet staring at him. It was the kind of bike with a custom job, something made to look ultra-aggressive. Snapping him quickly out of his head, Warren felt his nerves prickling. He just knew something was wrong. He watched the driver eyeing him like it was personal.

Like they knew what he was doing. Like they knew where he'd come from.

Through his rear-view mirror, he gazed back up at her apartment door, wondering if he should stick around. But the bike had disappeared, leaving him alone in the vicinity. Waiting a few minutes for something to happen—nothing did, except the sun getting higher on the horizon—he shook his head, trying to convince himself that it had been nothing. It was just his guilt.

But he just wasn't sure if it he was more guilty for fucking around with her or for leaving.

Chapter Fourteen

Warren

The Southern Californian blistering sun had finally risen over the long stretch of grass in the local park. The hot summer temperatures were already mounting, causing sweat to bead on Warren's chest as he ran after a soccer ball. His opponent was ruthless, never giving him a second to breathe.

What else should he expect from a six-year-old girl?

"Warry!" Katy's joyful yelps came from behind him as he raced her to the ball. "I'm going to get it!"

Despite what nagged at the back of his mind, Warren put on a big grin, ready to teach her a thing or two about competition. He wanted to give her his full attention, even if his mind was divided and working against him. He and Katy—they only had a certain amount of time together.

"Not so fast, kiddo."

His skilled footing found the ball before her, kicking it back her way so she could send it toward the net. They played a game of soccer where half the time they were on the same team, half the time they weren't. Although it was a little confusing, he didn't make a big fuss over the rules of the game. He was just out to have a couple of hours of fun. Seeing her every day, usually twice a day, was the only thing that kept him sane when he was off tour.

He watched her run, giggling as she kicked the soccer ball down field.

"Come on!" she called back at him, her pink cheeks flashing under the sun. "You're too slow!"

He pushed off, chasing her, closing the distance between them. But then something unexpected happened. She accidently shot the ball to the side, and it rolled down the grassy mound onto the sidewalk. Without hesitation, the little girl ran after it, trying to grab it, getting dangerously close to the road.

"No! Katy!" Warren stormed forward.

But she didn't listen.

"Katy!"

In a full sprint across the grass, he lurched into emergency stress mode as he saw her little frame teetering to catch the ball that was dribbling down the sidewalk, nearly falling into the street.

"Stop!" Everything inside him was shattering as split-seconds felt like minutes.

Fuck.

He closed the distance as fast as humanly possible, like she was in grave danger. Just as she tried to get the ball from the gutter, he lunged. Snatching her body, curling it into his own, he felt his heart hammering out of his chest. He buried his face into her curly blonde hair, struggling to breathe. *Christ*. But it wasn't because of the sprinting.

"But I was just—" she started, confused.

Cortisol rushed through him, coiling around his brain. He knew an extreme stress reaction when he felt it. Even still, he held her tighter than life, thanking God that he'd made it in time. Thanking God she hadn't gotten hurt.

"I was just trying to get the ball," she said.

"It's okay. It's okay," he said. "Let's just play on the grass from now on. Let me get the ball if it runs away."

Mothers gently pushing strollers in the sleepy still of Monday morning were looking at him like he'd lost his mind. There was not a single car on the road. The local park and surrounding streets were dead quiet.

He had completely lost his shit.

Trying to recompose himself, he kissed her hair, knowing he had to get a fucking grip. It didn't matter if it felt all too similar. It wasn't the same situation, he reminded himself. He wasn't in Iraq. He was home. Katy was okay.

"Are you okay?" She patted his back. "Do you need to go see the doctor?"

"I'm okay."

He sucked in air, shaking it off, tightening her into his chest. She hugged him back, looking up into his eyes.

"I wish you lived with us."

"I know," he said, tucking a lock of her hair behind her ears. "Me, too."

"I can ask mommy?"

"Better not right now."

She gently ran her fingers through his hair, smiling and giving him a childlike peck on the cheek. He placed his hand on his cheek where she'd kissed him, closing his eyes so he could keep it with him forever.

"Can we keep playing?" she asked, pointing at the grass.

"Absolutely."

His face twitched as the agony from his scar coursed through his body. That's when Warren knew for sure that his scar was opening again, in a figurative sense. And he couldn't let that happen.

He tossed the ball back onto the grass, pushing through the pain to run after her and staying much closer for the remaining time they had at the park. He'd never be able to explain how much that little girl meant to him. He'd never be whole again, and he'd never forgive himself if anything ever happened to her.

* * * *

An hour later, Brooke rose from her faded blue lawn chair as Warren walked Katy up to her home. The curly-haired youngster beamed from ear to ear, holding her soccer ball on her hip as she walked up her small grassy lawn.

"Mommy!" Katy lunged forward, hugging her.

Brooke embraced the little girl, sending her inside to wash up before snack time. Once they were alone, Brooke turned to Warren, her face solemn.

"Does she know you are leaving in a matter of days?" she asked, adjusting her messy brown ponytail.

"Not specifically," he admitted.

"Come on. Don't just disappear." The disappointment on her worn-out face was undeniable.

"I know. I won't."

"It was really hard for her last time you were gone. She needs to be prepared."

Warren folded his arms, settling comfortably into numbness. Brooke stared at him, as if she knew exactly what was running through his mind. It was probably in hers, too. The truth he wanted to forget was that if he kept leaving, maybe one day he wouldn't come back. Or, he'd be coming back in a body bag.

The vision of Geoff flashed across his mind, and he found himself stumbling forward. As if she felt it, tears welled in her eyes.

"Five years today. You know that, right?" she questioned, driving a searing knife into him.

A knife that even he could feel.

Silent, Warren ran his hands over Brooke's shaking shoulders, pulling her into his chest. He didn't know what else to do.

She continued through a cracking voice, "Sometimes I just get so fucking angry. Why him? Why us?"

"I know. I'm sorry."

She ran her hands over her face, as if trying to wake up. There was one thing Warren knew. She was so strong. Hell, just thinking about everything she'd been through…

"I'm always here for you guys," he reminded her.

"Really?" she fired at him, pushing him away. "Because you haven't been here much the past five years. You didn't even show up to his goddamn funeral."

The words cut deep.

But Brooke didn't understand. She didn't want to understand.

He stepped back, and Katy came out to say goodbye. He forced a smile, which she seemed to know was false. He tipped his ballcap and took his leave, not wanting to prolong it.

He'd fucked up, and he knew it.

The problem is that some fuckups are unfixable.

* * * *

Warren returned to work as he pulled through the military training facility up in Wrightwood, running on too little sleep. In the higher-altitude mountainous area, the desert air brought him back to Iraq—perfect training conditions for what they had to do on their next deployment.

Maybe it was his pent-up anger, maybe it was his frustration, but he was planning on fucking delivering some hard-ass training, regardless of the pain he was in. By the end of the day, everyone was going to be suffering just as much as he was. He was going to make these boys perfect, whether they liked it or not. He was going to teach them what it meant to never give up.

Warren zipped up his hoodie, fresh from his place, slinging his modified shotgun over his shoulder. He was the type of guy who liked to research and purchase his own equipment, giving him a little stockpile at home that made him look like he was prepping for the apocalypse. Thinking about it a little more, he realized how that could have freaked out Alisa.

The master chief was meeting him in the office that morning to go over where they were at and readiness levels for getting at the next high-priority target. Warren moved into the compound's office, a small building with top-secret access. No cell phones were allowed. No landlines. In fact, the building had been outfitted like a safe—keeping their discussions impenetrable.

"Chief." Master Chief Rose turned to greet Warren as he walked in.

They were alone.

"Sir." Warren nodded at the man he'd worked with for a long time.

They'd been through a lot together. They'd seen a lot of shit and suffering. They'd also seen a lot of wins.

The master chief motioned for Warren to sit, so he did so, sliding his guns off onto the side table. He'd be needing those later.

"I'm going to cut right to it," the master chief started. "I have been informed that there was an incident over the weekend."

"There was," Warren confirmed, sitting confidently in the cheap chair.

"You punched one of your petty officers?"

"I did."

"Care to explain?" Master Chief Travis Rose's eyes widened as he looked around the room in disbelief, a shine emanating from his receding hairline.

Warren stared down the master chief, angrily sucking his teeth—the first show of emotion he was willing to express. He'd thought of exactly what to say all weekend, but by that point, he found himself too goddamn incensed to keep it cool.

"Petty Officer Gaudet made a disgusting racist comment, and I reacted." Warren leaned forward, hot red flushing up his neck, thinking about how his subordinate had deeply disrespected Alisa. "I want him formally disciplined."

The master chief narrowed his eyes, showcasing wrinkles that promised experience. "Write up a report with the full story, and we will proceed with disciplinary measures. We are zero tolerance here."

Warren rapped the chair's arm with his knuckles in a tone of finality and moved to get up.

"Wait." The master chief motioned for Warren to sit. "This isn't over. I also have to deal with the fact that *you* punched him... You outrank him, you are his leader — and you assaulted him."

"And I'd do it again. Harder."

"And '*you'd do it again*'?" The master chief tilted his head in incredulity. "And this is instilling confidence in your leadership? You know very well that I should be disciplining *you* as well for that. You are trusted with the well-being and safety of the platoon, your crew. I can't have you punching your men when we have better ways for handling this type of shit. You *know* this."

Warren remained still — silent and unapologetic. He wasn't going to back down from what he'd done. The guy needed an ass kicking far worse than what he'd given him. It had gotten so damn personal.

"I did what I did. I don't give a fuck," Warren finally stated, keeping his words curt and cold.

"This isn't like you. In all the years we've worked together, I've never seen you crack." The master chief pushed on, dropping his tone to ask. "Are you burning out?"

"*No.*"

"This next deployment —" the master chief started, but immediately stopped as Warren's glare turned deadly.

"What about it?" Warren snapped.

"Chief, in the last five years, you've spent more time on deployment than on home soil—by a landslide. You've gone longer, further, harder than any other man in the platoon—or in the SEALs, for that matter. At what point does a man burn out? At what point do you need to stop?"

"Never. I'll *never* stop. Failure is not an option."

"I don't want to lose you, like how we lost—" But he stopped.

Warren tensed, thankful for the sudden suspension.

Moving on, the master chief let out a fatigued sigh, flipping open a file in front of him on the desk.

Picking up a memo from the top, he then locked eyes with Warren. "I don't want to lose you. The Navy doesn't want to lose you."

"You won't."

"Willing to sign on it?"

Warren quirked his eyebrow, realizing where they were at.

"Look... Your review is in. You're eligible for the biggest retention bonus, given your level of service." He tossed the paper over the desk to show Warren the cash amount. "All you have to do is re-sign."

Warren's eyes flashed up to his master chief, absorbing exactly how bad the Navy wanted him to keep going.

Chapter Fifteen

Alisa

Alisa sat in front of one of the most brilliant doctors in the hospital, trying to not think about the fact that it was Thursday. She still hadn't heard from Warren — not since he'd snuck out of her place days ago. What had happened to their deal?

"Alisa, did you hear my question?" the doctor asked.

The pointed words drew Alisa back to reality. Dr. Roske leaned back in her office chair, adjusting her brown glasses on her fair nose. Loose curly blonde hairs stuck out from her temples as she observed her student.

"I'm— I'm sorry, Dr. Roske," Alisa said.

"Are you familiar with fusion imaging? Have you studied that yet?"

"Um, yes," Alisa started, nervously tightening her navy-blue blazer. "I'm more comfortable with magnetic, but I'm working on my knowledge of fusion as well."

The radiologist flipped through a patient's scans on the screen. It was yet another on-the-job residency aptitude test.

Alisa heard her cell vibrate in her bag and a panicking part of her mind debated if it was Warren. She felt her fingers twitch to get it but stopped herself.

"A lot of radiology is really witchcraft," Dr. Roske explained, pointing at the screen. "What do you see here?"

"I'm not sure," Alisa said, trying to concentrate. "Maybe, inflammation—"

"What?" Dr. Roske cocked her head, assessing her student. "It's a glioma, of course."

"Right."

Alisa squinted as the doctor outlined the ill-defined boundaries.

"Look… This is quintessential radiology," Dr. Roske said. "Half the time, you'll find yourself looking at ghost apparitions, trying to write some sort of report on what it all means. Everything comes down to your professional opinion."

"I-I completely understand," Alisa stuttered, folding her hands professionally in her lap. "I'm eager to pursue this in my residency."

She bit her lip, screaming at herself to be smooth.

"Well, it's a long journey to get here." The doctor shot her a skeptical look. "After you are licensed, after your basic residency, you'll need years and years of specialist training, but you already know that?"

Alisa continued nodding in agreement. "Yes, Doctor—this is something that I'm prepared for."

She waited, prickles on her skin as an awkward silence flooded the space between her and the doctor. Dr. Roske assessed her, seemingly judging her words. Alisa shifted in her seat, trying to look as serious as possible but knowing her mind had been elsewhere all week.

"I really want this," Alisa said, trying to make her sales pitch. "I really want to be in radiology."

"Okay," Dr. Roske started slowly, narrowing her eyes at Alisa. "So, for the residency, I only have two spots available. It's very competitive."

"I know," Alisa responded. "I am aware."

The doctor crossed her hands on her knee, clearly trying to formulate the right words. Alisa knew what was coming next.

"Surely, a young woman like yourself would prefer to be working more directly with patients as opposed to here in the back office?" Dr. Roske's light blue eyes shot her student a challenging look but one that Alisa was used to getting. "Radiology is really not for most people."

So, she gave the doctor a dose of raw honesty.

"I'm not suited to work with people—or children, for that matter. I've never been very good at the softer touch, the bedside manner thing," Alisa explained, chewing her lip and looking back at the screen. "I'm not a people-person, but I'm good at medicine. I'm good at science."

It was hard admitting the truth, but she needed the doctor to understand. Alisa wasn't going to be able to be the well-loved doctor, receiving chocolates and Christmas cards from their patients, or the doctor who played funny games with the kids, making them all laugh their blues away. All her years in med school had taught her that she wasn't cut out for that.

"You are better with people than you give yourself credit for, I'm sure," the doctor suggested, but pushed forward with the conversation.

"This is my path," Alisa said.

"You are so young. How do you really know your path?"

"Trial and error."

And I'm tired of embarrassing myself.

Alisa shifted in her seat, but Dr. Roske's desk line rang, cutting the conversation and prompting her to take the call. A conversation ensued between her and a surgeon. Alisa watched in awe, knowing that someday soon, that was going to be her.

Bright rays of sunshine danced on the doctor's face, warming up the small office. After a scorching weekend, LA's heat was only rising. That afternoon, they were already in a record high of heat and smog. Alisa had seen the worst of it since she started taking extra shifts in the ER. There were a lot of cases of serious heat stroke and dehydration coming in these days.

As Dr. Roske's conversation carried on, Alisa clued in that she had a spare minute. That part of her brain obsessing over why her phone had vibrated took control. Exhaling in defeat, Alisa slipped her hand down the side of the chair toward her bag, fishing for her cell phone. Though she kept her eyes on the doctor, her mind was somewhere else entirely.

When she'd woken up in bed alone on Sunday morning, grasping for Warren's hard, warm body, she'd lied to herself, pretending that it didn't hurt that he wasn't there, that he'd just disappeared. She justified to herself that there were many reasons he'd leave without saying goodbye. She promised herself that she'd hear from him, that it wasn't over.

But then, she'd seen the check he'd left for her.

And she'd felt that.

She pulled her cell into her lap. A rush of cutting disappointment, yet again, coming over her, Alisa saw that there was nothing from Warren. Though, there was a text message from someone she was not so excited to hear from.

Dean had written.

You going to be at the airport tomorrow? I'm arriving after dinner.

Alisa inhaled sharply, her nostrils flaring. She slammed back a text message to him, fear mounting.

I think so.

You could sound a little more excited. It's been a while.

Backtracking, she started typing but deleted it. It sounded too guilty. Her brain was spinning. Dean sent another message right away, clearly suspicious.

Something's going on with you — and I'm going to find out what.

Alisa felt screaming anxiety rushing through her body, taking in Dean's words. She felt tears springing to her eyes. Something cracked inside her in the absence of Warren's protection. *He said he'd keep me safe.*

As Dr. Roske's phone conversation became more involved and she pulled up more images, she placed her hand on the phone's receiver.

"My apologies, Alisa," Dr. Roske said, excusing her. "Take a break. Let's come back to this."

Alisa hauled up her bag, nodding politely at the doctor and taking her leave. Her knees nearly rattled together as she galloped out of the office, down the staircase in the hospital and outside for some fresh air. Or, what she imagined would be fresh air.

After all those years in LA, she should have known better. The air was hot and smoggy, and immediately she had to shed her blazer, exposing her creamy sleeveless blouse that was too thin to be worn on its own. She peeled off whatever she needed to stop feeling dizzy.

Dean knows. He fucking knows.

Sweat beaded on her chest, the air too thick to breath effectively, so she made a break for her car in the parking lot. Of course, that wasn't a solution. The old, beat-up lemon was a thousand degrees and practically melting under the coastal sun, and it didn't have air conditioning. Even still, she jumped in, needing to be sheltered and alone, manually rolling down the windows in front then turned on the engine.

How could he know? He has been nearly three-thousand miles away.

In all the years, she'd never gotten the feeling that Dean was keeping tabs on her. Watching her. But, then again—she'd never done anything except school and work. *Not much to keep tabs on.*

Digging in her bag, she grabbed for her cell again but found her fingers grazing on a sharp corner of something. She gazed over, seeing it was just the corner of the folded-up check Warren had issued her. *Damn.* Eventually she was going to have to make a decision— cash it or tear it up.

Alisa leaned forward, closing her eyes and resting her head against the lava-hot steering wheel, praying.

"Why did I have to meet you?" Her face twisted as she thought of Warren running his lips up and down her throat. He was the only man she wanted. *Needed.*

Warren had changed everything. He'd made her feel like she belonged when she was with him — like she wasn't so socially stunted, like she could have a man like him.

Yet, every day that had passed since he'd left, reality had become more and more bleak. She didn't even have his number to track him down. He'd always called her from a blocked ID. What was she supposed to do — show up at his house and demand answers? She shook her head, sucking in breath as she pulled the car out of the parking lot.

Dean was coming home, and everything was going to go back to the way it had been.

"I can't do this," she whispered to herself, feeling a stray tear run down her cheek. "I can't — "

Her future life burned through her mind as she began the slow crawl home. The afternoon traffic back to her apartment nearly drove her crazy on a good day, let alone a day where she was unable to focus on anything but the aching feeling in her chest. She wanted to be home, she wanted to be outside, she wanted to be at work — but at the same time, she didn't want to be anywhere.

As she rolled into the parking lot at her apartment complex, she drew out her cell again, desperate to see if that time — maybe, just maybe — there would be something from Warren. Maybe he'd finally gotten off work, maybe he'd finally thought of her. Her hopes were high to see any sign of life from the man who had claimed more than just her body.

"I just need answers," she said to herself, trying to justify a thought that had been percolating in her mind for days. "Why did he leave?"

It was well into evening, and there was no doubt he would be home—wouldn't he? Where did he work, anyway? Her mind trailed to that very secretive looking facility outside of Wrightwood, and how hush-hush he'd been about it when she'd probed him. He had some connection to that place.

Her face twisted into tears as she sat back in the driver's seat, her hand on the door to get out. She flitted her sad gaze up to her small, lonely apartment—a place of solace and peace, a place where she had found refuge for years, a place where Warren's scent still lingered. Like a scalpel piercing through her chest, she felt the blade turn and her esophagus jerked. *His damn masculine scent.*

Then, her cell rang, stopping that thought. When she jumped to check the caller display, her stomach sank when she read the name—*Dean Teller.*

Exhaling, trying to collect herself, she answered politely.

"Alisa." Dean's frustrated voice came through the line. "What the fuck is going on?"

"*Nothing*—are you ready to come back?"

"Hell, yeah," he said. "But you know what? I'm getting worried, Alisa. You haven't been very good, have you?"

"*What?*"

"Don't play games."

"It's not what—"

Dean cut her off. "I'm not an idiot, Alisa. You're different."

"I just— I have my final exams next month. I'm stressed," Alisa sputtered.

"Our deal had pretty explicit terms." Dean talked over her. "And I don't think you've been honest with me."

"No, please—"

"Don't lie. I have eyes everywhere."

Alisa opened her mouth to argue but nothing came out. Nothing ever came out. That's always how it went with Dean. She bit her lip, shaking her head. He was going to fucking kill her.

His tone grew more aggressive, more accusatory. "Something is up. You better hope it's not what I think it is."

"Dean, *please*."

"You know what happens next, Alisa. Play stupid games—win stupid prizes."

And with those parting words, he ended the call. Alisa was left gawking at her phone, trembling and tormented. Her thoughts spiraling, a creeping sensation crawled up the back of her neck as she heard a loud noise. Gazing up, a blacked-out custom motorcycle rolled down the street in front of her, the loud boom of the muffler drowning out anything else.

A male driver with a fully black helmet and a neck tattoo cocked his head to obviously stare her down. She just couldn't deny that he looked like the type of guy the Dean would hang out with, like he was someone in the club.

"You're imagining things," Alisa whispered, but the bike slowed down in front of her for no apparent reason.

She freaked out, jammed her car into drive and sped out of the parking lot in the opposite direction.

Under stress, under threat, she felt panic erupting up her throat. Peeling down the boulevard, tears rolling down her cheeks, she didn't know who to be more angry with — Dean, Warren or herself. The only thing that she really knew was that her house of cards was crumbling. She wasn't safe. She needed help.

She had to find Warren.

Chapter Sixteen

Alisa
Four years before

Flipping over the envelope in her fingers, Alisa melted into the back stoop of the tiny home she shared with her mother to a symphony of ambient noise from her LA neighborhood. Ambient noise that she usually found soothing had grown to be nothing more than an annoyance. Then again, by that point, almost everything irritated her. Blame the sleep deprivation, the endless nights holding her mother's hand in the hospital or the stress— Whichever way, she was on a hair trigger.

She stilled, only moving to slide her finger over the corners, trying to feel where they grew sharp. Maybe she needed it to hurt. Maybe she needed to not feel numb.

Alone, her preferred state, she sat on the small stoop that led out onto a cracked, fenced-in concrete pad where her mother's car was parked—like anyone would steal that beat-up car, anyway.

The crisp edge of the white envelope nearly sliced her finger as she grazed it, an omen for what she knew was inside. There was no mystery. The resulting drop in her stomach was the only thing she'd allowed herself to feel all day. Emotions had grown dangerous since the morning she'd woken up completely orphaned. It had only been a few days, but she suspected she'd never get used to the new reality.

Sucking in a reluctant breath, she slowly tore at the envelope opening, knowing there was no point of waiting any longer. It wasn't like avoiding it would make it go away. Her naked toes digging into the sagging wood step, she pulled out the paper housed inside, feeling the dry air of LA burn a little in her throat. The cheery bright colors on the letter did nothing to quell her unease. The bill, like many others, was well past due.

"I've been doing everything I can," Alisa said to herself, taking in the large sum at the bottom.

Just one other thing she couldn't pay.

"Everything?" A masculine voice appeared from the alley beside the red brick house her mother rented.

Her head cranked to see...Dean Teller, the dark-haired boy who lived down the street and grew up with her. She hadn't seen much of him lately. It had been a while.

"Dean—" she gasped, like she was seeing a ghost.

He swished toward her in a black leather jacket, peeling off his too-cool shades. He shot her a look that was purposeful and tough. A scar running down his jaw was fresh, a reminder of where he'd been.

She continued, surprised, "You're back...already?"

"Time flies, Alisa."

"Indeed."

She folded the bill, stuffing it in the envelope, hiding it away. There were things she didn't want anyone to see.

Watching him cross his arms, Alisa didn't miss one fact. Dean was not the boy she'd grown up with anymore. A handful of years in the Marines, he had grown up quick. His recent tour in Iraq had made him a man.

"Sorry about your mom," Dean said, flat-toned. "She was a nice lady."

She dropped her gaze, wishing only to count every tiny pebble at the bottom of the stairs and to get away from his pitying gaze.

"Happened fast, didn't it?" he continued.

Alisa nodded, biting her lip.

"Need any help?" he asked.

She shook her head, the bill burning beside her. She damn well needed help, that was for sure. She was losing the house and was being hounded for everything else they owed. Cancer had cost more than just her mother's life. It was costing her own, too.

"Alisa," Dean pressed, "look at me. You're not fooling anyone."

She flickered her gaze up, still silent. His face held stern, unapologetic. She knew him well enough to know he had an agenda. He'd always been like that.

He carried on, "I know what's happening here. I know you need money. You need help."

"I don't know what you've heard —" she started, but he cut back in, his gaze trailing up and down her perched form.

"Don't bullshit me. We both know." His arms dropped from his chest, and he reached inside his jacket.

That was when she caught the wording of the badge on the breast. *Deadeye MC.*

"Is that some sort of bike gang?" she probed, peaking her eyebrow, desperate to change the topic.

Pulling out his phone, he chuckled. "Ah — just a little thing me and the guys put together in Iraq. It's nothing."

She narrowed her eyes at him, questioning. What was he up to?

He pointed at her with his phone. "Do you have anywhere to go at the end of the month? I can put you up somewhere."

She found herself folding her arms protectively. "I'm fine."

"Where are you going to go?"

She tightened her arms around her ribs, holding on for dear life. The truth was…she didn't know.

A pause found them, which he seemed to savor as he drank her in. Nearly curled up in front of him, he apparently sensed her vulnerability. He was practically salivating.

A sly grin crossed his lips. "You don't have a plan, do you?"

Her eyes grew hot. He wasn't wrong. And she was close to being screwed.

"Look… Everything has just happened so fast," she pleaded for her self-respect. "I haven't had time to even think."

Not even about how she'd just been accepted to med school. The school sure as hell wasn't going to pay for her to attend, and getting a loan was nothing more than a pipe dream with her credit.

Dean licked his lips, focusing on her, like she was the last unicorn on earth. He knew something.

"Alisa, you don't have to do this alone. You need help."

She exhaled, confessing, "Dean, I have no one, nothing. No one can help me now."

"Not true."

"Then who?"

He stepped forward, throwing out his coarse hand to her. "Me."

Chapter Seventeen

Warren
Present day

The sun had long set over his training camp, but Warren didn't care. All the guys had gone home long ago and were probably having dinner with their families. Warren had had girlfriends before. He knew what those final moments were like before a big tour.

Hard. Heartbreaking. Lots of anticipation.

And that's why Warren had reluctantly agreed to the master chief's request to let the guys have a long weekend. Though it was only Thursday, they'd trained hard enough that week. It was as good as it was going to get, the master chief had said. Let them all go to Crash's wedding the next night and blow off some steam.

Warren reached into his gun case, storing the customized rifle he'd had purpose-built for the mission, locking it up. It was kind of like his baby.

Maybe he'd be the only guy on target practice all weekend. Maybe he'd be the only one camping out in the middle of the desert, with dummies of high-priority targets for company. But he didn't mind.

That's where he was at home.

He paced to the front of the compound, not far from where the HMMWV — or Humvee — was parked. They had a handful of different vehicles driven up here for some of the more technical aspects of assault training. But tonight, that HMMWV was going to be his camper. He'd already pitched a small tent in the bed of it — the type of tent that he could ditch the top fly and watch the stars at night. It was hot enough that he barely needed anything anyway — just a cot and a net to keep night crawlers away.

Solemn, solitary, he focused on the few tasks he had left to do for the evening before trying to find something else to keep his mind off things for the rest of the night. Yeah, to say his mind had become addicted to fantasizing about the taste of her skin would be an understatement. He couldn't get a fleeting thought of Alisa through his mind without his cock throbbing in angst. To say he wanted to fuck the shit out of her would be...

Well, goddamn accurate as fuck.

Things had just gotten complicated. He didn't have space for complicated.

Pivoting to turn back to the office, he saw a flash of headlights coming off the gravel road in the distance. Immediately, he was thrown out of the temporary peace he'd attained. His spidey senses tingled, wondering what the fuck it was all about. Sure as hell, someone showing up randomly wasn't going to be good. As the car repositioned itself in front of the gate, he heard a buzzing at the radio in the office. He felt irritation rising up his neck as he realized that whoever was there was trying to get in.

Marching inside the office door, getting to the radio console, he pressed the button.

"Can I help you?" he grunted into the box, keeping it distinctly unfriendly.

He waited for a second, still seeing the headlights outside the gate.

Finally, a response.

"Warren?" An anxious feminine voice crackled through the line.

Alisa's voice.

"*Christ*," Warren snarled, buzzing her into the gate and marching out of the office.

His temporary peace was kicked aside, replaced by a blaze sparking in his chest. What the fuck was she doing? He should have known her damn curious eyes had caught on when they'd driven by the place together.

Shit, she's bright.

As his heavy boots hit the packed dirt, he stopped dead in his tracks, crossed his arms and watched her old beater drive down the gravel driveway. His mind spun with questions, including what the hell he was going to say to her. Within seconds, she was parking right in front of him, shaking like a leaf as she got out of the car. And despite the fact that it looked like she was suffering from heat stroke, with her cheeks flushed and skin glistening, she was undeniably the hottest piece of ass he'd ever seen.

For the first time all day, he felt that aching pain in his back, deep in his scar—a reminder of what mistakes cost.

"So, this is where you work?" Alisa broke the silence in the desert night air, approaching him in the dim moonlight.

"You shouldn't be here," Warren said, struggling to temper his growing anger.

"We need to talk."

"No."

"Warren," she let out, flickering her dark eyes at him. He felt her hostility, her aching.

"You need to leave," he pointed back at the gate, unwilling to get into it. "We don't even tell our families about where we go, what we do."

Alisa's face twisted as she snapped back, "So that's how these guys all cheat on their wives then, huh?"

"That might be some guys, but that's not me," he growled, unprepared for her assault. Though, he knew he should have expected it—given the way he'd left her.

"Oh, right—you're the good guy, aren't you?" she flipped back sardonically, rolling her eyes.

He felt his jaw tighten, his shoulders flexing. His body wanted to do things that his brain didn't.

She continued, lashing out, "Mr.-fucking-perfect, huh?"

Warren tightened his arms across his chest, knowing exactly where it was going. As she got closer, he inhaled her seductive scent but couldn't miss the redness around her eyes. *She's been crying.* Clenching his jaw, he knew he'd caused those tears. The truth was painful, and she'd clearly come all that way to let him have it.

"Why the hell did you leave without saying anything?" she demanded, stepping forward to point at his chest.

"Because I'm the good guy."

"That's what you keep saying," Alisa said, but then took in a deep breath, seemingly collecting herself.

When she pivoted, he felt her demeanor transform in front of him, less attacking and more real. She curled her long black hair over her shoulder habitually.

"You shouldn't be here," he repeated.

"But you're the good guy, aren't you? That's why I'm here."

He cocked his head, assessing.

She added, "I'm here, standing in front of you, asking…"

He had to stop her. "Asking for what?"

He felt her draw back in surprise, eyes widening. The way the moonlight reflected in her wet eyes nearly bowed him then and there.

She took in a deeper breath before finishing her thought. "I'm asking for more. I'm asking if we could be more."

"What do you want me to do with that, Alisa?" He opened his arms, flashed his hands into the air and his tone grew angrier by the second.

"I took a risk," she said.

"We both did."

"But you aren't in the same situation as me." She flickered her lashes at him, pleading — that type of pleading that lit him on goddamn fire.

"I can't give you more. I can't give anyone *more*." He motioned to the facility. "I'm fully committed to this. I'm leaving again soon, and I'm going to be gone for a long time."

"I just—"

"And you've got that." He pointed at the ring hidden underneath her creamy tank. "That's what you are committed to."

He let that message sink in, taking a step back. Yeah, he felt the *fire* between them…the lust. But that was what he knew he'd have to do. The second things got complicated, and he knew it would come to that.

"*Warren*…" She chewed her lip, blinking her eyes to keep in all in.

He quickly countered, laying down the law, "There's not a chance in hell that this can work. We both knew this."

"But—"

"This was never going to be anything more."

His words were met by a red flush flowing up her neck. A tear rolled down her cheek, as she shook her head in pure loathing. He took another step back, creating space between them, grumbling to himself.

"I should have trusted my instincts."

"And what instincts were those?" She lashed out as he backed off.

"To stay away."

As his words hit, he spun and marched away, knowing he couldn't watch her fall apart. He couldn't—because he couldn't do anything about it. Shouldn't. Wouldn't. That was the way it had to be. There was no other option. She had to accept that.

He had.

"Warren, *stop*," her increasingly incensed tone trailed behind him as he turned. The way she said his name was nearly his undoing. "I need you to listen."

"I can't," Warren called over his shoulder, motioning back to the gate.

The only thing worse than hearing her cry was hearing nothing at all. Silence hit him hard as he marched away, moving through to the motor pool to the HMMWV, where his makeshift tent was. He shook his head—willing to hear her get in her car and drive away, willing her to listen to him one last time, willing the idea of Alisa wiped clean from his head.

But his engorging cock had other ideas.

As he got to the HMMWV, adjusting the straps on the side of the bed to secure the tent, he heard the telltale patter of female steps behind him. A rage rushed through his body. She didn't know what she was doing to him, what she was putting him through. He was seconds from detonating.

"I told you to fucking leave," he snapped, turning to face her.

"I need help."

"Help?" he drilled. "What kind of help?"

She blinked her big dark eyes up at him and slid her tongue across her shaking lip, searching for words. He knew she had run out of them. He knew…because it was the same for him. The anger in her face was palpable—something he felt deeply. She pursed her lips as if to say something, but he found himself sliding his hand up her neck once again.

"You're asking for trouble," he growled at her, deep and threatening, gripping her jaw.

"I'm already in trouble," she said.

"And you want more?"

"Let me have it."

With a dark groan, he grabbed her body, drawing her fast and hard against his frame. He wasted no time claiming her mouth again with his, reminding her that he set the tone and pace…not her. Dancing his tongue with hers, he tasted her broken dreams, her spent wishes.

"I'm not the guy for you," he grunted as his pulled her neck up to his mouth, letting his teeth trace down the sensitive flesh. "I have nothing to give you."

"Then just give me *this*," Alisa pleaded, losing herself in his grasp, sinking into his mouth.

It was a bargain he couldn't refuse, not with her sexy, lithe body pressed up against his, and his cock angrily thumping in his pants.

Damn, he had to have her.

Chapter Eighteen

Alisa

With the desert breeze catching in her hair, Alisa felt Warren's grip on her. He kissed her so deep and thoroughly that she started feeling dizzy. They'd been there before. She knew how it went.

Alisa had really enjoyed his kiss that last time, but things were already at the next level. In control, he demanded her surrender as he tasted her. He forced her body into his, gripping and holding her where he wanted. Her mind ran wild with fantasies about what he was going to do next, driving a tingling sensation up her thighs. He pulled away A dangerous sheen spanned his eyes, ready to make her plead for it.

"You want this?" he asked.

"*Please.*"

The subsequent feeling of his hands all over thundered desire throughout her body.

"You want more?"

"Please, just be the man I need tonight," she said.

"Against my better judgment."

He kissed her again, deeper, lapping up the sweet taste in her mouth before drawing back—teasing her with his delicious lips to no end. She tilted her head involuntarily as he pushed her jaw up to get better access to her neck, biting at it, shooting pain and pleasure down to her core. It was damn clear. He was as hungry as fuck.

And he wanted to take her down.

Alisa stirred in his arms, aching for him in ways she couldn't explain—aching for him in ways that had forced her to drive all the way up here.

"Tell me how you want it," he said.

Alisa bit her lip, passion and lingering anger burning her eyes. His grip only got harder, impossible to run from. She liked that feeling, liked to see the alpha breaking out of him. She liked to submit to him. She knew very well what she craved, but she'd never thought of sharing it with anyone…except him.

"I want you to want me so bad that you won't take *no* for an answer," she blurted out as he grazed his teeth up her neck, finding her ear.

He kissed all the way back to her mouth, kissing her hard and deep with a lot of tongue. He kissed her how she wanted him to fuck her—without apology.

She continued spilling her darkest thoughts. "I want you to push me against a wall, take me for your own—rough and angry. Even if I fight you, you just need to have me…"

"Is that your fantasy?" He exhaled, hauling her ass up in his hands, pulling her increasingly wet crotch up against the fabric of his pants.

"Yes—"

"To take you how I want it, whenever I want it?"

"*Yes*," she confessed.

She ran her hands up his muscles, feeling every defined swell and bulge. Sinking and surrendering into his strength gave her a sense of security she never had.

"I can do that."

"Oh my God, Warren — *please*."

A growl escaped his mouth as he picked her up, throwing her over his shoulder, moving them both into the bed of the HMMWV. Inside the small tent, he slammed her body down on a cot, ripping off her pants and tank. In just her underwear and bra, his tough gaze evaluated her, running his hands up her soft, trembling thighs.

He tore off his shirt, kicking his pants and boxers to the side of the bed, revealing his jaw-droppingly gorgeous hard body and harder cock. She sat up to lean forward, grasping for his cock, needing to touch and taste the pre-cum glistening on the head. But he thumped her back onto the pillow, working his hands up her thighs to her panties, mission-focused. In one fell swoop, he ripped them off, tearing the lacy fabric. Her mouth dropped open as the pain ricocheted through her body, but then he found her bra — tearing it off just as viciously.

"Aren't you going to fight back?" he growled.

She grinned, pushing back on his chest as hard as she could. He easily overpowered her, seeming to savor every second of it. Breathing heavily, his cock bouncing in hardness, he gripped the gold chain around her neck that housed her engagement ring.

"*This*," he grunted, fury in his face.

She had no time to respond. He'd already yanked on the chain, breaking it and throwing it across the bed of the truck. A clinking sound echoed in the small space as he dropped his head to grasp her breasts, tasting and biting each nipple in turn.

As he sucked on her tits, any thought of what he'd just done left her mind, and she quickly found his rough hands drawing lower down her abdomen, teasing her once again. That was what she was growing to love about Warren. He helped her forget, to live in the moment. Her trembling thighs practically shook in anticipation, needing his body to graze her pussy, needing to feel his cock.

God, she felt so turned on. It was unbelievable.

The more she writhed underneath his mouth, the harder he strapped her body flat on the cot, sending a clear message. He was going to do what he wanted to her. That gave her a sense of security she couldn't buy.

"Aren't you going to tell me to stop?" he growled as she moaned underneath his mouth, grazing down her tummy toward her hairless mound.

"Please stop," she uttered so damn unconvincingly.

"Don't fucking move, you little slut."

With his wet, heavy tongue, he traced down the wet slit, exposing her throbbing clit.

"Oh, God." Alisa turned as she squirmed, the intensity too much. She needed to orgasm more than she ever had in her life.

Gripping her hips hard, bruising her sensitive skin, he angrily pushed her bucking hips down and feasted on her pussy. Licking up and down her clit, swirling his tongue all around it, he groaned with her moaning. The rhythm he found was intoxicating, making her delirious with desire.

"Warren, *please*," she pleaded, nearly crying due to how badly she needed it. "Don't do this."

Her attempt at fighting him off was laughable. He sure found it amusing. She wasn't fooling anyone. He tightened his grip on one side of her hip, shooting pain up her side, and used his other hand to find the opening of her pussy, driving several fingers inside her. It seemed he was going to make her pay for her bad acting.

"You're *my* slut now," he growled as he drove her closer to the edge. Her abs tightened as she gripped his gorgeous auburn hair.

"I'll only ever be a slut for you —" she gasped as he found a particularly sweet spot.

Fingering her faster, hammering that spot that she loved, he flicked her clit relentlessly with his tongue, giving her no break and demanding her orgasm to flow. She was so goddamn close it hurt, and his insistent touch only drove her closer to where she wanted to be. The pain and pleasure he made her feel were too damn good, and that's when the epiphany hit her. He made it okay for her to feel. He made it okay to surrender. Because he was going to keep her safe. As that realization planted in her brain, she felt herself crying out his name again and again, begging him for something...anything.

Begging for more.

She intertwined her fingers in his hair and pulled him closer into her. While he was still pumping his fingers inside her with her nearly over the edge, he turned his head and bit the inside of her thigh, at first playfully, then harder — until she screamed. God, she loved it when he made her hurt. His intensity drove her well over the edge, feeling everything in her body shake violently as some crazy orgasm crested, unlike anything she'd felt before, releasing her juice all over his fingers. He wasted no time, growling in hunger, as he grabbed her body to rip her off the cot. Switching them, he dropped his body down, lying on his back and hauling her smaller frame to straddle him. Still unsteady from her insane climax, she locked eyes with him. He kept his fingers on her clit as he worked her down to his big cock.

"Ride me," he grunted, holding her body to keep her upright.

He slid her body down his cock, feeling every inch opening her pussy more and more. It was so goddamn intense that she buckled forward, her tits swaying in his face.

They'd stopped being civilized and became animals, fucking each other into a goddamn raw state. Never in her life had she experienced something so fresh, so passionate. Her lust for the man was through the roof — or, through the peak of his military tent.

He sucked and bit at her breasts once again as he fiercely rocked her hips back and forth over him, his heavy cock buried deep within her pussy. She opened her mouth to find breath, but she was simply breathless, the feeling of being so full completely foreign to her.

"*Harder,*" he ordered.

Unrelenting, he moved her hips faster, taking his cock deeper and deeper. She groaned loudly, hearing the antennae at the front of the HMMWV bouncing as he fucked her relentlessly. The truck's suspension was tested as he growled, his cock throbbing and pulsing inside her. He was just as close as she was — her second orgasm growing closer to the surface. Multiple orgasms had never been a thing for her, but he was making it one.

She'd never had a man so perceptively hear her body, understand her deepest desires.

Falling forward, her hair forming a private tent over his face, she kissed him in a way she'd never kissed before, tasting herself on his mouth. Losing herself in the moment, she whispered everything onto his lips as they rapidly played and danced with each other's tongues.

"I've never met anyone like you," she said.

"Me neither."

"I'm so into you."

He growled loud and long, punctuating it with profanity as his muscles tensed, his body flexed, and his cock pulsed harder than ever before. He was hitting the apex.

"Me, too, *fuck*—" he yelled as he came inside her.

Heaving for breath, she let herself fall on top of his chest, wrapping his arms around her. He held her tight, close, like he was never going to let her go. It was a promise. Their inhalation became synchronized, and she closed her eyes, trying to enjoy the temporary slice of paradise that she'd been given.

And she knew that she'd never forget him.

Never.

The intensity of the thought, of the moment, flushed a strange response up her face—tears involuntarily springing to her eyes once again. She wasn't the emotional type, but something about Warren just drew every emotion out of her that she never knew she had. He made her…warm and fuzzy—two things she didn't think she was or could be.

"Why'd you come here?" he asked.

"I guess—I just had to know."

"And do you *know* now?"

"Yes."

She chewed her lip, afraid to confess. Classic Alisa resigned to hide her emotions, but just then, she was too sated to prevent it from happening. A few tears strayed, falling onto his chest where she laid, breathing with him.

He reached up and felt her cheek, felt her eyes. "Are you crying?"

She sniffled, wanting to deny it, anxiety lurching — *what a way to ruin the moment.*

But Warren didn't reject her, chastise her. Not at all. In fact, he responded just by squeezing her into him tighter, holding her so close that she could hear his hammering heart. They lay like that for a little while, to the point that she felt them both drifting into a peaceful place, into the paradise she felt with him.

To Alisa, it just felt like home...being held once again against his solid chest.

Chapter Nineteen

Alisa

Alisa curled into Warren, inhaling that intoxicating scent for the last time. She didn't know all the rules he played by, but she'd gathered he'd get in a lot of shit for fucking her in the back of the military vehicle.

"We can't stay here," Warren said, breaking the silence.

"I figured." She traced down his defined ab muscles, feeling him suck in breath at her touch.

"I would drive you home, but you can't leave your car here, either," he said.

"I get it. I'll be on my way." Alisa tried to get up.

He pulled her back into him, staring her down. "*Stop.* I'll follow you home, of course. Make sure you get there."

His chivalrous offer stirred her.

"You don't have to do that," she said.

"Yeah, I do. I've seen your engine."

A grin spread across her face at his playful comment. He knew better than anyone how questionable her car was — liable to break down at any time. In return, she enjoyed teasing him, playfully running her fingers up and down his chest.

"When are you going to cash the check?" He exhaled as his abs flexed at her barely-there touch.

She chewed on her lip, not knowing the answer. "I don't know."

"Do it in the morning. Seriously."

"Maybe."

She could tell he was going to challenge her, but the way she twirled her fingers up his masculine skin, admiring his naked chest, he seemingly couldn't get the words out. She was turning him on all over again. His cock even started twitching again, and she was tempted to grab it for a second round.

"We really have to get out of here," he said.

He squeezed her in harder, purposefully demobilizing her. Breathing in her hair, he kissed her forehead in a way that screamed *you mean something to me*. Then, he released her, getting them both off the cot to grab discarded clothing. He sorted through fabric, pulling on only his boxers and jeans. After he tossed her pants and tank to her, she dropped to her hands and knees, searching for the broken chain.

"Looking for this?" he asked.

She looked up, seeing him dangling the chain with the ring. Something awkward settled between them. A reminder. Timidly, she stood, reaching out and taking it from him. She didn't miss the crackle in his eyes as she did. She tucked the necklace into the pocket of her pants, never leaving his gaze.

Flipping his crumpled shirt over one shoulder, Warren then turned to jump out of the tent, silent and serious. As he leaped out, she saw that same long scar on his naked back—the one she'd seen at his pool. It was a reminder of how little she knew about him.

Following him, she found herself standing beside him in the packed dirt as he yanked his shirt on. He bent over beside the Humvee. She ran her fingers up the side of his back where the scar was, close to it but not touching. Even in the dim moonlight, she could see it wasn't well stitched. She could have done much better, even as a student.

"How did you get this?" she asked.

He shot up immediately, brushing her off—trying to stifle the wincing in his face. His pain was clear, and his expression warned her not to go there, not to bring it up. A little surprised, she stumbled back as he motioned to her car back near the entrance.

"How long did it take you to drive up here in that shitbox?" he asked.

A little smirk crossed her lips as she replied, "A lot longer than how long it took you to drive me up here for the engagement party…in your big, fancy truck."

Warren stopped, grabbing her to him one more time. The stars glimmering overhead, a gentle breeze rustling the Yucca trees behind them, he held the small of her back, pulling her into his embrace. She trailed her fingers up his biceps and shoulders, then grazed the stubble on his neck and chin, like she was trying to memorize him. He said he was leaving soon, and she could only guess he'd be going far, somewhere inaccessible. He couldn't easily come back, couldn't be there if she needed him. She'd be alone again, trying to protect herself.

He dropped his head to give her a kiss, slow and sweet. Caring. Wishing. But *apologetic*. She felt a strange magic, like that moment belonged in a movie.

Then he moved back, pulling his keys out of his jeans.

"Ready?" he asked.

"As I'll ever be."

"I have to leave once you get home," he explained.

"Wasn't this supposed to be seven days?"

"That was the idea."

Alisa took in a deep breath, mustering courage, processing thoughts. Feeling a little out of it from the sex and the heat, she stumbled to get the words out, but she eventually did.

"What happened? Why'd you drop the check and run?"

"Alisa, it would be all fun and games until someone gets hurt," he said. "We jumped in too deep, too quick. It was a mistake."

"Are you afraid of hurting me?" she asked.

"Yeah."

"Don't be. You can't hurt me," she lied.

"I can," he replied, "and I will."

He crossed his arms. She found herself nodding, too dazed to argue. Something in the back of her mind set off alarms, trying to get her to say something. He opened his mouth to continue, but stopped himself, then nodded at her curtly.

"We'd better get going," he said.

"Okay."

He pivoted and marched toward his truck, leaving her leaning on her car. She pursed her lips to blurt out more, but she fell mute. The way he had gazed so intently into her eyes just threw her off, making her cave back into herself. Everything she'd struggled with at the hospital splashed across her mind, along with other words screaming like a hurricane, throttling her to speak up for herself. *He doesn't understand. I need help.*

But she just watched him walk away, knowing she had to let that be their grand finale...as unceremonious as their beginning.

* * * *

As Alisa made her way back to the city, watching Warren's truck through her rear-view mirror was both agonizing and comforting. Part of her wished she could abandon her car off a cliff and jump in with him, settle in with him and never have to face her real life again. She tried to focus on driving and stop thinking about him.

Music didn't help her mind get off her confused, conflicted feelings, and the long trip down from the mountains only made her insane. She just felt so powerless, stuck between a man she couldn't have and a man who had her under his thumb. The feeling of being so powerless only exploded as she pulled around her block.

Emergency vehicles and displaced residents lined up in front of her building on the street. Firetrucks. People clutching blankets. Cops. That was all she saw at first.

Then she grasped what was happening. Her building was on fire. She yanked the car over to the side of the boulevard, watching flames licking the sky. It wasn't hard to deduce. Her apartment was the epicenter of the fire, complete charcoal by that point.

She jumped and shrieked as her driver's door whipped open, a dark figure leaning into the car.

But she let out her breath when she realized it was Warren.

"It's on fire!" she cried. "What the hell is going on?"

Warren pulled her from the car, deadly serious. He wrapped his arms around her shoulders, holding her protectively against his chest. He paused, his head like a periscope—looking all around. She felt something breaking inside her, watching everything she owned going up in flames and smoke.

"When you said you needed help, Alisa, what did you mean?" he asked, staring down at her. "Were you fucking serious?"

"Warren—"

His grip on her tightened.

"Do you actually need help, Alisa?" he asked. "Is this for real?"

"*Yes.*"

He spat profanities, shaking his head in disbelief. He shot his gaze around again, seeming to take in every detail.

"What type of help do you need?" he pressed. "What type of trouble are you in?"

He stood firm, waiting for her reply. But she had too many words rumbling through her head. She felt stunted, unable to connect. It was the same social problem she always had when under stress. He grew visibly frustrated as his grip tightened to assess her. She just felt like she was in a different world.

"You need to talk to me," he said. "This is serious now, Alisa."

"I'm trying—"

"Try harder. *Fuck.*"

Then a police officer approached them from the side, his pock-marked aging face illuminated by the blaze. Warren's clutch stiffened on her shoulders, dragging her into him. *Defending*.

"Ma'am—do you live here?" the cop asked in a croaky voice, his notebook out as he walked toward her, clearly judging.

"Yes," Alisa said.

She tried to add more but felt herself choking. Words would not come out. Her home was on fire. *I've lost everything*.

Slowly she started sliding downward, losing balance. Warren heaved her up, holding her strong and tight against his hard frame, not letting her fall. He was her support. Hot tears poured down her cheeks as he spun her face into his chest, absorbing her anguish. She grew numb.

As she buried her tears into Warren's chest, all she could hear was the cop asking Warren questions.

"When was the last time she was home?" the cop asked.

"I don't know."

"But she's been with you?"

Warren replied slowly, "Yes—we've been up in the mountains for most of the night."

"Are you...together?"

"What does that mean?" Warren's tone grew distrustful.

"I think you know what I mean."

A strange pause unfolded between the two men. Warren held her tighter, silent.

Eventually, the cop continued, "She can't enter the premises, even once they get the flames out. Does she have somewhere to stay?"

"Yes," Warren confirmed, his hand reaching out to take something.

"With you?" the cop pushed.

Warren remained quiet, shoving something into his pocket.

The cop grunted, concluding, "That's my card. You'd better call me tomorrow."

Alisa pressed her eyes shut as she thought of the few things she'd still had of her mother's as well as her textbooks, her med notes... Why the hell had it happened?

Warren ushered her forward, but she stumbled, buckled and nearly fell. He wasted no time in picking her up, getting her bag from her car and settling her into his truck. He was in control, and he was moving her to safety. It only reaffirmed everything she'd come to believe about him.

Sitting in the passenger seat of his truck, she caught his expression as he jumped into the driver's seat. A troubled look had taken over his features — a look that told Alisa that something was very, very wrong.

Chapter Twenty

Warren

Warren didn't expect to be leaning over his bathtub at half past two in the morning, but there he was — a wet cloth in hand. He dripped hot water down Alisa's shaking back, warming her, reviving her. She remained curled up, her head resting on her knees — frozen, scared.

And she had damn good reason to be, he griped silently to himself. Someone was clearly after her.

"Should we call someone for you?" he probed, studying her reaction. "Your fiancé, maybe?"

Her back muscles noticeably flinched as he said the words, telling him everything even as she remained silent. He grabbed the bar of soap, lathering and washing her arms and shoulders, massaging the tension out of her.

"Seems weird that you're not calling him," he said.

"What do you want me to say to that?" she whispered, her trembling voice barely reaching his ears.

"Is this what you meant when you said you needed help?"

He let the question linger, trickling soapy water down her delicate back. He wanted her to respond but wasn't sure she was fully with him. She was so goddamn shaken.

So he employed every tactic he knew.

As he kneaded, he enjoyed how smooth and soft her skin felt under his calloused hands. Bathing her was nearly the distraction he needed to stay cool. But it wasn't enough to take his mind off the burning urgency of the matter. Dogged, he pushed on.

"Tell me about him."

"What do you want to know?" Her dark eyes flitted up to him, looking at him for the first time in a while.

"What type of guy is he?"

"Not like you," she admitted.

He found a knot in her back, working it, giving her space to elaborate…and she did.

"He's an asshole." She closed her eyes, shaking her head as she slowly peeled upward from her position.

"Yeah? And why are you marrying him?"

"I don't want to," she said too fast, then chewed her lip.

As she averted her gaze, she unconsciously told Warren something. She didn't want to talk about it. That was exactly the moment when he really needed to know the truth about her engagement. Something was clearly very wrong.

"Talk to me." His tone grew darker, more urgent.

"It's complicated." Alisa let out a long exhalation. "It started as one thing and turned into another."

"What does that mean?" Warren asked, trying to keep her talking, get her to open up.

She shook her head, biting her lip, absent. "He must know. He *must*. My apartment... Was that a threat?"

"You tell me. What does he know? I'll help you."

Haunted, she gazed at him. "No one can help me now."

Warren arched his eyebrow, completely taken aback. At first, he had just been trying to get a sense of who her fucking fiancé was. But, by that point, screaming alarms were going off in his head. *I'm a fucking idiot. Why didn't I see it?*

His thoughts darted to the loud blacked-out bike he'd seen driving by her place, seeing him exit her place — then the cop asking weird questions. She was in serious trouble. He'd played stupid games with her. It was all far worse than he'd ever thought.

He reached out, gently holding onto her chin and turning her face to look at him. He studied her, trying to understand.

"Has he hurt you?"

Her lips trembled again as the words came out of his mouth, and she immediately ran her hands over her face, shaking her head. Something told Warren she was shaking her head because she didn't want to answer, not because she was telling him 'no'.

And nothing — fucking nothing — lit a goddamn fire inside Warren like the thought of someone he cared about being hurt.

He found his hands gripping her more tightly, afraid she would slip away. She slumped over, all that brightness and energy fading. Whatever her secrets were, Warren knew they were fucking dark. Any man that would hurt a woman…

Goddamn.

He growled, "I need you to tell me everything."

"I'm scared, Warren." She shook as she said it, and he knew he was trying to get blood from a stone. She was too deep into shock to confess.

"What's he going to do to me?" she mumbled.

"Nothing."

"How do you know?"

"Things have changed. You're under my protection—now that I see what's up." Warren's thoughts flashed to his tickle trunk of big-ass guns in the basement.

She grew silent again, shaking her head, leaving him to stew and brew dangerous plans. He knew how to kill, knew how to be stealthy, precise and untraceable. He wasn't against killing for a cause—and he owned that. SEAL training had taken a hold of a part of him so deep that he'd never be able to purge the natural warrior in him.

First, he had to take care of his ward. It was clear that Alisa was mentally and physically exhausted. It was clear that she'd broken down, she was traumatized and she couldn't take anymore. The mind could only take so much. He knew what his job was. He needed to get her to bed, get her some sleep and give her brain a break.

Unplugging the soaker tub in his master ensuite, he pulled her unsteady body up, her naked form tempting him once again. But he knew he couldn't be that guy. That was exactly what he was trying to get away from—taking advantage of her. She was too damn vulnerable for anything else that night, even his thumping cock.

Wrapping her in a towel, he dried her and plunked her into his big comfy bed. He readied himself to head downstairs to sleep on the couch, trying to live up to his own standards of being a decent fucking guy, having some semblance of honor, when he felt her stirring in between the sheets.

"Stay," she said in a small, pleading voice. "Please."

Warren let out a breath, knowing that was a bad fucking idea. But, how could he say *no* to her long, gorgeous frame and her sweet, loving face? He hesitantly settled in behind her, holding her tight to his chest, breathing promises into her hair. She intertwined her smooth silky brown legs with his, reinforcing everything he had come to realize.

I could never hurt her.

Any man that hurt women wasn't a real man.

That night, Warren barely slept. Wild scenarios running through his mind, he buried his face into her hair, wondering what the fuck was happening. His heart banged against his chest as his cock ached, pressed up against her tight ass. The growing anger pulsing through his body told him he was on a knife's edge. Everything that was complicated already had just gotten ten times worse, and he was goddamn concerned as hell. 'Pent-up' was an understatement by that point. He was in a fucking cage. And all he wanted to do was break out of the prison he was keeping himself in.

Hours of thoughts brought him nowhere, and he blinked open his bleary eyes to see the sun on the horizon once again. Thankfully, a peaceful Alisa was still fast asleep in his arms, in his bed.

And thank God it was finally a new day.

He slowly edged away, knowing he had to get a change of scenery to figure something out—before his tightening balls forced him to pin her down and have his way. As he sat up in his bed, looking down at her sleeping body, curled up and serene, he realized that image would be burned in his mind for the rest of his life. There was something just so damn captivating about her.

Every time he looked at her, his veins pulsed, reminding him what he really wanted.

Her.

He flexed his jaw as he swiftly left the room, leaving her alone to rest. The woman didn't need to be attacked in her sleep. When he checked his phone in his kitchen, his slowly awakening brain realized what day it was.

"It's fucking Friday, of course," he groaned to himself. *The day of Crash's wedding.*

Warren ran his hands over his face, wondering why the hell he subjected himself to sleep deprivation when he wasn't even on tour. Why the hell did he keep punishing himself? He scoffed at the thought, knowing the brutal answer. And that's when he grabbed his earbuds out of the drawer, throwing them in to start his morning workout—the only thing that made him feel sane.

Sweat. Pain. Fatigue. His autobiography would have to be titled *Relentless Pain and Hardship*. The harder he pushed himself, the more he felt in control, the more he felt like he was living up to expectations of himself. A perfect SEAL. A perfect leader. *No mistakes.*

The morning rolled on, and the sun rose higher. Warren found himself panting for breath in his driveway, sucking in hot air, after a series of intense rounds of cross-training in his empty garage. He thought about the cop and when to call him. The fire at Alisa's apartment was in no way an accident, he was sure. And that meant one thing only — someone was after her. To scare her seemed more likely, given the perfect plant of the cop asking questions right after.

Warren had no doubt in his mind that the cop was dirty, part of the larger plot to get after her. Warren trusted no one, assuming the worst right off the bat. He was never wrong about people.

And now — what to do about it?

He settled on trying to call the cop mid-morning or midday. He'd already flung out some fact-finding texts to his friends — friends who had other friends at LAPD. Everyone had friends.

He could get to the bottom of things on Alisa's behalf, shielding her from it all. He knew he'd be better at it. And he had the whole weekend before shipping out. In that time, he could help her find a new place, help her figure out her life so she'd be safe while he was gone. He had lots of friends to help with that. But, before he could ruminate further, a call came through his earbuds.

"Yup," Warren answered, seeing it was a blocked caller, likely someone from work.

"Chief." Master Chief Rose's voice came through the line.

Something in his tone told Warren it wasn't going to be a good call.

"Sir."

"I'm at the compound," the master chief said, pausing before continuing. "I see a tent on the back of a Humvee...but no one in it. Well, at least — not *anymore.*"

Warren stifled a groan, knowing exactly what his boss fucking saw. The man was damn clever, perceptive. *Knowing.*

"Look—" Warren started, knowing he'd tried his best to clean up the cot and the truck, but it had been dark and he had been trying to hurry the fuck up.

"No, no." The master chief stopped him, changing course. "That's not what this is about."

Warren paused, letting silence hang for a second until the master chief continued.

"This is about something that has become very clear to me. You have been behaving different this past week. Very different. There's something going on with you, Warren."

"I know," Warren admitted, grazing his teeth on his lip. He wasn't going to lie.

"Take a textbook SEAL—exemplary in every way— and suddenly, out of nowhere, he's making bad decisions. Is he trying to throw away his career or is he going through something?" the master chief said. "I ask myself—this is a guy who's deploying shortly on a high stress, maximum difficulty mission...*and* to lead a platoon. So, as your commanding chief, I've got to ask you—what the fuck is going on?"

"I don't really know." Warren exhaled slowly. "I met someone."

"A woman?"

"Yes, a *fucking* woman," Warren snapped, then checked himself, shaking his head. "But don't worry... I got this."

There was a pause on the line, then the master chief said, "I've never seen you like this before...and I've seen you with girlfriends."

"This girl is different. *Very* different."

"Fine. I need to meet her."

"Not happening," Warren concluded, shaking his head.

"You aren't bringing her to the wedding today?"

Warren knew there was only one right answer, so he remained silent.

The master chief continued, "You're not going to tell me that you aren't planning on going. These men, your crew — they are good guys. They need to see you show up. This is *your* platoon. You have to set the tone for morale."

"I don't do weddings."

"You are today. Bring her. It'll be fun. Do you remember what *fun* is?"

"No."

Warren let out a frustrated noise, growling at his boss. A fucking wedding was the last thing he needed. Command staff could be so fucking meddling sometimes. That was not how the fucking weekend was supposed to go. Warren had important shit to do, problems to solve.

"Christ, I hate to issue this as an order." Master Chief Rose laughed.

"Don't."

"You need a swift kick in the ass. I've never had a better man working for me. No chance in hell I'm losing you now, after everything."

Warren recognized that the box was shrinking. "Look... I'll see what I can do," he finally said.

"Good — Let's have a drink tonight and figure this all out."

Warren ripped out his headphones, irritated. He had better things to do than go to a fucking wedding. What a goddamn waste of time. Marching inside in search of a cold glass of water, or Scotch, his peripheral vision caught an attractive woman gliding down his stairs.

He glanced over, sweat beading down the side of his face. Alisa smiled at him, tugging on his black T-shirt to cover her pussy, guilty and bashful.

"Good morning," she said.

"Morning."

God, she looked so fucking hot. Hot—and as vulnerable as hell. And that was exactly the moment when he realized he had no choice.

"We need to get you a dress."

"Why?" she asked.

"Because you are coming with me to a wedding today," he said and checked his watch. "We leave in three hours."

"*What?*"

She leaned over the railing, trying to get a better look to see if he was joking. He wasn't. He held his ground, needing that distance. His entire body throbbed to get closer to her, but he knew better. He didn't need to make matters more complicated than they already were.

"I don't think I'm up for that," she said.

"Doesn't matter, unfortunately."

"I don't get a choice?"

"I have to go, and I'm not letting you out of my sight." He made a seesaw motion with his hands.

Alisa looked like she wanted to rebuff him, wanted to counter—but she didn't. She crossed her arms.

"I don't like this."

"I don't care," he said, grabbing his cell. "Let's get you a dress."

Looking like a lost fawn, she gripped the railing for stability.

"I'm going to need more than just a dress, you know," she said.

"What's your suggestion then?"

She looked left and right, exhaling. "Look... I'll call Maria and get her to drop me off some supplies, since apparently she loves dressing me up."

"Dressing you up—?"

"Yes, exactly."

The look Alisa gave told him something—and his mind immediately wandered to the first day he'd met her, all dressed up in next to nothing. He felt his cock harden just thinking about those fucking shorts and how much he'd wanted to rip them off her, how bad he'd wanted her from the second she'd bent over in front of him, dusting his wood. Fuck, she could dust his wood all day long.

He needed to push Maria a big tip or at least drop a five-star web review, if she'd been behind the shorts.

That morning, his cock saw no relief, aching to the point of pain when Alisa turned and sauntered back up his stairs, emphasizing that she had nothing on underneath the T-shirt. Revealing *everything*.

"Damn," he grunted.

He watched her ass bounce as she crested the top of the staircase. If she was trying to torture him, she was doing it right.

He was growing rabid. Whatever protein shake he'd lined up for after his workout seem paltry compared to sucking up the sweet juice off her pussy. His rough hand gripped the countertop before him, trying to prevent himself from following her.

Cool it, big rig. You've got work to do.

Warren paced about his house, focused on getting shit done. His mind oscillated between two things—

work and her. He couldn't rid himself of the question of what the hell Maria was going to dress her up in this time. Was she responsible for the shorts? Why? Hell, he didn't even give a shit anymore. He just wanted to see Alisa's perfect body wrapped up in something that he could unwrap — or rip apart. His appetite for her was only deepening, growing harder and harder to control.

Maybe she'd get her fantasy after all. He was losing the ability to listen to the word 'no' in his head.

The more entrenched he got, the more invested he was, the more he felt like protecting her was second nature. He was inadvertently giving her more than he'd planned.

At the time they were due to make their exit, to make their drive to the wedding venue, Warren stood in the front hall, adjusting his navy-blue suit. Suit, but no tie. He was an open-collar type of guy, the white of his dress shirt highlighting how dark he'd let his tan get over the summer training. He'd never really looked at himself like that before, never really thought about it — but he wondered what Alisa saw.

He saw a hard-edged SEAL — a workhorse, like one of those Clydesdales. He saw a man who'd gotten gritty, dirty and bloody, and had never really got it all off, not even when he'd come home. He saw a man who had stopped living a life and had started living like a machine.

He saw a man who didn't stop.

Can't.

Then he heard high heels hitting the hardwood floor at the bottom of the staircase down the hall. His eyes darted over to Alisa, and he was forced to inhale sharply when he drank her in. He saw a woman in his house who only had eyes for him.

Maria had not disappointed.

In a strapless golden gown, long on one side, but short enough on the other to reveal her long, silky leg, she stunned him. Literally, *stunned*.

"Christ," he grumbled, adjusting his watch as she floated toward him.

Her long black hair, shiny and coifed, curled around her. Her bright white smile hit him hard, and his hands shook with need. All he wanted to do was lunge forward, rip that fucking dress off and —

"You okay?" She grinned at him, knowingly flickering her lashes.

He smiled back, readying to say something too clever, but then his gaze dropped once again to her chest, seeing something that spread bitterness in his mouth every time he saw it.

That *fucking gold chain* around her neck, that damn engagement ring nestled between her delicious breasts. He observed that she'd temporarily secured the break in the chain by leveraging the gold clasp to keep it all together.

The contaminated symbol didn't deserve to rest against her skin, he sneered silently. The sight wiped whatever smile had been there right off his fucking face. Why she'd bothered to fix it at all, he had no fucking clue. Why couldn't she just dump the fucking thing? The gold glinting back at him, mocking him — it immediately put him in a goddamn fucking mood.

Fuck.

"Let's go." He turned, marching toward the door.

After yanking it open and turning to usher her through, he kept his face emotionless as she walked past, chewing on her glistening lip as she was probably trying to see through his armor. The only thing Alisa didn't know yet was that his steel was impenetrable. No one got in.

Because five years before, he'd thrown away the key.

Chapter Twenty-One

Alisa

"Oh, thank you," Alisa said as she received a glass of fizzing champagne.

The server nodded curtly before moving with his tray to the other partygoers.

Feeling out of place, she stood apart from Warren in the lush garden. As beautiful as the wedding ceremony had been, it hadn't been a pleasurable experience. Maybe it was the bride, reminding Alisa of how close she'd come to marrying Dean, or maybe it was Warren, reminding her how unsettled everything still was. He had been so hostile with her since they'd left his house.

She sipped the golden bubbly in her flute, trying to calm her nerves, as she watched a seemingly relaxed Warren chat with the men in his crew like nothing had happened the night prior — like she wasn't melting in anxiety on the verge of a breakdown. Absolutely terrified. Alone.

Isolated.

Warren was right in front of her but a thousand miles away, all day giving her nothing but one-word replies. For a man who'd once drawn a deep, intimate passion from her, he was making her feel like she didn't belong with him.

Alone among a sea of strangers grouped together after the wedding, she waited impatiently for the dinner to take place in the upscale Southern California hotel that had a beautiful view of the Pacific Ocean. Truly, the whole thing was picturesque, like the bride had clipped the experience from a highlight reel. Alisa chewed her lip, looking around — knowing she should be enjoying the moment more and spending less time worrying about the flipping sensation in her tummy.

It didn't help that her phone had vibrated too many times with messages from Dean. She pulled out her cell, looking at the latest threatening tirade. He promised he was going to find her.

She examined her situation, the rising frustration at her fate. The only person she wanted to talk to was someone who could tell her when she could go back to her apartment so she could try to salvage anything she could — or someone who could tell her what the hell had happened in the first place. Playing nervously with her lower lip, running it along the flute, she felt a shadow loom over her.

She gazed up, sinking back under Warren's ferocious glare. His blue eyes had hardened to stone, driving chills up her spine.

"Don't answer him," he said.

"I'm not."

He reached out, plucking her cell from her fingers, turned it off and shoved it in his suit pocket... unapologetic. She parted her lips to argue, but he gave her a 'don't fuck with me' look, halting her.

"Are you the only person allowed to make calls?" she asked.

"Who do you need to call?"

"Maybe the cop from yesterday," she supposed. "Maybe I need answers."

He cut her off. "I'm handling that."

"Care to share, then?"

"No."

She nearly dropped the flute and her clutch at once. "*Warren*."

"Leave it with me," he said.

"This is *my* life."

Her gaze flitted around, only to then give him a certain stare when she was sure no wedding guest was watching them in their little corner of the garden.

"Alisa, I'm not playing games today," he snapped, eyes narrowing on her.

"Me neither."

She didn't miss the flush hitting his cheeks as his gaze intensified on her, darting up and down her body. Goosebumps crossed her chest, as if he'd grazed her with his fingertips.

She pouted her lips to say something back, to keep him there, but he shook his head, pulling away. Then he did what he'd done all afternoon. He moved a few feet away to talk to someone else, close enough to keep tabs on her but far enough to make that distance as clear as day. Mere feet between them, she felt like it was a chasm. A canyon. The Grand Canyon.

And she once again stood alone, trying to shrink into the flora so no one would see that she wasn't talking to anyone—that she didn't know anyone, that she didn't belong, that she was an imposter. Unseen, no one approached. And maybe she wasn't so upset about that, feeling less than equipped to be charming.

As cocktail hour transitioned into dinner, held outside the hotel on an elegant stone patio, Warren did what a date was expected to do — escorted her to their table, poured her wine, helped her do whatever she needed. But his stone gaze barely connected with hers. He played his role well enough, but she grew more embarrassed by the second, wondering if everyone else at their table saw what was so glaring to her — that they weren't together. They were so separate. She was there for one reason only, and it wasn't romantic. It wasn't intimate. It was pure business. Transactional.

The more wine she inhaled at dinner, the less she cared that she had an early shift at the hospital the next morning. That wasn't her — a dedicated med student. She'd never shown up even slightly hungover. But she'd grown distracted.

Slowly she was forced to admit that the wine wasn't helping, but she kept hoping it would. It would kick in any second, make her feel *less*. Because, at that precise moment, she was feeling a hell of a lot more than she'd ever felt since...

Well, since mom died.

Alisa suddenly pushed back from the dinner table, folding her napkin on her half-eaten plate.

Warren turned to her. "What's up?"

"I'm fine," she said, chewing her lip in that way she did.

She smiled politely at the other guests at the table, excusing herself as the ocean breeze caught her hair. Then she made a break for it.

The garden around the corner, overlooking the long sandy beach, seemed like a good place to be alone, an easy escape from the nearly concluded dinner. She picked up another glass of something bubbly as her heels clicked on the stone patio, sending her quickly around the corner of the hotel.

Entrenched in a canopy of gorgeous trees, she let out the pain that she'd been holding since Warren had first frozen her out. She was kind of tipsy, really freaked out. She was in crisis mode, living off pure adrenaline. Nothing felt okay.

She stationed herself at a stone bench that looked out over the ocean, inhaling the sweet scent of salt water as the sun gently settled on the horizon, taking a much-needed rest after a blistering day. The residual orange glow across the sky, polluted by the smog of the city, reminded her of her own life—what should be so beautiful, tarnished by toxins she felt powerless to stop.

"Good evening." A man's voice echoed through the space as he approached.

Alisa looked up to see a tall, lean man with receding gray hair and a clever face stopping a few feet away, waiting for her response. He swirled his snifter, motioning beside her.

"May I join you?"

"Yes, please." She nodded to the ample room on the stone bench beside her.

"I'm Travis," the man said as he sat. "I work with Warren."

"I'm Alisa."

"I've heard," he said, grinning.

A calm pause fell between them, and she realized that for a military man, he made her feel quite comfortable. He had the air of intelligence, the air of fatherly wisdom. She found herself turning, opening.

"I don't want this to come across the wrong way," Travis started, his eyes twinkling at he looked into her. "But, this afternoon, I've been watching, and I see the way he looks at you."

"Really?" she asked, hoping that was a good thing.

Travis nodded, knocking back the amber liquid in his snifter.

He continued, looking out over the sunset, "I've been in the Navy a long time. I've worked with Warren a long time. He's simply my best, and he deserves the best — but, he hasn't always been given that."

"What do you mean?" She leaned in, hanging onto every word, hoping to decode the enigma.

The nearly disappeared sun danced its final glow across Travis's face, illuminating the depth of the worries in his experienced face.

"Warren used to have a girlfriend, used to have a life — years ago," Travis said. "But, one day that all changed."

"Why?" She was nearly tripping over herself to learn more.

Travis just shook his head. "That's Warren's story to tell."

As soon as the words escaped, Alisa knew very well that it had something to do with Warren's scar. It just had to — She felt so much pain still in him, centering on that very spot — something still so unresolved, something that had never healed.

"Master Chief." A dark voice emanated from the entry to the garden, a warning in his tone.

Both of them turned to see Warren standing there, his arms crossed, not impressed.

Travis turned to Alisa, "It was a pleasure. Thank you for joining us today."

He shot her a charming wink before standing to shake Warren's hand, then promptly marching out of the garden. All Alisa could think of was — *will he ever tell me what happened?*

Alone in the dusk, Warren stepped forward through the shadowy garden, lit only by small amber lanterns. His glare never left her, watching her — ostensibly trying to piece together the conversation she'd just had. Despite the music and voices echoing from the other side of the hotel, all that Alisa could hear was the rustling of Warren's suit jacket as he walked up to her.

She sucked in air. It felt like time had stopped.

"You left," he said.

"I needed some air," she defended herself, matching his distance.

She saw his gaze dart down to the chain on her neck, and back up, emotionless. The ring between her breasts burned into her skin, screaming at her to say something. She reached down, pulling it up and toying with it in front of him.

"Is this what has bothered you?" she asked carefully.

"No."

His body stilled except his shoulders, visibly flexing — in fight mode. She nodded, hearing what he wasn't saying.

"This ring means something," she said, holding it up.

"No shit — it's your engagement ring."

"It's more than that. It's a reminder," she said. "A reminder of why I have to work so damn hard — to get out of the hole I'm in."

"The hole?"

"Please, Warren — there are things you don't understand. Things that have forced me to this point."

"Are you going to tell me about it?"

"Yes."

"When?" he demanded.

She exhaled. "Soon."

He paused, seeming to take in what she said, reaching to rub his chin. Her concession seemed to help. After a minute of silence between them, he took a seat on the stone bench beside her. The arctic hadn't defrosted yet, but she felt some of the iceberg melting, much to her relief.

Into the distance, he looked over the darkened sandy beach, seeming to listen to gulls and distant beachgoers still at it. She observed the man in deep thought, digesting and plotting. A part of her felt safer than she had in a long time, just knowing that finally she had someone on her side. Someone that was strong enough to make a difference.

Then Warren turned back to her. Alisa had to stabilize herself receiving his gaze, his *real* warm gaze, reminding her of everything she tried to forget with all that wine. God, he was stunning.

He scrubbed his jawline again, assessing her. "I have a lot of questions."

"I bet you do."

"Let's start with one."

"Shoot." She chewed her lip.

His gaze darkened, dead serious. "You don't love him?"

"Not a chance." She didn't hesitate, finding his arms falling around her instantly.

"Good."

He dragged her body across the bench toward him, stoking the fire.

A hard lump formed in her throat as she confessed, "I never meant to keep this from you. I just didn't know you cared."

Looking deep into her eyes, he held the back of her neck.

"I'm an all or nothing kind of guy. You're either in or out with me."

"So, am I in?"

He grinned, saying nothing — *killing her*.

Defeated, she sunk into his hold, feeling the icy distance melt between them. Then all she wanted was to feel his lips again, to feel his body over hers.

"I've said it before and I'll say it again," Alisa said. "You're nothing like my fiancé."

His teeth grazed on his bottom lip, that familiar flame in his eyes. "Not fiancé — He's your ex."

Drawing her face to his, he intertwined his fingers with her gold chain once again, reminding her how he'd ripped it off the night before, reminding her how he'd ripped everything off her in the back of the Humvee. Her thighs shook with the reminder of what he drew out of her.

"*Warren*," she whispered, images of his rock-hard body flashing through her mind, making her mouth water, her panties soak.

It seemed that he felt it too, admitting, "I shouldn't have wasted the seven days."

"We still have time."

"Sure 'bout that?"

Tension rose between them like a hot, springy coil. She shifted a little closer. He reacted, tensing his fist, with the unfortunate effect of snapping her poorly fixed chain once again, sending the ring clinking to the ground.

"Shit," he growled, jumping off the bench to catch it.

She gasped, lunging forward in her seat but stilled. In his thick fingers, he'd found the gold diamond ring, and he was kneeling before her on the bench. He raised it up to hand it back to her.

But they were interrupted.

"Oh my God!" A woman's high-pitched voice echoed from the entrance to the garden, less pleased and more just shocked. "He's proposing! Warren's fucking *proposing*!"

Warren and Alisa's faces snapped to see voice, realizing it was Jen in her full white wedding gown and accompanied by a growing number of onlookers. Cheers came from the group, congratulating them both.

"Wait! Has she said *yes*?" Jen pressed forward, clearly very drunk.

Not missing a beat, Warren slipped the ring on Alisa's finger, his gaze locking with hers. He shot her a nod, encouraging her to play along.

"Yes," Alisa responded, a little less convinced as she felt overwhelmed by the crowd rushing into the garden to see the spectacle.

As Warren pulled her up to her feet, he pocketed her broken gold chain. He held the small of her back as they greeted everyone. The attention had completely shifted from the bride over to them — and Alisa overheard shocked comments from the crowd.

"Warren's proposed? He must really love this girl."

"Who is she? He must have been hiding her."

"Thank God he's finally got a chick — maybe he'll lighten the fuck up."

Travis stepped forward through the crowd, grinning from ear to ear. He glanced back and forth from Alisa to Warren, that same mischievous twinkle in his eye, as if he really knew the truth but wasn't going to say it.

"Congratulations, you two," Travis beamed, motioning gracefully to back to where the dinner had been held. "Shall we celebrate?"

Tugging Alisa's body against his, Warren ushered her back to the wedding, where a dance floor had been set up. The wedding reception was just getting started. Toying with the engagement ring on her finger, it was at that moment that Alisa questioned... *Warren's not serious, is he?*

Chapter Twenty-Two

Alisa

"Do you still hate weddings?" Alisa whispered into Warren's ear as he held her close, slow dancing to a romantic song.

"Only when I'm forced to dance."

He glared at the sidelines where his guys had pushed them forward to have their first dance as a 'engaged couple'.

"You're pretty good in my books," she said, grazing the side of his face with her lips and still wondering what was going on between them.

"I'll show you what else I'm good at," he said, more threatening than flirtatious.

It was the type of threat that made her quiver.

She bit her lip, feeling the heat from being so damn close to him. "I'd like that."

Her brain spinning from too much wine and arousal, she let out a too-sexy moan into his ear, feeling his arms tighten as he heard her.

"Keep making sounds like that—" he started, sucking his teeth.

"Don't give me any power," she whispered. "You know I'll abuse it."

Her words were met by a low laugh. Finally, the song ended, and he drew her from the dance floor, on a mission. He tried to get them through the crowd, but they were stopped by a circle of younger-looking SEALs—his men.

"Chief." One of the guys handed shot glasses to him and her. "Congratulations."

Alisa hesitantly took the shot glass, full of something that looked like tequila. Warren sent her the sexiest subtle wink she'd ever received, practically making her fall into him and surrender once and for all. She shook her head a little, knowing her shift at the hospital the next morning was going to be painful. Her diamond engagement ring sparkled in the air as she shot the tequila back.

She couldn't help but make what she could tell was likely the most twisted, horrified face as the alcohol burned her mouth. Her watery eyes blinking, she realized that Warren had been watching her and was breaking down in the most uncontrollable laughter she'd ever seen. A deep booming laugh escaped his mouth, infectious and wonderful. The sight of his true, raw smile—ear to ear—was so damn endearing.

Alisa knew right then that she was some kind of *falling* for that man.

The young SEALs slapped Warren on the back, joking and beaming that they'd never seen him let loose before. Clearly, there was something to that. Warren hadn't been lying when he'd told her that his presence improved morale. Having the boss there, having *Daddy* relaxed there, drinking alongside the guys, seemed to make everyone so much more at ease.

Even Alisa found herself chilling out, chatting, more connected with other people than she'd ever been. It occurred to her that being next to Warren again, she hadn't felt awkward and unusual at all. She had started feeling normal — really fucking normal, like she belonged.

The music pumping and lights whirling, she knew she was having the night of her life. It wasn't too long after a second shot of tequila that she felt Warren's heavy paw on the small of her back, pulling her up to kiss him, much to the immediate cheers of the guys. Catching the look on their faces, it was obvious that no one could believe Warren had gotten engaged.

To the thumping rhythm, Warren moved her body, casually pushing her away from the crowd, out of the busy area. Laughter and voices disappearing behind them, he moved her around the hotel, looking for something.

"Where are we going?" Alisa slurred, letting out a girlish giggle.

As they hit a dark, secluded spot on the side of the hotel, Warren spun, pinning her body against the wall. He pressed right into her, and his intentions became damn obvious, along with the elongating hardness of his cock in his pants.

Alisa let out another shy laugh as he kissed up her neck, manhandling her to get a better angle at her ass. He squeezed her until she yelped.

"Shut up," he growled as he opened to bite her neck, ready to give it to her hard.

"I—" she gasped as he pressed his rough hand over her mouth, restricting her.

"You've been teasing me all night."

Releasing his hand from her mouth, he forced his lips onto hers, darting his tongue out to lap up her taste. She moaned under his touch, knowing that he was giving her a taste of that fantasy she'd told him about — the one where he made it feel a little dangerous, a little rough...

"You don't think there will be consequences for your actions?"

Silent, she inhaled as he pressed his mouth harder against hers. Just like her, he tasted like tequila and pleasure.

"This is what you get, now," he said.

So damn turned on by his authority, she melted a little in his grip, pliable to his commands.

"I'm going to show you how I like to fuck," he snarled, meaner than before, his lips curling in a grin as he kissed his way up her jaw.

Her eyes rolling back, she moaned as he kissed her harder and faster — the exact way she wanted his cock rocking inside her. She fumbled at his belt, desperately trying to rip open his pants, knowing her soreness from the night before would only bring her closer to climax faster.

But Mr. Perfect tore her hands away, always in charge, holding her wrists so damn tight that it shot pain up her arms. He was so fucking Dominant. Dear God, he knew what she liked already so well.

"Tell me to stop," he ordered as he moved his hands up the slit of her dress, finding bare thighs. He wasted no time in pushing aside her lacy panties to find the wet pussy that welcomed him.

"Stop, *please*," she pleaded, pretending to push his hand away from her crotch.

It was a role-playing game she'd never felt safe enough to enjoy with anyone else. But, with him...? He was about to enjoy all her bad acting.

"Safeword, again? I love hearing that word come off your lips." He pushed at her.

"Never."

"Say it."

"No."

His grin widened as he kissed her harder than before, growling with outright savagery. Hearing his insatiable grunts nearly drove her over the edge. But it wasn't enough. She wanted more. She wanted to see him unleashed. The heat up his throat hit his face, a deep, angry roar escaping his lips. Whatever fucking nice guy he was before, she could see that now all that pent-up anger from the day was rushing over him.

"You going to give it up?" He snarled into her ear, his fist intertwining in her hair, pulling it back until she yelped.

"Maybe."

"This is too easy."

She bit her lip, shooting him a feverish look as he found his way underneath her lacy panties again, feeling the increasingly sopping slit of her pussy. That first touch was fire. Her whole body felt electrified as he massaged her clit.

"Stop," she pleaded, her head pressing against the concrete wall behind her.

She tried to twist away again but was met by his strong arm. He wasn't going to let her get away.

"*Please.*"

"Not a fucking chance." He gripped her neck with his other hand, tightening his hold on it.

Alisa's eyes rolled back as he thrust his fingers into her needy pussy and pumped in and out. His masculine scent, mixed with alcohol and sex, engorged her. Aroused and intent, he flexed his shoulders and biceps as she ground her body against his, her breath turning rhythmic. The throbbing in her pussy was real — and it could only be remedied one way.

"Please...fuck me," she begged, breaking out of her role.

Her sudden demand was met by a cruel laugh. Clearly, he was damn entertained by her body writhing over his hand.

"You'd like my cock, wouldn't you?" He fumbled at his belt.

"Hell yes —"

"I love what a dirty slut you are."

"Just for you —" She bit her lip devilishly.

But the swift sounds of footsteps cresting the corner of the hotel had Warren drawing back from her, adjusting her dress so that they both looked normal. Or, at least not amid a heated make-out session on the dark side of the building.

A man's voice she recognized to be Crash's interrupted them as he urgently marched up.

"Chief?"

"What's going on?"

Warren squared himself to the groom.

Crash's well-trained eyes did not even dart to a clearly panting Alisa, remaining on task. "I need you to check something out."

Nodding toward the front of the hotel, on the opposite side than the wedding party, Crash remained dead serious. Warren seemed to get it, dragging Alisa up against him. Brushing her hair back, he issued clear and direct orders.

"Go back to the party," Warren said, stern as hell. "Stay with people. Plant yourself on a chair. I'll be back in five minutes. Five fucking minutes."

Confused, she pouted to counter, but he shook his head, telling her to stop. He wasn't taking questions.

Launching her toward the noise, he watched as she reluctantly sauntered down the path. Glancing over her shoulder, she clearly saw that he was making sure she obeyed. And once she turned the corner, re-entering the party, she gazed back only to see Warren marching to the front of the hotel with Crash.

What's going on?

She adjusted her hair, a little messy from their tussle. Watching him leave didn't help the aching feeling in her pussy, and she was more desperate than ever to have his body pressed against hers, preferably naked.

Hearing a cackling noise over her shoulder, she looked and saw Jen not far away, getting down on the dance floor with her bridesmaids. Alisa's gaze snapped back to where she'd come from. She bit her lip, knowing she should listen to him but needing to follow him.

Her drunken feet took her where her mind wasn't willing to go. Finding herself creeping along the side of the hotel, she quietly stalked to the front of the building, observing Warren and Crash standing there together. Then she realized that they were hovering over a blacked-out bike in the throes of a heated argument with the driver.

That bike... Alisa narrowed her eyes.

Then, she recognized it. It only took her intoxicated brain a little longer than it would have normally to diagnose the situation. Yes, she'd seen that bike before—right in front of her apartment...before it had been burned to a crisp.

She felt chills creep up her arms, realizing what that could mean.

At that precise moment, the bike peeled off, the driver shouting out something threatening at Warren.

She stumbled back as Warren and Crash spun and began marching toward the exact spot where she stood. She shook, her eyes darting left and right for a place to hide. The flora wasn't welcoming, full of cacti. Knowing Southern California, she was liable to get bit by a black widow if she tried it.

It was too late. Warren spotted her, stopping feet from her. He crossed his arms with more than just a disapproving look. He stared at her like she was the last unicorn on earth. She could see that something had really pissed him off. The air had grown as serious as fuck — and he wasn't playing around anymore.

"I'll see you back at the party." Crash nodded at his boss, quietly taking his leave.

The resulting silence between Warren and Alisa was weighty. A light illuminating that corner of the hotel flickered above, the only movement in that ten-foot space.

She let out a long breath, knowing the conversation they needed to have.

Chapter Twenty-Three

Alisa

Alisa stood in front of Warren, shaking like she had feverish chills. Sweat beaded on her chest, the heat wave never relenting. Her mouth grew dry in anticipation of what was to come. He wasn't happy, and she didn't expect that to get any better.

"What the hell are you doing? I told you to wait back there," Warren started.

"Has he found me?" she asked.

"What do you think?"

She played nervously with her lip, which was only met by his darkening face.

"You're constantly putting yourself in bad situations," he said. "Do you have any idea who could be hiding in these bushes?"

His words hit hard, and the underlying implication wasn't missed. But she was an independent type. She'd gotten herself that far. She had to step forward.

"So, what happened?" She put her hands on her hips, straightening her spine. "Are you going to tell me?"

"No." Warren snarled that savage growl in his throat.

Alisa pulled back, grasping at the broken trust between them. "First, you won't tell me what the cop is saying, and now you won't tell me about what happened with this guy? Why not?"

"I'm protecting you, since you are incapable." His voice cracked, and she saw the anger in his eyes.

"I *am* capable."

"Not from what I've seen, doing dumb shit that'll get you killed. From now on, I handle things," he said.

Her mouth dropped open in complete disbelief. She felt the fake-engagement ring digging in, reminding her how everything was on his terms.

"I'm not a passenger in my own life," she said. "I'm a solutions-oriented woman."

"Then offer solutions."

Anger exploded in her mind, and she shakingly shot out her hand. "I'll have my phone back now, please."

"Not if you think you're going to call *him*."

"I'll call who I want to call—" she started, but quickly regretted it. She bit her trembling lip, trying to stay strong in front of Warren's abject intensity.

After a brief pause, he reached into his suit pocket, yanked out her cell and threw it at her.

"Prove me wrong."

Then he watched her as she turned it on, clearly hearing all the notifications pinging—someone clearly trying to get a hold of her. They both knew who that was. Her face twisted as she saw Dean's name scattered across her screen.

He was back in LA.

He was demanding her presence.

She looked up at Warren, burning in her eyes. Why did it have to be so complicated?

"Why are you doing this?" she asked, feeling tears rushing to her eyes.

"You gave yourself to me. You're mine to protect now."

His eyes drifted down to the engagement ring she wore on her finger, the ring he'd slid on.

"We both know this isn't for real," she said, twisting the ring, peaking her eyebrow at him.

"And why's that?"

Staring, he leaned in, his hand thumping against the wall beside her. She sank as he trapped her underneath him yet again. She felt her eyes suddenly sting, hating the truth.

"You'd never marry me."

"Why not? What is the fucking deal with you?"

Her lips pouted, fraught. He didn't get it. Shaking her head, she closed her eyes.

"It's time for you to tell me what the fuck is going on with your ex," he said. "What I need from you is information. I can't protect you if I am blind."

"What? You want his address?" She shook her head fitfully. "You'd just do something we'd both regret."

"I don't give a flying fuck. I'm in charge now. I'll make you tell me what I need to know...by any goddamn means necessary."

The way the last words came out, she knew it was a threat. Goosebumps prickled up her thighs just thinking about how he'd punish her, torture her, hurt her...and she'd *love* it.

"Please, don't do this —"

But he cut her off, dropping his head to give her one more hot kiss.

A kiss that would be her undoing.

He dominated her easily, her own spine buckling into him as he took her mouth, kissing her deeply. He took over all her senses. All she could taste, hear, feel...was him. She moaned, needing the feel of his tongue against hers, but then he abruptly yanked back, leaving her breathless.

Warren looming over her, not letting her go. He was going to torture the full truth out of her. She didn't want to tell him, but she couldn't fight him off anymore. He was going to see her for what she really was.

"Speak," he growled, deeper and more threatening than ever.

"I'm—" Alisa started, clearing her throat. "I'm indebted to Dean. He paid— He paid for *everything*."

"What does that mean?"

Pressed against the hotel wall, she blinked rapidly, focusing only on his deeply concerned icy blues.

Swallowing thickly, she confessed, "When my mom got sick, I paid for her medical bills with all our money. I had just been accepted to medical school. She was so happy that I was going to be someone. But I had nothing left to pay tuition."

She paused, licking her lips, watching Warren's stone-cold face.

"And there was Dean, offering to help me out," she said. "I shouldn't have, but I took his money. He made me feel like he wanted to take care of me at first, but then things got scary. He got obsessive, controlling. His help came at a big price."

Warren's face flinched as she said it, and she knew the worst was happening. Alisa's gaze fell to the ground, a shameful blush heating her face.

"How much do you owe him?"

"Hundreds of thousands," she said.

"*Fuck*. How does a guy like that have money to pay for so much?" he demanded.

"I don't know."

"Alisa, do you really not know, or do you not *want* to know?"

She remained silent, shaking her head and averting her eyes. She could get killed for what she really knew, so she'd never say it. Dean wasn't on the right side of the law, and neither was his money.

When she looked back up, she saw that Warren's gaze had slid down to the ring, seeming to realize the implications. He sucked his teeth, pulling back. She saw that fury crossing his face, sensing it was directed at her.

"One thing I can tell you—money is money," Warren started, crossing his arms as he stood back. "At no point do you ever have to sell your soul."

Then Warren said something that totally surprised her.

"I'll pay your debt."

Her mouth dropped open. "Warren, that's too much."

"Call him. Break it off…whatever dumb deal you have. I'll write the check."

"And then? You deploy?" she asked, dumbfounded.
"Sure."

"You realize it's not just about the money. He's that psycho-obsessive type. You leave, and I'll be left here, dealing with him. Alone."

"I'll make sure you're safe when I'm gone. You won't have to worry about a thing." He seemed as confident as hell.

But still... She cocked her head in confusion, his promise just not good enough for her. How could he even say that? He'd be a million miles away.

Pulling up contacts in her phone, she searched for a phone number. What she had to do. It had just become crystal clear.

"Call him," Warren ordered. "End it."

She hovered her finger over a contact, and she gazed back up at him.

"I'll break it off with him if you stay with me," she said.

"You want me to quit my job?"

"No, just stay back this one time. Stay with me," she pleaded. "Just once."

"I made a commitment. I can't do that," he said. "But what I can promise you is just as good. My friends will watch over you."

"No. Warren, all I have is *you*—someone menacing enough to scare this guy. He won't stop. He won't give up. I know what he's like." She exhaled, shaking her head.

He didn't reply, just stared at her in response.

"It has to be you," she said.

But he'd run out of responses. That was when she knew her options had run out. There was only one thing she could do to stay safe—find her own way.

"You're right," she said, bringing the phone to her ear as it started ringing. "There are people watching me, following me, threatening me, maybe even trying to kill me—"

"What are you—?" he started, a vein pulsing in his neck, but someone answered on the other side of the line, drawing Alisa's attention back to her phone.

"Maria," Alisa spoke into the phone, "any chance you could come get me?"

"I'm not letting you out of my sight." Warren stepped forward in all his authority, commanding her. "Not a fucking chance."

Alisa turned her nose up to him, holding her ground. "Then don't deploy. Stay with me."

"I don't do ultimatums."

The way his cold eyes narrowed on her told her what she needed to know. So, she had to protect herself. She had to leave Warren. Being with him was distracting and dangerous. She'd regroup and forge a new path—solutions-oriented.

"Yeah, I need to stay with you tonight," Alisa replied to Maria on the phone.

Twisting the diamond ring on her finger, it was at that very moment that she knew beyond a doubt that Warren's proposal had just been another fantasy playing out between them, as unreal as it was temporary. Their seven days had concluded—and he wasn't going to give her any more.

She was on her own.

Chapter Twenty-Four

Alisa

After a long, fitful night, Alisa sat in front of Dr. Roske once again in her office — though the tone had shifted for the worse, if that were even possible. Dr. Roske flipped a pen in her hand, cautiously observing Alisa.

"You didn't make it in yesterday," the doctor said.

"I wasn't scheduled."

"Yes, you were — in the ER."

Alisa cocked her head back, shocked. *What?* Putting the pieces together, she realized that she'd accepted a trade from another student. Smacking her palm to her forehead, she exhaled shakily.

"I'm so sorry. I got caught up—" Alisa started.

"It's not like you to miss a shift, but you did. I'm hearing you've become more and more distracted lately." Dr. Roske's intensity was palpable.

Alisa chewed her lip, knowing there was more to the story. All the doctors talked.

"They were really short-staffed," the doctor said. "Dr. Zucker isn't pleased."

"It's not going to happen again," Alisa promised.

"But, if it does?" Dr. Roske questioned. "I know the hospital demands a lot from doctors, but the truth of the matter is that lives are in our hands. We must prioritize our commitments."

"I'm committed. I'll be here."

"I hope so." The doctor flipped through a folder, raising her eyebrows.

Alisa realized her name was on it.

"Has the board considered my residency?" Alisa asked.

"Your name has come up, but the timing has not been good, not with you missing in action. Dr. Zucker carries a lot of clout in this hospital."

Alisa started fidgeting nervously, unable to process what was happening. Everything she had worked so hard for had just got lit on fire.

The doctor leaned forward. "Alisa, you can do great work for a long time, but people only remember the most recent. Take my advice and make sure your most recent work is flawless, if you really want this."

Alisa took a deep breath, praying to God. The doctor dismissed her to finish off her shift in the ER, knowing she had a lot to make up for.

* * * *

Hours and hours later, after a long day, Alisa sat in the setting sun on Maria's tiny stone patio. Paranoia drove her to constantly scan the landscape, listening for any loud engine—motorcycle or V8 truck. Though it was damn hot out, she shivered in her borrowed clothes, anticipating the worst. She fidgeted, checking the time for no reason.

Maria lit a cigarette, leaning against the door. Her purple hair catching beams of light, and she furrowed her brows as she clearly assessed her young friend. Alisa drew the creamy sweater tighter around her, twisting the ring anxiously.

"I've never seen you wear that ring before," Maria said.

"I just started last night."

"Why?"

"It's hard to explain," Alisa said.

Alisa smoothed out her sweater's fabric, looking for wrinkles that weren't there. She was just anxious, fretting, feeling like everything had become so impossible.

"Are you going to call him?" Maria asked.

"Which one?"

"Warren, of course."

Alisa arched her eyebrow at her. "Maria, why did you want me to clean his house? And why the hell did you send me…in those shorts?"

Maria's eyes twinkled with that same conniving look that she'd once given Alisa. She leaned back, shooting Alisa a motherly expression, like she cared more than Alisa could ever understand.

"Maria?"

Finally, the businesswoman let out, "I knew it from the minute I met him. He's strong, determined and protective."

"So, you were trying to set me up with him, then?"

"Maybe," Maria grinned. "In a way. Warren is the type of guy who might just save you from the mess you're in."

"No one can save me, Maria. I made my bed long ago," Alisa relented, saddened. "I don't have a choice now."

"You always have a choice."

"I'm scared," Alisa admitted. "I've got big problems, and it's only a matter of time before I'm in a body bag, buried in the sand behind Dean's clubhouse."

"Like I said, Warren's the type that can save you. He's a scary beast. Does he know about Dean's club?" Maria asked.

"Not really."

"You have to tell him. He needs to understand the depth of Dean's criminality, and he needs to know where to find you if you go missing." Maria smashed the remnants of her cigarette in the tray on the bistro table, coughing.

"Warren and I...it's over."

"It's not really over, Alisa. Come on."

Alisa just shook her head, unwilling to get into the extent of their argument from the night prior. Warren wasn't always going to be there to protect her. It was a harsh reality that she wasn't prepared to accept.

She couldn't ruminate on it further because her cell vibrated. She pulled it up—seeing an email from Dr. Roske.

I've managed to get the board to review your residency application again. They want you to come in for an informal conversation, a coffee chat. Can you come in right away?

Alisa quickly typed back and sent it.

I'll be there in thirty minutes.

Getting up from the chair, Alisa checked the time again. "I've got to get to the hospital. This might be what I need for my residency."

"Okay." Maria spun to open her door. "Just let me get my keys."

Waiting, Alisa stood at the edge of the patio, reflecting. Life had changed. She could feel it. There was no going back.

She was almost at the end of a long journey. Exams and residency — the only things that had mattered to her for so long — were almost there. She was lucky enough to be on the cusp of becoming a physician, if she got her residency.

I just have to survive that long.

She chewed her lip, dropping her gaze to the grass in front of her, tracing the outline of the ring on her finger. *Can I get out of this?*

She shook her head slightly, knowing the deeper truth — the truth she was unwilling to admit to anyone, barely even herself. Being engaged to Dean had felt like a safety net for so long. She'd been okay with it for most of her studies.

"But I was wrong," she whispered to herself.

"Ready?" Maria clambered out of her place. "This is so exciting!"

Alisa nodded, and the two women made their way to the street where Maria's car was parked. Alisa felt a sense of comfort in being with her boss and friend. Back to the only semblance of normalcy in her life.

Opening the door to Maria's car, Alisa heard someone calling her name over her shoulder. It was a croaky, masculine voice that she'd heard before.

"Alisa Kelly."

She spun, realizing it was a cop, one she recognized. In plain clothes, he was holding his badge up to her and Maria.

"Alisa Kelly," the cop reiterated, marching toward them.

She immediately recognized his pock-marked face. He had been the cop at her apartment complex when it was on fire, asking Warren questions.

"I'm Alisa," she said slowly.

The cop stopped a few feet from her.

"Alisa Kelly — you are under arrest for arson."

"Arson?"

Her mouth dropped open, and she stumbled back. She grasped at the car, trying to find stability.

"What is this about?" Maria demanded, trying to shield her.

It didn't matter. The cop lunged forward, flinging out handcuffs. Panic shot through Alisa's body as she realized what was happening.

"You're under arrest. I'm taking you into the station for questioning." He gripped Alisa's forearm so she couldn't run.

"No," she blurted out, stunned. "This can't be right."

The cop secured handcuffs on her, then yanked her toward him. He wasted no time in hauling her body across the pavement.

Maria stood there, shocked, clearly unsure what the hell to do.

"Maria —" Alisa yelped. "Please, do something."

"Shit." Maria darted her eyes left and right, her hands outstretched.

Alisa knew there was nothing that could be done as the cop pushed her toward his brown sedan.

"You have the right to shut the fuck up," he assured her, opening the door and cramming her into his back seat. "In fact, I'd prefer if you did just that."

"What—?" she gasped as the door slammed in her face.

She shook as she watched him pace around the car and get into the driver's seat.

It didn't seem right to her, but she felt like she had no choice. She obeyed, fearful of what would happen to her if she didn't. He was a cop, right? He could hurt her.

She bit her lip, feeling a flush of anxiety shooting through her as the cop peeled down the street, taking her to the station. As they barreled down the boulevard, it seemed the one time in LA when traffic was nonexistent. Alisa wished congestion had been heavy.

It didn't take Alisa long before she realized that he had bypassed any natural route to the police station. *Where is he taking me?* Her fingers tightened on the door handle, and as they rolled to a stop, she tried to heave it open.

But the damn child locks were engaged—and she realized she was stuck. She was helpless.

The cop shot her a threatening look through the rear-view mirror.

"I wouldn't do that if I were you."

Her mouth quivered, and she covertly tried to grip her cell phone in her purse. *Warren.*

"Or that." The cop jerked the car over to the side of the road, lunging back to slash her purse from her hands.

"What are you doing?"

She screeched as he hurled her purse on the floor. She scrambled, realizing she was in for a fight. Everything in her body tensed as she tugged as hard as she could on the door handle, even kicking it, like that would do anything.

"Please...don't hurt me," she cried, watching the man clamber over the console with a murderous look on his face.

"Come here, little kitty."

"No!" she screamed as he jumped onto her.

Overpowered, she realized exactly was he was doing as he intently gripped beneath her ears, behind her jaw. The pressure increasing, the bloodflow to her brain decreasing, she felt it coming on. He was expertly putting her out.

The last thing she remembered was realizing that she was never, ever going to get a residency in radiology.

* * * *

Alisa woke up under a blanket, a warm ocean breeze wafting her hair. Coming to, she realized she was at the top of a dune overlooking a beach and aching all over. Instinctively, she grasped at her clothing, making sure it was all still on her body. It was.

Panting in sheer panic, she sat up, trying to understand where the hell she was, what time it was and what the hell had happened to her. Surprisingly, she felt...largely unviolated. They hadn't hurt her — yet.

She gazed down the beach, unwilling to recognize it for what it was. Who was she kidding? She knew exactly what was happening. And if her fears were correct, she was out of LA.

And she was far away from any help.

No one could save her.

Letting out a long, desperate breath, she closed her eyes, wondering what the hell to do, if Maria had called Warren for help or if she'd ever see him again. Now, more than ever, she needed him. She let her tongue dash out across her lip, thinking of him—thinking about how he'd kissed her, of how he'd touched her. She already missed him like hell.

"Looks good on you, the ring," someone said from above.

She opened her eyes to find Dean farther up the dune. He offered her a hand.

"It's been too long," he said, a lock of his dark hair dropping onto his brow over his black sunglasses. "*Alisa.*"

Pushing back in the sand, she fumbled her way up into a seated position, her eyes darting around the deserted beach, desperately looking for—

"Looking for someone?" Dean challenged, turning his head as he adjusted his leather jacket—his neck tattoo stretching as he twisted.

She shook her head, her eyes wide open, trying to pretend everything was okay.

But it wasn't.

He crossed his arms, settling into a chilling stance as he stared her down.

"I'd ask you if something was wrong with your phone, but I know that's not the case. I know you've been ignoring me. I know you've been trying to run."

"Dean," Alisa said, and she tried to push herself up and farther away. Finally, up on her feet, she saw no one at all on the beach that could help.

Dean pulled down his dark sunglasses to get a better look at her, his smirk telling her everything. It was like the cat that got the mouse. Alisa knew what was going to happen next. His anger lingered only one shade under the surface. She knew that anger. Instinctively, she recoiled.

"Where are you going?" he asked, watching her shuffle back from him, creating space between them. "We're just getting started."

"Dean, you don't understand," she whispered as she stumbled backward.

But he followed, quick and fast. He grabbed her, heaving her closer to him, grinning down on her.

"I think I understand well enough. It's time we went over the terms of our deal once again."

"What do you want from me?" she sputtered anxiously. "What have you ever wanted from me?"

"Come on. You know the answer. *You* are what I want."

He ran his hand, partially blackened from the engine grease off his motorcycle, up her throat.

She trembled in pure fear, recognizing that unstable look in his eyes. He was a man who killed people — but not like Warren. Dean killed people for very different reasons.

He wasn't honorable. He wasn't serving his country.

"So, what's it going to be?" Dean asked, examining her throat as if she were a prize. "Should we make it official?"

She hoped to God he wouldn't notice the bruising from Warren's biting. But he did — running his fingers along the exact place where Warren's teeth had claimed her. Dean *knew*, she realized, watching the man's pupils dilate. That competitiveness was rising within him, and he wouldn't be outdone. He wouldn't be taken for a fool.

She closed her eyes, shaking her head — wishing it all away. She was immobile in his arms, crumbling. Breaking down.

"Dean, please — I can't."

"You aren't going to say 'no' to your man, are you? After all I've done for you?"

Your man. The words burned. She flashed her gaze at him, a warning.

"Let's stop pretending. All you ever wanted was to control me."

"Shut the fuck up." He brushed her hair from her face, then threw her forward.

Alisa stumbled in front of him, crying inside. She'd known it would come to this...eventually. There had never been any other way.

Dean's final words confirmed it.

"The reverend will be here soon, so we better get you pretty."

.

Chapter Twenty-Five

Alisa

Alisa drew the creamy sweater closer to her form, wrapping it tighter around her, as she watched the cop who'd kidnapped her casually chat with Dean halfway down the beach. She knew without a doubt that Dean had the guy on his payroll. That was how he got what he wanted — by throwing cash around.

Warren's questions came to her mind, and she chewed her lip, unable to admit it, even to herself. But she couldn't lie to herself anymore. A tear fell down her cheek, which she promptly wiped away. So many emotions roiled through her, and she was unable to accept how things had ended.

Dean trailed his gaze back up the beach, grinning at her. He didn't give a fuck about her deep discomfort — her hurt. His narcissism had grown everyday she'd known him, until it had exploded to levels she couldn't describe. He'd cheated. He'd lied. He'd manipulated.

The dirty cop motioned to the top of the beach where a man in a black button-up shirt was walking down the path from the clubhouse. *God, it's the damn reverend.* He held something in his hand — paperwork.

It all hit her. She was really going to marry Dean. She was really going to throw it all away.

The wind picked up, whipping her long hair around her face and body, and it promised some protection. She wouldn't have to show how she really felt. Not really. No one cared anyway.

The reverend looked up at her, smiling and beckoning her over. The dirty cop left, saluting Dean on his way out. Then — all eyes were on her.

The wedding march of death played on loop in her head. One numb foot in front of the other, she reluctantly strode down the sand, closer and closer to where Dean stood, watching her. Holding out his hand for her, he called her name. His flawless smile, poised and fake, would charm a snake.

As she found her spot beside him, the reverend clearly had no appreciation that she was under duress, and she didn't dare show it. He'd kill her…she knew it. She had no doubt it would come to that.

The reverend started his spiel, glancing down at the paperwork he had.

"Here we are on Sunset Beach," the man explained, "ready to seal you together in marriage."

The reverend went on, talking about vows of marriage and the legality of what he was about to do, his responsibilities and theirs. He promised a quick ceremony, seeming to misread Alisa's behavior for bridal nerves.

Pain stirred inside Alisa, knowing just how impossible it would be to save her now. They were far out of the city, and how the hell would anyone find her? Only Maria knew where the clubhouse was — perched at the top of the beach, a multi-million-dollar surf shack obtained by the proceeds of crime.

She closed her eyes, dreading her fate. She stopped hearing the reverend. She stopped feeling Dean's clutch on her. All she could think about was her mother — specifically, her mother on her death bed. As her mother had drawn her final breaths, she'd been so happy that Alisa was going to med school, so happy that she was going to be someone.

Alisa opened her eyes, listening and observing as they drew closer to the legal part of the short ceremony. Her hair blowing, the beach was still except for the strong wind. It made it serene, almost unreal.

Dean drew her closer against him, grinning as he spoke with the reverend, fondly recalling how they'd met, fondly detailing the course of their four-year 'situation-ship'. All of it was false.

She saw him for what he really was.

Her mother's proud face flashed before her eyes once again.

Then Warren's.

"I deserve better," Alisa whispered.

The way Dean's eyes flashed at her told her that he had heard her words — and he didn't like it.

"What was that, dear?" the reverend asked, leaning forward.

Dean's expression threatened — *speak, and I'll fucking kill you.*

Alisa opened her mouth but froze.

He really would kill her, wouldn't he? It was just a matter of time.

Yelling crashed through her mind. She should have never agreed to the deal. She'd always deserved better. She'd made a big mistake through all of it, but not the same type of happy mistake she'd made with Warren.

She backed up, peeling herself from his arms.

"What is this?" Dean kept his fake smile up, seeming to know that the reverend wouldn't marry them if she was under duress. "You okay, doll?"

"I—" she started but chewed her lip as his eyes changed to murderous.

The reverend looked back and forth between them, about to say something. But then, something unexpected happened.

"Y'all need a witness?" A booming masculine voice fired down the beach—a voice Alisa would never forget.

Relief washed over her.

Dean and Alisa spun in unison to find Warren barreling toward them. Alisa sucked in breath as she watched the damn fine SEAL stopping right behind them in all his dominant, confident glory. Arms crossed, his face cold, intense—he stared Dean down like he was ready to fucking kill him.

Alisa didn't doubt that he actually was.

Dean stepped forward to face the SEAL. Alisa never realized it before, but Warren was that much taller, that much more muscular. If she wasn't scared shitless, she'd actually be enjoying how wet he instantly made her—and how intimidating he was to others.

And how he'd shown up.

"We haven't met," Warren said.

"No, we have not," Dean responded.

Squaring themselves to each other, it looked like a goddamn duel. Alisa darted her eyes back and forth, realizing she was standing before a ticking time bomb.

Or a goddamn nuclear explosion.

"I'm Warren," he said, but did not give his hand.

"Dean," he replied. "Can I help you?"

Warren said nothing, flicking his gaze up and down Dean in disapproval. He sucked his teeth, the icing on the cake. His gaze traced the club patches on Dean's jacket, seeming to put all the pieces of the puzzle together — all the things Alisa should have told him.

Finally, after letting the question hang for too long, Dean asked it again.

"I said, can I help you?"

Warren finally replied. "*Sure*. You ride?"

Dean's mouth widened in a snarl-smile, and he shot back, "Sure."

The reverend seemed to take a step back, trying to understand what was happening between the two men, who were obviously squaring off. Dean realized that and grinned as if nothing were wrong, beckoning the reverend back. He played it cool — very cool, apparently unwilling to let the ceremony crumble to a halt.

"That's a military bike club." Warren nodded at the patches, seeming to know exactly what the *Deadeye MC* was, surprising Alisa.

She'd always thought the club was fringe.

"Yeah, Marines," Dean responded proudly, nodding at the marking on his jacket's chest. "Two tours Iraq."

"Cool," Warren responded, betraying nothing.

"Yeah, I've seen a lot of shit," Dean leaned back, putting his arm around Alisa's waist, pulling her into him as she squeaked.

His chest puffed. Clearly, he was engaging in a dick-measuring contest, much to Warren's obvious amusement.

"Lots of shit, huh?" Warren led him on.

"Fuck, I can't even count the firefights, man," Dean laughed, bordering on bragging, glancing back at the reverend. "But you know — chicks dig a vet. Iraq was a bitch — "

Warren cut him off, "Tell me about it."

His tone was obviously sarcastic, drawing ire from Dean, who was used to people fawning over him.

"You been to Iraq, buddy?" Dean scoffed, shooting him the side eye.

"More times than I can count."

"What — ?" Dean began to ask but cocked his head instead. "You military or something?"

"Something."

"He's a SEAL, actually." Alisa pushed Dean off, stepping away from him and toward Warren.

That meant something.

Dean's focus snapped to Warren and back to Alisa, a whole lot of *not good* flushing up his cheeks. The reverend cocked his head, starting to understand what was happening — and the dick-measuring contest continued.

"A fucking Navy SEAL, huh?" Dean sneered at Warren, then back at Alisa.

"Yeah, '*chicks dig a vet*'," Warren repeated the guy's words, deadpan.

Screaming inside, Alisa sucked in a deep breath, wondering if that was her moment—once and for all. She started walking.

"Where do you think you are going?" Dean snapped, lunging to her wrist.

Warren launched forward, chopping Dean's arm and sending him backward with ease, his body crumbling down into the sand, but the man bounced back up fast.

"Back the fuck up."

"She's mine." Dean's eyes grew dark, still holding back.

"Not anymore," Alisa squeaked.

Warren brought his arm around Alisa, and she twisted her ring in her hand. Dean readjusted his sandy jacket in a huff. The outline of the knife he packed along his ribcage grew obvious, as if he were sending a clear signal to Warren.

But, before anyone could say anything else, Warren turned, hauling Alisa with him up the beach. She didn't dare glance back, but in her peripheral vision, all she could see was an infuriated Dean flexing to fight and a startled reverend retreating from the beach.

Ushering her along, Warren's body language told Alisa that he was on guard.

And she was under his protection.

Chapter Twenty-Six

Warren

Warren kept going, marching up the sand, despite Alisa gasping for air as he dragged her forward. He didn't doubt her cardiovascular threshold. She was just in shock. He didn't blame her. For once, he was a little stunned, too.

He flickered his gaze down to the mouth-watering woman holding his hand for dear life, like he was extracting her from a war zone. He never wasted time in taking control.

"Thank God you came," she said behind him as they passed through beachy brush. "I didn't think anyone was coming."

"Yet, here I am."

He felt her quake, clearly not missing his insinuation.

"How did you find me?"

"Maria," he responded, continually assessing their surroundings. "She suspected Dean was behind it, the way that cop pulled you away."

He ushered her forward onto the street, where he'd left his truck. There was a lot more to that story, but they didn't have time to chat. Wasting no time, he wrapped his arm around her, heaving her into his truck. She yelped as he did, seemingly catching her off guard.

"Maria—" she started.

Yanking her seatbelt, Warren said, "So, he's a fucking biker? And this is his clubhouse? You could have filled me in on those details."

"I'm terrified to say what I really know, what I've seen."

"You didn't think it mattered?" he asked.

"Yes and no..."

As he buckled her in, he felt her body tensing and knew instantly what she was thinking. It had only been a matter of time. They'd been playing with fire. Shaking his head, he retracted, but when she placed her soft hand on his cheek, he was halted. The sensation of her gentle, tender touch threw him off, but not as much as seeing the look on her face.

"Thank you."

Tears flushed into her dark eyes. *Those goddamn eyes.*

Warren sucked his teeth, trying to get a grip. They still had big problems.

He growled, "I'll never understand why you'd throw your life away like that."

Her palm flat against his cheek, she angled his face to hers, her lips trembling. "I never thought I'd fall in love."

"Keep telling yourself that—and it will come true."

"I was wrong. I know I was wrong because—" But she stopped talking.

The way she trailed her gaze up and down his face, pursing her quivering lip—it hit Warren hard. He knew exactly what she was going to say next.

And he didn't want to fucking hear it.

Instinctively, he pulled back, perceiving danger. He wasn't wrong.

"Leaving so soon?" Dean called out from the bushes lining the edge of the beach.

Warren whipped around, squaring himself to her approaching ex, hearing her cry out behind him to get in the truck. She didn't want him fighting Dean. *Laughable*. Warren slammed the passenger door to the truck shut, and she didn't have a goddamn choice anymore.

He was going to handle things *his* way.

"I think we need to have a conversation," Dean said, cockily stepping up to him like they were evenly matched.

"Go fuck yourself."

Dean put on a show of making a surprised face, then snapped, "Ah, too fucking cool, huh?"

Then, Dean lunged forward, lashing out his knife from underneath his jacket and hacking at Warren. Warren defended, pushing Dean off, easily sending him backward. That seemed to only piss the guy off further, and he clutched at his knife.

"Coming at me with a knife?" Warren challenged. "Must be too fucking scared to fight me like a man."

"I ain't scared of nothing!"

Warren laughed. "How about you drop the knife, and we can see about that?"

The expression that crossed Dean's face betrayed the truth. The man was, in fact, scared of something.

"How about we make our own deal?" Dean said, circling.

Warren grew silent, standing strong, guarding Alisa in the truck. He wasn't going to show any sign of weakness. He knew he had a problem. His back injury and his scar had been screaming at him all day. He had to bite his cheek not to wince in pain.

Dean continued, trying to look tough. "How about I kill you — and get Alisa. Does that sound fair?"

"Keep threatening. Keep giving me cause."

He knew he could break the guy in half if he wanted to. He just needed a reason to make it plausible self-defense.

Overconfident, Dean jumped forward, slashing out with his knife again. Warren shifted to block him and punched him hard several times, winding the man and drawing blood from his face. Aggression was pumping through Warren's veins, and his training had him on autopilot. He knew exactly what to do.

Well, that was until Dean lunged forward one final time, and Warren's back seized. That was the moment he faltered. That split-second delay in defense proved to be the advantage Dean needed, catching his knife alongside Warren's ribcage toward his back, driving hard in that vulnerable spot.

His fucking scar.

Enraged and losing his cool, Warren grabbed at Dean's throat, holding him in mid-air with one hand while he punched the asshole into a state of semi-consciousness. He dropped the guy to the ground, and Dean moaned in pain.

"I'm going to do us all a favor because I'm a real nice guy." Warren opened his wallet. "How much does she owe you?"

"I don't want your fucking money," Dean said. "It's never been about the money."

"No, it never was. You just used money to control her, to keep her under your thumb. Not anymore."

"She's not getting away this easy."

Warren cocked his head, realization washing over him. Then, he let out a long laugh. Amused. He reached down, grabbed Dean at the throat and squeezed.

"She'll get away with murder, if I say so. And so will I," Warren said. "This is your last chance. How much does she owe you?"

Dean coughed up blood, grunting something about two hundred thousand.

Warren scratched two-hundred-and-fifty thousand on a blank check, rounding it up. In the memo, he jotted down—*Alisa's debt*. He folded up the check and tossed it down on Dean's chest, unceremoniously.

"Take it to the bank," he growled. "And stay the fuck out of our lives. She's mine now—and if you even so much as think about her again, you'll be face down in a ditch."

Shoving his wallet back into his pocket, Warren heard the distant roaring engines of motorcycles. As the sun dropped, Warren felt an odd chill—one he shouldn't feel given the heat of that LA summer. His instincts didn't betray him—and the distinctive noise of motorcycles grew closer, ripping down the Pacific Coast Highway.

Warren gazed over, realizing that the bikers were pulling onto the street, looking around. It didn't take

long before a few of the guys had caught sight of him —
standing tall over the bloody body of their boss.

"That's right," Warren grumbled to himself. "I
fucking beat your boss. Take a picture."

Satisfied, he jumped into the driver's seat of his
truck. He flipped the engine on, too impassioned to say
anything about the tears streaming down Alisa's face,
too furious to listen to her when she gasped that he was
bleeding through his shirt and too damn fired up to feel
where Dean had slashed him open.

"He called in reinforcements."

"What?" she panted. "Did they see you?"

"I don't give a fuck. We're done here." He hit the
gas, peeling to the edge of the parking lot where it met
with the highway.

"Where are you taking me?" Alisa whipped her
head to face him, seeming to drink him in.

His body shifted in his seat. The way her dark eyes
hit him... He gripped the wheel of the truck just to
ground himself.

"*Warren.*"

"Just trust me. I got this."

* * * *

I've stolen a biker's girl, Warren grumbled to himself
as he parked his truck in his garage.

Oh, he knew exactly what it was...after he'd seen
that fuck's jacket. There was no mistaking it. The
goddamn Deadeye MC — Warren knew about that club.
Vets mostly, some Army, some Navy — one of the
roughest military biker clubs. Started off good but went
to the wrong side of the tracks real quick.

"Should we head inside?" Alisa called over to him from the garage landing. Trepidation still coursed through her tone.

"Yeah," Warren said, stretching around his ribcage to feel the blood on his back.

"Are you coming?"

"I'll be a minute."

Even though he could tell she didn't want to, she listened to him.

And once she was gone, he made his way to the sink in the garage — cleaning out his wound.

The asshole had only caught him a bit. It was just a surface laceration. Removing his shirt, patching up the cut, he couldn't help but grind out a deep, guttural groan in agony, nearly falling over the sink. He clutched the sides as he felt pure pain ricochet through his back. His scar. His injury. He'd been doing everything he absolutely shouldn't be doing, making it so much worse than it had to be.

Sucking it up, convincing himself that it didn't hurt, he paced to the front of his garage. At his height, he was able to glare through the small windows in his garage door, keeping an eye on his quiet street. He was too fired up to be trusting. He had to have a plan.

Warren pulled out his phone, texting his friends — the ones who had left the SEALs and lived nearby. He needed a goddamn insurance policy — not for himself but for her. After a few minutes, he strode inside, finding Alisa standing at his kitchen island, her trembling hands trying to peel a banana.

"You must be hungry." Warren observed her every move, still processing everything she'd said to him.

"I'm tired," Alisa admitted, and only ate half of it. "And I shouldn't stay. I've missed an important meeting — for my career."

"It can wait."

She shot him a look. He wasn't interested in arguing.

"Whatever it is, it can wait. You can call them and reschedule. *Rest*. You know where the bed is," he said. His shoulder muscles twitched, and he felt the overwhelming need to protect her — to take care of her.

She dropped the rest of the peel and pushed away from him. She left in silence, but she had listened to him, climbing up the stairs.

Cracking the Scotch in his kitchen, he poured himself a heavy glass. Was that what it felt like to have a woman in his life? It wasn't just the alcohol burning down his throat. There was something else boiling inside him, something about what she'd said to him. He didn't want to think about it.

The Scotch seemed to agree with him, reminding him how far he'd come in such a short time with Alisa — How much she'd opened his eyes to what he was doing to himself. She'd been doing it to herself, too — self-medicating through work.

With the rim of the glass on his lips, a thought crossed his mind. Maybe he should tell her about his past, about how he'd got that scar. But then he shook his head, knowing exactly what would come of that conversation. It was nice and fine to tell him he was allowed to make mistakes, until she heard what he'd done.

Suddenly his phone vibrated on his countertop, snapping him back to reality. The highlighted screen revealed a call coming in from his boss, the master chief. Warren immediately picked it up.

"Yeah."

"Chief," Master Chief Rose said through the line, "there's been a situation. We are flying out at first light. Can you get to the airfield ASAP?"

The air in his kitchen grew thick, like time had stopped.

Warren leaned over the counter, just breathing, distantly hearing the master chief prompt him for his answer.

Chapter Twenty-Seven

Alisa

Alisa sat on the edge of Warren's bed in nothing but a towel. He'd saved her. He'd defeated Dean. Her mind was barely able to process how emancipated she felt — for the first time.

Hearing his heavy steps approaching, she flickered her gaze to him through the darkened bedroom as he entered and stood still before her. Her heart thumped so hard that she wondered if he could hear it.

"Hi." She searched up and down his stiffening body. "Do you feel safe here?"

His tone was different. She paused.

"I feel safe because you are here — " she responded slowly, tilting her head as she tried to understand him. "Because he's scared of you."

As the answer rolled off her tongue, she rose, letting the towel flow off her curves. It was time to show him her appreciation. The dim light of the moon cast over her breasts, seeming to stir him in the way she'd hoped. His teeth grazed his bottom lip, and she knew exactly what he wanted to do to her.

"What are you doing?"

"I need to find a way to thank you," she said, squaring her naked form to him, running her hand down her flat stomach, "for everything you've done for me."

But he said nothing, staring intently at her.

"Warren, what can I do to thank you?" she prompted, playful seductiveness in her tone.

He fell forward, gripping her waist to hoist her to him, feeling the side of her face with his other hand. It never ceased to take her breath away—with how hard and rough he was—and how much she loved that.

"Tell me." She grinned.

"I don't have time for games anymore."

Then he took her mouth with his, tasting her lips.

He kissed her hard, deep, moving slow then fast. Faster, still. She loved the way his tongue intertwined with hers, loved the sensation of his slick mouth manipulating hers however he wanted it. The moment was already overwhelming, emotion crashing over her. She sank into his arms, surrendering, getting lost in him. She was definitely falling.

He searched her mouth, her kiss, closing his eyes as he slid his hands up her back, more firm and needy than ever before. She moaned, tilting her head back as he kissed down her chin and neck, grazing his teeth. Already she felt drunk on the feeling of his dominance. Her body responded fast to him, getting wet in a snap.

He pushed her head to the side so he'd have better access at her ear and neck, continuing to taste and play. She'd never realized that ear was a wildly erogenous zone, and her legs literally shook as he held her tight, deepening the sensation. It felt for the first time like she wasn't ever going to lose him.

And if she did, she knew she'd lose herself.

He dropped his hands down her form, grabbing her wrists. "I didn't forget."

Before she could ask what he meant, he reached over to the chair by his bed, ripping off a tie that laid beneath the suit he'd worn to the wedding. It wasn't a tie he'd worn to the event, but she guessed he'd tried it on at some point.

Spinning her around, he kissed down the back of her neck, down her spine and tied her hands together tightly behind her.

She realized — *this is what he didn't forget.*

"I'm going to do whatever I fucking want to you," he growled, pushing her down so she fell over his bed.

She writhed as he shed his clothes and climbed behind her, running his hands up her thighs.

Whispering in her ear, he told her, "And you're going to fucking like it."

She felt the throbbing, bouncing of his hardened cock behind her. Nothing excited her more than the feeling that she drove him just as crazy.

Tied up, immobilized, she rubbed her face against the pillow, trying to find a comfortable spot to breathe. He pushed her face down harder, bringing her ass up into the air so her body formed a triangle. He ran his fingers up and down the back of her thighs. Her body could only respond by twitching with need and arousal, her pussy getting absolutely drenched. She needed to feel his touch…inside.

Pushing her ass back to plead, he slapped her cheeks hard — ferociously.

As she cried out in pain, he gripped her waist, reminding her, "I'm in charge. Don't fucking move."

She grinned as he followed the words up by spanking her again and again until she moaned in pleasure, literally twisting underneath him. The more she responded, the more she moved — and the more he gave it to her. He gripped her in a way that hurt — hurt so damn good. Bruising was a certainty, she thought as he angled her hips up, his hot breath coming in between her crack.

She felt him blowing a stream of air up her wet slit. Trembling, wanting to cry out and beg, he touched her clit, twirling his fingers around it and rubbing it just the right way. She was so goddamn aroused that she knew she couldn't hold back her reactions.

"*Warren*," she moaned as he pushed two fingers in her pussy, making quick work of sending electric shocks up and down her legs.

Then she felt his tongue.

He licked down her ass into her wet slit — and played skillfully with her pussy. He groaned as he did it, telling her how much it turned him on to pleasure her — and that he was doing damn well. He took no short cuts, taking as long as needed to build pressure inside her. She felt herself losing her mind, getting dizzy, as he drew her closer and closer to heaven.

"You didn't believe in love?" he snarled, in between licking her to pure paradise. "You sure?"

She pursed her lips to respond but could only scream out his name as he pumped his hand inside her harder and faster, driving her over the edge.

"Tell me what this is then," he demanded through heaving breaths.

Again, she couldn't put words together — too lost in what he was doing to her.

"That's too bad." He licked back upward, biting her ass cheek, pulling his fingers out of her. She whimpered as he did, needing more of that. Needing to be full.

"I need you inside me."

"Yeah?" He moved upward so that his hard cock was at a perfect angle with her pussy.

But he just teased her, rubbing his pulsing cockhead against her throbbing opening.

"*Please*, Warren."

He leaned forward, pushing up on her wrist bonds, making it hurt as her arms twisted up her back. She couldn't move an inch without the feeling that her arms were going to snap out of place. Completely vulnerable before him, he fit his thick cockhead into her opening, slowly. Panting, she couldn't push back. She could only wait.

Then he slid himself up her aching channel, pumping his cock into her.

Grabbing a fist full of her hair, he brought her face off the pillow, snapping her neck backward. With her wrists tight and neck back, he dominated her easily. He overpowered her. She was at his mercy.

Warren wasted no time thrusting his long, hard cock in and out of her deprived pussy. He held her down just how she wanted, finding the right angle to fuck her senseless. The way his cock hit the front side of her pussy, he grated against that exact spot where the best sensations came from. Nearly on sensory overload, she cried out his name again and again. The entire bed shook under what he was doing to her.

"I like hearing you say my name," he growled, fucking her harder and harder.

She moaned it again, his powerful thrusts driving her into the headboard.

"I'm going to miss that."

Alisa was too deep into a hard-hitting orgasm to truly register his words.

She let herself go, completely letting herself get lost in the moment — lost in her feelings for him. And it was at that exact moment that his cock thickened and hardened even more inside her, something she didn't even think was possible. Her climax grew, and she felt weakened, falling into the mattress.

He untied her, whipping the tie across the room, and flipped her underneath him, dropping his arms on either side of her. He hovered, opening her thighs to welcome him. Taking her mouth once more, kissing her deeper than ever, he pulled her knees up and situated himself between her legs. She felt his manhood throbbing in need.

But she also felt him wincing in pain. As she ran her hands up the side of his ribcage, she felt the bandage where he'd seemingly patched himself up from where he'd been slashed. Her eyes narrowed in concern, but he pushed her off.

Clearly pushing through the pain, he bent over, licking her nipples, teasing and playing with them with his mouth. Grazing his teeth along her skin, he feasted on her breasts, making her whimper in delight. She panted, trying to get a grip on reality — her mind literally spiraling. She just wanted to scream out how much she loved him — how much he'd made her fall in love with him.

She barely could believe it.

"Okay?" he checked, pushing his cock again into her opening.

She bit her lip, nodding passionately. Wrapping her hands behind his head, feeling his glorious auburn hair, she received his cock in her opening and his tongue in her mouth.

As the bedframe rattled underneath them, he rocked back and forth harder and harder as she called out his name again and again. Finally, the bedframe broke, the headboard sliding down—but he grabbed onto it, continuing to fuck her until she saw the heat rising up his throat. One hand on the broken headboard, one hand on her tender waist, he pumped into her as he growled intensely, savagely—yelling into nothingness out of both pain and pleasure. She felt him come inside her, drenching her already wet pussy in his seed.

Then he collapsed to the side of her, throwing the headboard onto the ground like he didn't give a fuck. Grimacing and heaving for breath, he turned to her, grabbing her into his arms, caressing her stomach. He drove goosebumps over her sensitive flesh, easily coiling more tension into her already-sated body.

She touched his face, seeing it contort under her fingers. She drew her hand down his ribs, sneaking toward his injury, blaming the doctor in her. He immediately slapped her away from it, his grip on her wrist tightening in threat.

"Don't," he panted.

"You're hurt."

"I know," he started, his teeth cutting along his lip like he was trying to find words to say something to her. "I—"

But then he stopped, shaking his head.

He pulled her into him, kissing her hair, kissing her forehead and cheeks. The way he touched her was loving yet apologetic. Then he pushed away, rolling off the side of the bed with a grimace of sheer agony. Standing up, he snatched clothes, whipping them on.

Then he walked out of the room.

As he disappeared, Alisa felt a sinking feeling in her stomach. She didn't know why—or what. She just knew it was there. Something was wrong. She didn't move, just listening to the sounds of the house. Where did he go?

When she heard him pulling something heavy out of the basement and opening the front door, she jumped up. What the hell was going on?

She grasped at whatever she could—his T-shirt. Unsure, she padded down the stairs, gazing toward the kitchen. But Warren wasn't there. Peering around the corner of the hallway, she gathered herself. Warren was standing in the front entranceway, already fully dressed, arranging keys on the front console.

"I got the call," he said without glancing up at her, working on aligning the keys perfectly.

"The call?"

"There's been a situation. I've got to get to the airfield."

He still didn't look up.

Alisa slid down to sit on the bottom step in complete disbelief, watching him from a safe distance, as if getting any closer would just make it hurt more.

"W-What do you mean?"

"I'm flying out in a matter of hours. I'm deploying tonight."

"Y-you can't," she stuttered as she felt her face flush with hurt.

"This is my job. This was going to happen."

"You knew about this?"

"It was going to happen sooner than later. We both knew." His tone remained stony, distant. It was the same Warren she'd seen once before.

"You can't just leave. I'm only safe because you're here. Without you, I have no chance." She descended into panic, realizing what was happening.

He shook his head that same way, as if unable to believe it either.

"I have friends to watch over you, like I said. You can stay here as long as you want. Here's the house key and the security code." He pushed a few things along the console. "And you have my check to buy a new car."

"Stay here?" she scoffed, her eyes wide with urgency. "As what? Your house sitter?"

"Alisa." His eyes darted up to hers for the first time, and she saw that he was in as much pain as her.

She wanted to push off the step, jump after him — but she didn't. She couldn't.

"I don't need your friends. I don't need your gated community," she cried. "All I've ever needed was you."

"I warned you that I couldn't give you more."

"Couldn't — or wouldn't?" she challenged.

He didn't reply, rotating toward the door. His focused face didn't quite mask the injury cut into his back.

"You are just going to leave? After that?" She nodded upstairs to his bedroom, where they'd both let themselves sink into each other until the pain didn't matter.

"I'm committed. I have no choice."

Alisa grew speechless, unable to process what the fuck was happening. He was really leaving. Her face twisted in hurt, her stomach lurching in ways she couldn't control.

He fired her one last look, nodded and strode out of the door. She impulsively jumped up after him, sprinting to catch the door before it closed.

"You must have a choice."

"That's not how this works." He didn't check back.

"You can't leave," she cried out after him, tears pouring down her cheeks.

He stopped on the front steps, glancing over his shoulder at her in the doorway.

"You can't leave, Warren—"

The world fell silent, still even.

She finally exhaled, "because I'm in love with you."

The way his throat and cheeks flushed, she knew he'd heard her. But he just shook his head and walked away, jumping into his truck. He said nothing else.

She then watched the man drive away. Drive out of her life.

They'd finally fallen apart.

As unceremoniously as we started.

She sank down into his doorway, watching his truck leave her sight, trying to suck in the night air for survival. Tears were an understatement. Ugly crying was more accurate.

She grabbed at her chest, feeling her heart palpitate—some sort of spontaneous supraventricular tachycardia. Or maybe her heart had just shattered. What was the prognosis for that? It was the first time she'd ever felt it.

But, then again, she'd known it was going to happen.

Chapter Twenty-Eight

Warren

Jumping out of his truck in the dead of night, Warren tossed his truck keys at one of the guys in the military airfield crew.

"I've got some kit in the back that I need to bring," he said.

The crewmember nodded, opening the bed of the truck to pick apart Warren's pelican cases. This time, Warren was bringing his latest plate armor. He'd invested in a custom job to keep his back safe, unable to afford any further injury.

Warren marched with purpose toward the hangar, ready to prep before the rest of his crew arrived. A somber mood hung over the airfield as he entered the staff building, knowing that early emergency deployments were hard on everyone, especially guys with families. The least he could do was get shit ready for them.

Swiping into the secure building, Warren dove into action mode. He got into the locker room. He whipped off his shirt, readying to hit the showers. He needed a fucking cold one — anything to wake the fuck up and rinse off the scent of her. Yeah, he could still taste her in his mouth, something he didn't want to remember.

The tall mirror hanging over the counter in the locker room reflected his snarling face. Warren ran his fingers up his unshaven jaw, rough and angry.

Turning, he threw down his pants, twisting to grab his belt. The pain in his back soared, unstoppable... unforgiving. He grimaced again, knowing it was the dumbest idea to fuck the shit out of Alisa with a fresh wound, even dumber than deploying with it.

He edged toward the mirror, checking the bandaging job he'd done. His massive back tattoo came into focus, the memorial he'd got to remind him but had tried to forget. A date sprawled across the top was unforgettable — five years ago, almost to the day.

Geoff.

His mind wandered to all the other men he'd lost.

"You've damn near lost yourself along the way," he said.

Or maybe I already have.

Determined, he spun to the showers, willing himself to keep going. If there was one thing he had to do, it was to never stop. He was never ever going to sit with his fucking feelings. He was never going to open up that locked vault.

Not a goddamn thing could make him.

* * * *

Hours prepping for deployment poured by as quick as a cup of coffee. It wasn't hard for Warren to stay on task once he was in work mode. The boss had said — "*shipping out at first light.*" They'd gotten an insanely good lead on a prime target and couldn't waste it.

Once dawn crested, Warren heard more and more guys arriving to deploy. Being a more senior operator, he always was first there, last to leave. That's how he showed he cared.

Marching out of the building, he assessed the situation on the ground. Kitted up, he'd donned his tactical pants, along with boots and a shirt. He critiqued and questioned what was done and what needed to be done. He personally was ready to rock.

Up ahead, Master Chief Rose popped out of the hangar, urgently motioning for Warren to get closer. The C-17 Globemaster III, strategic transport aircraft, was warming in the distance. Guys in fatigues were already running up the back ramp, adjusting cargo and kit. The tempo was mounting. People were readying. It was going to be a wild one.

He wouldn't miss it for the world.

Warren felt his phone vibrating in his pocket. As the early beams of morning light hit his face, he noticed that Katy's mom had sent him a text — responding to what he'd sent her a few hours ago.

You're deploying now? Katy's just waking up. Want to have a call?

Sucking in breath and knowing it was going to be damn hard, Warren hit the video call button on his phone. He hated those moments.

"Good morning, sweetheart," he said into the video call, seeing little Katy's blonde curly hair completely disheveled as she snuggled beside her mom.

"Good morning," she said, pursing her sleepy mouth.

It killed him already, He could see it in her eyes. Disappointment.

"Are you leaving?" she asked in a tiny voice.

"Yes, for a little while," he explained, then tried to reassure her. "But I'll be back. I'll always come back."

Her lip quivered, and she started tearing up. "Daddy said that, too."

Warren felt his throat tightening, seeing Alisa's face as he left her. He went blank and felt cold. Brooke took the phone from Katy, speaking reassuringly to both of them.

"It's okay, Katy. He will be back soon," Brooke said, turning the camera to her. "Warren, we should probably make this one quick."

"Okay."

Brooke turned the camera back to the little girl, who was starting to hyperventilate.

"I love you so much," Warren assured her, hearing people calling for him in the background. "I'll be back before you know it."

"Promise?"

"I promise," he said with a confident smile that he didn't feel, coinciding with an ugly realization.

He'd already missed so much of her life. How much more was he going to miss?

Then Brooke ended the call, texting him that she would do her best to work with Katy on the situation, asking him to keep in touch.

Struggling, Warren put his phone away, unable to even think of calling Alisa. He couldn't take anymore. Gazing over the airfield, he sucked in dry, desert air. He liked that air.

He settled back into work mode...into focus. As he marched toward the plane, signaling to his crew, he felt a sense of comfort settling into his chest. Warren turned to see Master Chief Rose standing nearby in fatigues.

"Chief."

"Sir." Warren nodded amid the busy scene on the tarmac.

"Your retention bonus was approved," the master chief said. "Commensurate with your rank and amount of service, a fresh two-hundred-and-fifty thousand should be sitting in your account this morning."

Warren pretended to laugh at the quip, nodding his head in understanding.

"It's a small price to pay," the master chief continued, "to have you sign up for another five years of service."

The truth was that it was a small price to pay to get Alisa out of debt, Warren thought. To get her safe. That retention bonus was going to be withdrawn nearly as soon as it was deposited.

"If I wasn't in service, what the hell would I be doing?" Warren shrugged.

His attempt at humor was met by a dark look from the master chief.

"What about a life? What about *her*?"

Warren shook him off. "Guys like me — this is all I've got. This is all I'll ever have. My brothers are out there, fighting. I need to be with them. I need to be fighting."

"I don't believe that. Neither should you."

"I've got to do this." Warren motioned his chin up at the plane.

"You are *choosing* this life."

"I don't have a choice anymore."

Warren knew that he'd made his bed. He'd issued that check, taken that bonus. Things were already in motion that couldn't be stopped. He was going.

He turned to march to the plane. No one understood why he'd chosen to go back to that same place, deployment after deployment—why he kept fighting, why he couldn't let go.

Warren motioned orders at his crew. As he drew closer to the plane, he stopped dead on the tarmac, glaring around. He always did that—one more look at his home soil in case he never came back.

Stomping up the plane's ramp, he addressed his men, getting guys settled. Then, he signaled to the airfield crew to draw the ramp up. It was time. They were ready to go. The plane's engine roared in preparation.

For the first time in a thousand deployments, all he could think of was how weird it was leaving when, for the first time, he was realizing how much he meant to a few key people back home—Alisa and Katy.

They love me.

He felt something crack in his chest, forcing him to buckle forward. Shooting out his arm, he growled at the airfield doorman.

"Wait." He motioned to stop the ramp.

Chapter Twenty-Nine

Warren

"What the fuck is going on?" Master Chief Rose stomped up the tarmac to where Warren stood.

Keeled over, Warren grasped at his chest. He couldn't tell what was in more pain—his back or his heart.

"Get the med kit," the master chief ordered a guy to the side. "Is this a fucking heart attack?"

"I'm fine," Warren said through clenched teeth.

"You're not fucking fine. What's the goddamn problem? Can you breathe?"

"I'm getting on that pl—" Warren couldn't finish his sentence, wheezing through the last word. He felt his cell vibrating. He whipped it out, seeing a missed message from Brooke.

Katy had a little tumble. She's fine but keeps crying for you. Do you have a minute for a short call again?

"Christ," Warren said, reading the message several times. Whatever phantom knife was digging through his chest just twisted, splitting his ribs. His guilt was driving the pain...he knew it. The message from Brooke only drove him further — to go to Katy, see her in person one last time.

"What the hell is going on with you? Is this for real?"

Warren looked up, locking eyes with his boss. "It's my conscience. I've got something I need to do."

"I can give you an hour."

"I don't want to leave my guys in the lurch. We've worked damn hard."

"They'll be fine — because you trained them right. You'll be no good to anyone dead. Go get it done then get your ass back here."

Gripping his cell, Warren glanced over his shoulder at his team. Half of the guys from his team were on the ramp, watching, waiting. He grasped the concern in their eyes.

"Let's do this," Warren said, spinning toward his truck.

One hour. Don't waste time.

* * * *

Throttling down the highway, moving faster than he should, Warren listened to Brooke's line ringing and ringing. She wasn't fucking answering, and he was losing it.

Finally, she picked it up.

"Warren, sorry. Aren't we going to do this by video?"

"Look... I'm coming your way. Is Katy okay? What the fuck is going on?"

"She took a bad fall down the stairs," Brooke said, breaking into tears. "I think I should take her to be seen."

"Call the fucking ambulance!" he growled, nearing snapping his steering wheel in half from stress.

"No, Warren, Katy doesn't need an ambulance."

Katy's crying intensified in the background, burning into Warren's chest.

"I can't fucking fly there," he said. "Jesus. She needs the ER."

"No, she does not—" Brooke started.

"Yes, she goddamn does."

"She just needs *you*."

The way the word rolled off Brooke's tongue told Warren everything about the situation, reminding him of his inherent failures.

"She's only ever just needed you."

Brooke's final words hit him more slowly than the last, making him feel sadness he never noticed before.

"Got it," he replied solemnly.

His jaw clenched so damn tight, he thought his teeth would snap. The image of Katy falling, crying for him and him not being there—it was killing him. The image of leaving the plane behind didn't fucking matter anymore. She was more important.

The morning started to become a haze. He was operating on high octane stress.

Once Warren finally got to Katy, he picked her up and assessed her. He had already decided on the way that he had to take her to the hospital and packed both mother and child into the back of his truck. Goddamn head injuries were a bitch. He wasn't fucking around anymore.

His stress levels were off the goddamn charts as his truck was barreling back down the LA boulevard. Parking his truck at the hospital, he re-evaluated the little girl that he swung into his arms, re-checking her curly blonde hair for blood. Brooke stood behind him as he focused, seeming more than willing to let him lead.

The time ticked by — and he knew he wasn't going to make it back in an hour. The master chief was shooting him messages, asking what his status was, but Warren hadn't replied.

"Are you sure you can see normal?" Warren asked the little girl as he jogged toward ER, holding her tiny body tightly against him. Guilt had already consumed him.

"Yeah." She winced into the sunlight.

Brooke kept up right beside them, fumbling in her purse, probably for insurance information.

He ripped off his shades, placing them over Katy's eyes, serving to make her look like an adorable bug. He knew what it felt like when your head was throbbing and the sun was burning. He'd been there many times.

Crashing into the ER, he called out to the front desk staff.

"I've got a child that needs attention, stat!"

Nurses rushed around the desk to assess her, pulling a hospital bed from the side, asking what was going on.

"She fell down a flight of stairs." Warren's shaking tone surprised him. "She whacked her head."

As he placed her on the rolling bed, Katy started to cry, clearly overwhelmed by the situation — likely more overwhelmed by Warren's sudden frenzy. He was fucking losing it. Nothing the staff was doing was fast enough. It didn't matter that she tried to assure him. He wanted a goddamn doctor to sit down right in front of him and promise him the kid would be fine.

His cell vibrated in his pocket for the hundredth time. He didn't have time for fucking messages and didn't give a fuck anymore.

"Do you need to leave?" Brooke asked.

Katy's gaze whipped back and forth between him and her mother, surely trying to process.

"It's okay," Warren assured Katy, trying to compose himself.

He gripped her hand as the staff rushed them to one of the rooms in the ER where the doctor would see them.

Once in the room, the nurses started checking her vitals, scanning her over and testing for serious injury.

"Are you the father?" The nurse paused.

"Not exactly," Warren replied.

Brooke and the nurse exchanged glances.

Warren fumbled to explain, but the nurse had moved on, talking to Katy. Through tears, Katy answered the nurse's questions, one by one, but fell apart, unable to cooperate any further. Her wrinkling face broke out in a sob, calling for Warren.

"Katy" — Warren leaned down, grabbing her up to him, holding her against his chest — "you've got to answer. I know it's hard but — "

"Her heart rate is rising," one of the nurses called out into the hall, beckoning her colleagues.

His phone vibrated angrily in his pocket. He didn't miss Brooke's challenging gaze, as if she knew.

Katy started hyperventilating.

"She's in shock," Warren snapped, feeling her head for a lump.

How hard did she hit it? Is she going through delayed response? His military field training kicked in, aggressively pushing the nurses aside. He needed to take a leadership role. They weren't doing enough for her.

"Sir, we need access—"

"No!" he yelled back, holding the crying child to him.

He had to fix her. She was slipping away. Her cries grew louder, gasping for breath. He could feel her struggling to breathe.

Fuck!

"Christ, Katy—stay with me." He felt something strange coming over him, like he tasted sand in his mouth.

Iraqi sand.

His own vision blurred. "Please, Katy."

Katy's endless tears pushed him over the edge, the beeping on the monitor drove him to the brink. He was fucking losing her. He was holding her tiny body, and she was dying in his arms.

She was dying.

A weird wetness came over his right cheek, but his spinning mind was unable to place what exactly it was. It felt like the cold scope of a sniper rifle pressed into his cheek, having just slid down his face. That sensation, holding Katy to his chest, his mind flew rapidly to a time he only saw in his nightmares.

Warren looked around, realizing he was on the top of a crumbled building in Iraq.

It was midday, and the sun scorched the back of his neck, which was covered partially by a keffiyeh. *The wind had blown part of the fabric off his neck and jaw, but he didn't dare move to adjust. His finger was flexed on the trigger of* his sniper rifle, locked dead on the doorway of the building where his high-priority target was situated.

He was alone, still as hell, and hadn't moved for hours. He waited and waited…and waited. A grayish grit circulated in the air, moving all around him, getting into his nose and mouth. It was like a shit dust and tasted the same. The unforgiving climate threatened the outsider, making it clear that he wasn't welcome.

"Whiskey Charlie, you sitting tight?" He heard the voice of his leading chief, Geoff, through his earpiece.

"Ten four," Warren muttered back, keeping his voice low despite the blistering gusts at the top of the five-story building in the heart of the Iraqi city.

"When he comes out, you engage. Don't fucking hesitate. I'm right down here."

Warren waited, knowing his crew was around the ground level, preparing to assault the already-crumbling building. The only thing that kept them waiting was that they didn't know exactly how many people were inside. Geoff had seen the worst and was resolved on minimizing collateral damage when possible. If they could take out the target and only the target, it would be a flawless mission.

He adjusted the scope, ensuring it was perfectly focused on the door to the building where the target would be exiting. Walking up and down the busy street, he observed women in black cloth, other men and a young child running after a well-used ball on the ground.

"Get out of here, kid," Warren griped, looking for the kid's mother.

It looked like a little girl, no older than four or five years old, in torn clothes. Then he saw the mother – all in black – she was bartering with a merchant a little up the sidewalk, not realizing her kid was running rampant after the ball.

A beat-up car sped through the street, and Warren's nerves screeched into high gear. *That fucking kid was going to get hit*, he breathed to himself. **Fucking hell**.

"There's movement in the window," Geoff said. "Any second now."

Warren's black-gloved finger tightened on the trigger, and he sucked in his breath, holding it. He could hold his breath for a long fucking time, if needed, but hoped to God he wouldn't have to.

And he didn't.

The target, a tall Iraqi man in traditional garb with a Kevlar vest on moved out of the building, snarling as he looked around.

"Engage! Engage!"

Warren didn't expect the body armor and repositioned to get the guy's head. But the guy turned slightly, and Warren missed his first shot.

"Fuck," Warren grunted and immediately refocused, taking a second shot. "Shit!"

The second shot hit — the target's head spun and hit the ground. Warren observed splatter against the wall of the building and pavement. But then he realized — his first shot had landed.

The kid... The kid chasing the ball. She was lying on the ground, covered in blood.

He'd just fucking killed a kid.

"Fuck, fuck, fuck," Warren said, thrust into emergency mode.

Grabbing his rifle, moving as fast as he fucking could down the outer stairs of the building, he lunged toward the front of the building, finding his team already storming it.

Warren saw his body moving toward the kid who was bleeding out on the ground. He saw the bright red blood. He was kneeling down. He was over the kid. He was trying to stop the bleeding. He was huddled over, holding her tight to *his chest, exposing his back completely as his plates rode upward. Yelling out over the explosives and gunshots, he couldn't admit he'd already lost her. He didn't want to tell himself the truth. Her mother was screaming. Geoff was yelling into his ear to get the fuck out. Bullets were raining down on him, hitting him in the helmet and hitting the kid's body in his arms.*

He was hyperventilating. He'd just fucking killed a little girl. Nothing else mattered, and his mind disconnected from the war zone he was in the center of.

"No!" he yelled out at the street, that same cold feeling running down his cheek. "Fuck!"

Then he felt a painful slash up his back — way underneath his plated armor. He choked, unable to breathe. An enemy had taken advantage of his vulnerability, sending a hunter's blade so damn deep into his flesh that he'd undoubtedly caught organs. Coughing out, Warren's grip tightened on the little Iraqi girl, as if they could die together — as if he could always be there for her, as if she wouldn't have to die alone on the side of a shitty, blown-out street in Iraq.

Then everything went black.

Warren prayed he'd died.

He prayed that he could take her place—and that she could live.

But he woke up empty—his arms as empty as his heart—in a hospital bed. He woke up to the sounds of a woman's voice, coaxing him out of it.

"What's going on in here?" He heard a familiar feminine voice echoing through the room, drawing him out of whatever state he was in.

Lying on his side in a hospital bed, holding nothing to his chest, he looked over his shoulder, immediately shocked to see Alisa standing there, sporting green scrubs and a high ponytail. A badge on her shirt read

'Student'. He lay there, stunned. *What the fuck is going on?*

"Holy shit," Alisa said, seeming to realize who the real patient was.

Alisa maintained a chilling presence. Professional, confident. It's not that the nurses weren't, but something about Alisa was markedly different. As she called over to the nurses, he heard her being told that Brooke was holding Katy in an adjacent room. Then, Alisa focused only on him — her patient.

He felt every ounce of oxygen get sucked out of his chest, like the room had turned into a vacuum. He was darting his eyes back and forth between Alisa and the nurses moving into the hall, and the moment became so goddamn surreal that he questioned his lucidity.

Is any of this even real?

As Alisa checked him over in the hospital bed, Warren edged himself up, leaning on his elbow.

"We need to check her oxygen level," he slurred, watching Brooke holding Katy in the next bed. "Is she breathing all right? I can't find blood on her head —"

Alisa cut him off. "Just let us handle this."

She flashed a warning to him.

His cell vibrated again and again in his pocket, warning him that something was going down. His time was almost up. He had to get back.

"Look… With all due respect —" he said, continuing to try to get up.

"No." Alisa stood her ground, chopping him in the chest, pushing him back down. "I'm the medical professional, and you are *not*. Lie the fuck down."

But, as she pushed him back, that familiar slashing pain shot up his back, and he felt like he was going to pass out.

"Fuck." Warren grimaced, clutching at the bedrails for dear life.

He couldn't breathe.

Chapter Thirty

Alisa

"It's okay," Alisa assured the broken man lying before her. "It's okay."

Her rapt concern for Warren's well-being helped push aside the deep hurt he'd caused her just hours before. A million questions flooded her mind, but none as important as—what the hell was happening to him now? Alisa's ran her gloved hand over Warren's ribs. To her lightest touch, he winced, shrinking away from her.

"Fight me, and I'll inject you with something that'll make your dick fall off."

"Sounds kinky," he said. In a mix of fear and amusement, he angled himself to give her access.

"Shut up and let me do my job."

She yanked his shirt all the way up, running her gloved hands up his back. It was the first time he'd ever let her do that—touch his scar.

"Warren, what the hell is wrong with you?"

"A lot."

His grimacing didn't stop and worsened as she pressed on certain parts.

"We're supposed to ask if you have a latex allergy before we touch you," she said, kneading an area. "But I already know you must have one."

He shuddered and turned his head to her. "How?"

"Because you never wore a fucking condom."

She pushed his shoulder to give her a better angle at his back. *God, this scar is deep.*

"I get the impression you want to hurt me," he said. He clenched his teeth.

"*Do no harm.* Unfortunately, I took an oath."

Cool, angry, all she could think about were his boss's words—and that something had happened to him—something bad enough that he kept that demon close to his heart to that day, something that he'd refused to fucking tell her because she was worthless to him.

"Who's the kid?" she quizzed, trying to change the subject.

"She's the daughter of a guy from work."

"And are you *with* the mother?"

"With?"

"You know exactly what I mean."

Warren opened his mouth to reply, but the door swung open.

Dr. Zucker came in, gesturing to Alisa. "I'm assessing the child. I'll get you help for this."

"No, I've got it."

"Are you sure?"

"I'll handle him."

Alisa glanced back at the door, seeing a handful of nurses and Dr. Zucker watching her intently. She gritted her molars, determined.

"Just shut the door," Alisa called at the staff before turning her attention back to Warren.

Wiping sweat from his brow, contorted in the hospital bed, he gazed up at her.

"What the fuck are you going to do to me?"

"I don't know," she mused, her gaze intensifying. "Maybe kill you."

He let out a laugh before coughing.

Alisa circled around the bed. She had to get at all angles.

"Did you get stitched up in a military hospital?"

"A field medic." He coughed as she explored. "In Iraq."

Alisa snorted. "That'll do it."

Observing how the sutures had been done, though years ago, she shook her head.

"A knife wound?"

"You got it."

"I used to think you were Mr. Perfect," Alisa said, shaking her head. "But you aren't Mr. Perfect. You're just afraid of being imperfect."

"Ah, free therapy. Is there a two-for-one deal on today?" He smirked, relaxing under her touch as she gently massaged his side to determine where the pain was coming from.

"Funny guy."

She prodded at a particularly rough spot. Warren let out a long, slow breath, and she knew she had him where she needed him. The expression on his face tempered her. As angry as she was, he drew something out of her. It got her biting her lip, whispering down her most important question.

"What happened, Warren?"

He seemed to reflect on her question. She saw him drawing his fingers over his pant pocket, grasping at the outline of his cell. She faintly heard it vibrating and could tell he was deciding whether to get it or not. She'd been there before, knew what was priority. She leaned back, waiting for him to walk out on her, get after what was most important to him.

But he didn't walk out.

He dropped his hand from his pocket and locked eyes with her. The expression on his face was something she'd never really seen in him before.

"Alisa, I'm going to tell you a story. But, afterward, you're not going to want to talk to me again."

"I don't want to talk to you again now, so what's the difference?"

"*Alisa.*" He turned, his ice-blue gaze pouring into her, catching her off guard.

He wasn't playing anymore.

She leaned back, trying to understand. Hadn't she already told him the bad stuff from her own life? What could possibly be worse?

They both paused, giving him space to continue.

And he did.

"Five years ago, there was a bad op. Things went sideways," he said so quietly that it was nearly inaudible.

"Okay?" Alisa slowly removed her gloves, listening.

"Alisa, I get reminders. Your ring—a reminder. This scar—it's a fucking reminder, too."

"Of?"

"I shot a kid in Iraq," he said, shaking his head. "I fucking killed her—"

But his voice seized, seemingly unable to continue. *Is he choking?*

Alisa stumbled backward, grabbing at the IV drip for stability. Though, being on wheels, it did not prove helpful. Her stomach turned, trying to understand what he'd just told her.

"Oh, fuck."

He let out a long, haggard breath. She felt that.

"Katy's dad—Geoff, he ran that op. He ordered me to take a shot. I shouldn't have, but I did. A bullet went haywire. It was a goddamn accident, but I killed her."

"God—" she started.

She locked eyes once again with Warren. That same look flushed over his face—the same pained look he'd given her before he'd walked away the night prior. And she knew—the weight he carried was far heavier than he'd ever let on.

"Geoff blamed himself."

"Where is he now?" she asked.

"He killed himself"—Warren looked up at her, his face pale—"when we rotated home."

She froze.

"You have survivor's guilt," she said.

"It's not just that. It was *my fault*. Neither of them had to die."

"Are you sure about that?"

"Without a doubt," he said, his expression unmoving.

She caught a feeling of the war fighter's spirit, his hardened soul. A chill shot up her spine, giving her a shudder she couldn't repress. She'd seen it in him before but never as pronounced. She opened her mouth to reply, but nothing came out. This was a man who'd seen death like she'd never know, even as she worked in the ER. The difference between him and her was that she worked to prevent death, while he worked to cause it.

His jaw flexing, he narrowed his eyes, awaiting her response. She leaned back, trying to find a place for her hands.

Then a knock came at the door, and the nurse peered in. "Dr. Zucker wants to know if you are planning on looking at the girl after he is finished with her."

"Yes—I'll be right there," Alisa responded.

Chapter Thirty-One

Warren

Warren lumbered out of the hospital bed, following Alisa into the adjacent space where Katy and Brooke were. He tried to relax, his mind racing with questions about what had just happened — and what Alisa was thinking. For the first time, Alisa was so damn cool that he was failing to read her as she jotted notes at Katy's bedside.

Brooke nodded to him that she needed to go deal with the front desk for the insurance. She was asking him to watch Katy in her absence. He stood over the bed, taking a deep breath while Katy fiddled with the TV remote for cartoons.

He took the brief moment to slide his cell out of his pocket, seeing all of the messages he'd missed. Not only had nearly every guy on his team sent him something, but he had a whack of missed calls, most from the master chief. It had been well over an hour, and he was late to return to the tarmac. They all thought he was dead, clearly. He quickly fired off a message to his boss, letting him know he was alive, and fingered through the words received from the guys. What shocked him was the level of support. Guys weren't pissed he'd bailed. They were genuinely concerned about his well-being.

A man who introduced himself as Dr. Zucker waltzed in, rubbing hand-sanitizer all over his hands. He motioned at Alisa to have Katy sit up on the bed.

Warren reached down to hold Katy's hand, helping her, reassuring her, but he was thwarted. Alisa stepped in between them, nodding to the chair beside the bed.

"You can sit there," Alisa said.

"What?"

"I said — *sit down.*"

The sound of Dr. Zucker scribbling on a notepad in the background was the only noise in the room.

It took him a second, but Warren relented, sitting his ass down on the chair, sucking in a shallow, stressful breath — and giving Alisa space to work. Watching the scene unfold before him, it was clear that med student Alisa wasn't as soft as the woman he'd become used to, but in that moment, he didn't want soft.

Warren shifted, getting more comfortable, watching Alisa work. Slowly, putting the pieces together, he learned something about her. This was her — as professional and focused as he was at his job. She was like a Navy SEAL in medicine. He got that.

His senses started returning to him, and he acknowledged that it was all, in fact, really happening. Alisa was really triaging him, triaging Katy, taking control of the scene — *leading* the scene. Other health-care workers stood back in the doorway, nurses and doctors alike, watching her manage the critical situation. In one fell swoop, she'd not only taken charge of the child but calmed the increasingly aggressive adult — *him*.

Taking another deep breath, he saw Katy enjoying Alisa's attention. Alisa handled Katy in such a way that was both clear and comforting, punctuated by her sheer confidence...sheer competency. Whatever stress had boiled up in Warren was going back down. He reached to his cheek again, trying to figure out what he felt on his skin. It was like the cold barrel of a sniper scope.

"She hit her head?" Alisa asked him. "That's what you told the nurses?"

"Yeah, she fell down the stairs."

"Did you see it? Did you see where she hit her head?"

"No — she was at her mom's," he explained.

"Okay," Alisa replied, lowering Katy down onto the bed, resting her head on the pillow. "There you go. Just relax."

"Am I going to be okay?" Katy asked in a tiny voice, still a little anxious.

"Let's see," Alisa said as she lifted up both of Katy's arms.

Alisa continued, "Can you hold my hand — really tight? Yes, just like that."

Katy obeyed, squeezing each of Alisa's hands.

"Can you turn your head from side to side? Yes, perfect." Alisa analyzed quickly, seeming to check for discrepancy in muscle response.

"Looking for paralysis?" Warren chimed in.

"Shut the eff up," Alisa shot at him.

Warren's mouth dropped open. Dr. Zucker's eyebrows rose to the high heavens. But all anyone could hear was Katy giggling at Alisa's profanity and mumbling something about the swear jar.

A grin crossed Alisa's lips. "You think that's funny?"

"Mommy always swears," Katy whispered, as if she were telling a big, bad secret.

"I like your mom," Alisa said. "I want you to tell me what you see."

She held up different objects, making Katy giggle when she held them right in front of Warren's face. He played along, batting away the stethoscope dangling in front of his nose, like he was truly annoyed. He wasn't. He was damn glad Alisa was warming up.

"Now, I want you to tell me what you hear."

Alisa proceeded to make a few silly animal noises, which resulted in roaring laughter from Katy. In fact, it got Warren laughing as well, and he nearly forgot about the status check messages from the master chief.

"Yes, it looks totally fine. Don't worry," Alisa finally said, patting the child.

Dr. Zucker nodded in agreement, snapping his notebook closed and leaving the room.

Then Alisa spun to Warren, assuring him. "She's going to be okay, as long as she doesn't hang around you for too long."

The words ricocheted in Warren's mind. *She's going to be okay.* Hearing Alisa say it, it sank in. And he realized that it had never been as bad as he'd thought. Retracing his steps through his mind, Warren self-assessed that he had just completely lost it. The fear of a child dying in his arms... He recognized his trigger point.

"And...now, are *you* okay?" Alisa asked him, hanging her stethoscope back around her neck.

Her focus drifted up and down his face, analyzing whatever he'd felt on his cheek.

"Yeah, what is—" He touched the cool spot again, then realized *exactly* what it was.

For a split second, he had felt like Katy was dying…in his arms. For a split second, he'd faltered. A cool rogue tear had fallen from his eye. Stunned as hell, he pulled his hand back from his cheek, hovering it in mid-air, his gaze drifting up to Alisa as she watched the realization wash over him. That's what crying felt like. Her clever eyes saw through him, maybe more than he saw through himself.

"I won't tell anyone," she whispered, shooting him a knowing look.

A grin crossed his lips, along with the overwhelming desire to reach out and kiss the knowing look off her goddamn flawless face.

"Sit tight," Alisa directed, surprising him yet again with how cool and collected she was—certainly in comparison to how he'd been.

He had to give her credit.

As Alisa strode back to brief the nurses and doctor, Warren admired her from a distance, holding Katy's hand beside him, squeezing it in reassurance. He looked back down to the little blonde girl who looked so much like her dad. Warren couldn't count the times he'd been on an operation after that, deep in some hellhole, wishing that God had taken him instead.

He tightened his grasp on Katy's little hand, her baby blue eyes, just like his, blinking up at him. The way she licked her bottom lip told him she was trying to think of the right words to say something. He reached over, brushing a tear off her apple-shaped cheek. Something about being with Alisa had opened him up to what was really happening inside him — a storm of sorts. A storm of his own fears.

I'm allowed to make mistakes. I'm allowed to be human.

He let his teeth graze his lip as he thought of the words that had never left him.

He darted his gaze back to the door where he saw Alisa jotting notes in a chart as she spoke with the doctor about a different patient in the ER. Even after everything that had happened the night prior, the past week, he had to sit back and admire how she had maintained a completely professional demeanor throughout the whole scene, not breaking the depth of their relationship to anyone.

And that was a relationship he wasn't prepared to let slip away.

Not with a woman like that.

"I don't want you to go back," Katy said, breaking into his thoughts.

"I know." He caressed her hand, turning his full attention to the child. "I don't want to go back, either."

"Can you stay home this time?" she asked in a tiny voice, the same question she'd asked too many times. "Please."

Warren watched her little eyes fill with tears again, knowing how he'd failed her. When he'd come back from that tour, with his slashed up back that had one hundred stitches in it, he'd had more scars deep inside that had needed to heal. He knew it would be impossible to forgive himself for all that, for everything he'd done and failed to do, but at some point he was going to have to reckon with the fact that he was pushing Katy away.

He had to forgive himself for his mistakes.

He owed it to Geoff to watch over his little girl. He owed it to Brooke.

"Katy, I love you," he whispered to her in his gruffy voice.

"It's okay. I love you, too."

Her little red pout trembled, but he stopped her. "I'm sorry I kept leaving."

Somewhere along the line, he realized that he'd been lying to himself.

"I'll stay." He offered her a caring smile, knowing he was changing his life without even having a plan. He just knew he couldn't let her go, not anymore.

She reached up with her little hands, embracing him. He sank into her, knowing that he was doing things that for a long fucking time he'd never thought he could do. And as he refocused on Alisa in the distance, he wondered how to get her back and how to make their fake engagement a *real one*.

* * * *

Being discharged from the hospital had been bittersweet, Warren thought as he walked out of the main doors with Alisa by his side. He told Brooke to wait with Katy inside. He was going to grab the truck and pull it around for them. It was weird being at a civilian hospital but weirder having to hide his hardened dick for a good portion of it. Alisa gave him the type of warm and fuzzies that used to scare him.

He gazed over at Alisa, still a little quiet. He knew exactly what was going through her head, everything still so unresolved. He squared himself to Alisa. He was damn happy not to be in the ER anymore, damn happy that everyone was just fine, but was twisted up letting his chick out of his sight again.

"You sure you can't leave?" he asked.

She shot him a look. "No, I have to finish my shift. I just got here."

"When are you done?"

"Never."

He felt his chest tightening. He moved into her. "We need to talk."

"I can't right now. Look... I'm serious." She waved her hands, stopping him in his tracks. Then she lowered her voice. "I don't want to cry today, Warren."

He gritted his teeth, knowing that pushing wasn't going to do him any favors.

Letting out an exhausted breath, Alisa reached into her pocket. She pulled out his house key, trying to hand it to him.

He refused to take it.

"It's your key. I'll stay at Maria's while you're gone," she said.

"I'm not leaving." He tightened his fists.

"What?" Her head cocked, and it was clear that she was confused. The key dangled from her finger between them.

"I'm staying."

"I don't understand."

Her lips parted, searching for words. He laughed, too amused for the moment.

"I don't know how else to explain this to you. I couldn't be any more specific. I'm not leaving. I'm not getting back on that plane. Master chief thought I was having a heart attack on the tarmac and has convinced himself I'm a broken toy. He's offering me med leave, getting off this deployment."

"And?"

"I'm taking it."

"But...your troops?"

He ran his hand through his hair, reflecting on the issue. "Look... I don't feel good about abandoning them, but I've just got a bunch of messages from the guys worrying that I'm dying, supporting me staying back."

"You weren't having a heart attack," she said, her eyes wide. "I would have picked up on that."

"I know. I wasn't, really."

"Then, what?" She tripped on her words. "Psychosomatic pain?"

"What? Come on. You're a doctor. Can't you figure it out?"

He shook his head, knowing full well he almost broke his own heart. He was seconds from letting that ramp draw up, hauling ass back to the battlefield, never to look back.

"I'm not a doctor yet," she explained. "My final exams are next month and I'm hoping to be a radiologist."

"Alisa, I didn't know that's what you were gunning for."

"You didn't ask."

"Things are starting to make sense now."

She stepped backward, one foot closer to the entrance to the hospital. He followed her, hearing Katy giggling in the background, apparently finding their cat and mouse game amusing.

"I have to go," Alisa asserted.

"Come over after your shift. We have unfinished business."

She chewed her lip, unconvinced.

A group exited the hospital doors, pushing them aside. Warren knew he couldn't linger. Then Katy's giggling stopped, but he was too focused to think.

"Just come," he said.

Alisa flashed her bright eyes at him, but he didn't miss how they grew concerned. Deeply troubled. His spidey sense tingled, and he spun to see a man in a leather jacket who was stomping up the sidewalk. *Dean.*

"What the fuck is this?" Warren said. He planted himself firmly and squarely between the threat and the woman he would die for.

"Didn't think you'd get rid of me that easy?" Dean replied, reaching into his leather jacket. "She's mine."

He pulled out a gun.

Onlookers screamed, jumping aside. Suddenly, the situation felt like a duel, a standoff. Warren felt underprepared with no weapons but his fists.

"Cool it," Warren said. He motioned for Dean to stop but the man inched forward.

"She's not yours. I don't care what the fuck I have to do—"

"Stop. I don't want to have to kill you, but I will."

"Who's holding the gun?" Dean's unhinged grin was telling, the bruising and swelling on his face almost disfiguring him. He pointed the gun right at Warren, his finger on the trigger.

Purely on instinct, Warren dove toward the man, wasting no time. The gun fired but Warren caught Dean in the torso fast enough, driving him to the ground. The distinct echo of a bullet hitting concrete reassured Warren. A short scuffle led Warren to gain the upper hand, seizing the gun, aiming it at Dean.

Warren moved to arrest the man but lost his grip on his jacket. In a flash, Dean bounced back, whipping out a long, ugly knife from the inside his jacket — the same type of knife that had given Warren his scar, the type of knife he'd never forget. He dove at Warren, the knife out.

Warren pulled the trigger. He had no choice.

He'd seen the life go from a man's eyes many times but never had it been so personal.

As the blood pooled behind Dean's head on the concrete, Warren took a step back, wishing he were alone. He felt the unmistakable touch of Alisa, running her hand up his back, the only warmth left in his body. A part of him wanted to ball up and just fucking cry. It did not feel good to kill. Never did…even to protect.

He stiffened his mouth and turned to Alisa, checking to confirm she was okay. She was okay. *Everyone* was okay.

"Warren," Alisa said, but stopped. She choked up, looking back and forth between the menace that had haunted her life lifeless on the concrete and Warren.

She didn't say anything. There were no words left to say. He felt that.

Warren leaned down and kissed her, trying for a sweet, promising gesture. It was over as quick as it had started. Sirens in the background drew them apart once again. Staring into her eyes, he knew his decisions had been right. There was no turning back to his old life, but he wouldn't want to anyway. She was the only reason he still felt anything at all.

"Come find me," he said. "I need you." He ran his hand down her cheek, brushing aside a tear.

Someone called out in the background. "Alisa… Alisa!"

She chewed her lip as people rushed to the scene. She took a step back, then another. To the calls of her name, her gaze turned downcast, and she shrank back to the hospital doors. The last glimmer he saw in her eyes told him more than she would.

He'd take that.

* * * *

Mission-focused, Warren marched up Brooke's driveway, holding Katy against his chest. Thankfully, she hadn't seen what had happened, and he didn't have to stick around giving statements to cops for too long. It had been cut and dry. He wasn't happy about what had happened, but he couldn't deny a weight had been lifted, knowing that he'd neutralized the threat to Alisa for good.

All he had to focus on was the rest of his scrambled life. He had about seven hours to get ready for what he was going to say to Alisa. He had to apologize, and he had to make it good. That was, if she even showed up to his place. She wasn't all that committed when he'd asked her. He didn't blame her. It had been a fucked up twenty-four hours.

He let out a haggard breath, stopping at the top of Brooke's lawn.

Brooke took Katy in her arms, holding her little girl tight. For the first time in a long time, Warren knew exactly what he had to say. It was a morning of truth. He'd started with Alisa, and he could continue the trend with Brooke.

"Hey, girl." Warren ran his hand through Katy's curly hair. "Can you give me and your mom a minute?"

Katy nodded, kissing her mom and popping out of her arms. Brooke patted her as she ran into her house, ready for a real breakfast. Turning back to him, they seemed to both inhale at the same time. It was time to have a hard conversation.

"When's the next flight?" Brooke quizzed, seemingly ready for the worst.

Warren let it out, "I'm not going back."

Brooke's mouth dropped open. "What?"

Her disbelief didn't surprise him.

"It's done. I'm sticking around." He nodded, reassuring her. "For this deployment, anyway."

He paused, still nodding, thinking about everything. It had taken him a long time, but he'd finally figured it out. Her brows furrowed, as if she didn't believe him. Hell, he barely believed himself.

"Come on," she whispered, shifting where she stood.

"Brooke, listen. There's something I need to tell you."

She leaned in, her bright eyes blinking curiously.

It wasn't easy but he continued, "I didn't go to Geoff's funeral —"

Then he paused, exhaling slow. He kept thinking about that long, ugly knife that Dean had pulled out. She tilted her head, waiting. God, it was so fucking tough.

"I didn't show up to Geoff's funeral because —" he finally choked out — "because I had to pretend he was still around."

I had to pretend he isn't dead.

Her eyes welled up as he said it. The truth landed hard.

"Jesus," she whispered, blinking rapidly.

He sucked in a breath, thinking about all the guys he'd lost along the way. "I said I'd never go to a funeral ever again — not Geoff's, not any of the guys. I have to pretend they are all still around. I just can't —"

But his voice cracked, so he stopped. Those guys… They were his family. They were his brothers. His sons. They were everything. He'd lost too many. She nodded, understanding. That look of compassion nearly killed him. But he made himself stony once more. He had to. He wasn't about to let tears roll out again.

"I'm sorry, Brooke. I really am."

She lunged forward, burying her head in his shoulder. She broke. "God, I miss him so much."

He smoothed back her hair. "Not a day goes by where I don't wish I'd have done something different. Anything. I wish I could have saved him. I should have."

She just sobbed into him before taking a deep breath, pulling back and touching his cheek. She stayed silent, but her demeanor changed. He felt a softness from her that he hadn't seen in years. Everything was changing.

"I'm a different man now."

"We are all different now," Brooke agreed. "And that's not always a bad thing."

A pause fell over them. He considered her words. Things were happening in his life that he'd never expected — like, falling in deep.

She continued, "My best advice to you, Warren? If you love someone, tell them. Tell them every fucking day."

Damn.

He leaned in and kissed her hair, apologizing for every last thing he'd ever done.

"That's what I'm about to do, Brooke."

All he could think of was Alisa.

Chapter Thirty-Two

Alisa

Alisa glanced at the clock in Maria's car as she rolled up to a certain house in a certain gated community. After everything that had happened, there she was again, looking up at the dark bedroom window where she'd lost herself. Shaking already, she opted to park on the street in front of the house, since there was no chance in hell that she was going to stick around.

"Just give him back his key and be done with it," she said aloud to herself as she got out of the car.

With Warren's house key burning in the palm of her hand, she strode toward his house in her green scrubs, still unchanged from her shift. The way she saw it, there was no point in getting dolled up. It wasn't going to change anything.

The setting sun cast her shadow on his front door as she approached, ready to knock. She fidgeted for a minute, debating whether to ring, knock or just go in.

He'd kind of told her to do the latter. Second-guessing herself, she knocked before opening the door, stepping into the cool entryway of his gorgeous home. The scent of his home encased her, already too familiar. It was pleasant and warm. She fought it off, like an unwelcome invitation.

"Hello?" she called out down the empty hall, seeing no one.

Her voice echoed off the hardwood and slate walls, vacant and stony. She was late, but she assumed he was still expecting her. *Right?*

"Warren?"

Then she heard his heavy steps coming down the stairs. She coiled and twisted in pure anxiety, anticipating their final moments and the words she'd built up in her mind. But the second he turned the corner, smoothing back his freshly washed auburn hair, firing that icy blue gaze at her, she forgot everything she was going to say.

Damn.

"Hi." She folded her arms tightly, hugging herself into a turtle shell.

"You're late." He betrayed no emotion, just studying her.

"I had a meeting after my shift."

"About."

"Dr. Zucker offered me a residency," she said. The reality of it hadn't even hit yet. "He said he didn't need anything else to convince him after he saw me with Katy...and you. He said I've got a bright future in pediatrics if I keep doing what I did."

"Holy shit—congratulations. That's great," he said. "Here? At this hospital?"

"Yes."

They fell silent. Alone, once again…after everything. She had to bite her lip to prevent it from trembling, her emotions still running high. He stationed himself not far enough, leaning against the wall, continuing to assess. It bothered her how cool he was. He needed to be more upset, like her.

But he was not.

Stoic, solid, he stared right back, as if to see what she would do, if she would break first. He just reached up, rubbed his chin. The masculine sound of his calloused hands scraping over his rough stubble nearly drove her right into him.

Maybe she was being childish, but she held her ground, watching him, getting angrier by the second. It wasn't just about how he'd left. It was about how angry she was at herself, how desperately she wanted to sink into him but couldn't. She couldn't allow herself to.

"About last night—" Warren started.

She cut him off, flashing her eyes at him. "Look… I have no words for what you've done for me, what you did for me today. You protected me. You saved me. I don't know what to say. I'm speechless."

"Don't say anything," he said. "Just come here—"

"No, I can't. It's been way too crazy. This fling? This romance? Neither of us are any good at this. Let's just stop while we are ahead."

He remained motionless, waiting for her to continue.

Too anxious to pause, she confessed, "I feel like I've been shattered into a million pieces, and that's just after a week with you. My whole life has changed."

"Is that a bad thing?"

"I—" she started.

"Yeah?"

"I don't know. My life has been a certain way for so long, and you just show up and break everything."

"You don't like change," he said.

"No."

"Neither do I. I don't change."

"But you have, haven't you?" Alisa asked.

Warren pushed off the wall and stalked forward, watching her intently. She had already lingered too long.

"Sometimes things need to be broken," he said. "I paid off Dean, you know. Paid your debt. The Navy issued me a retention bonus, and I dropped it on him. I told you I'd take care of it."

He did that...for me? She froze at the door. She hadn't really put it all together. It had been rapid-fire on all sides, and she'd had little time to process. But, still, she had already made up her mind. She found the door handle and tugged on it, cracking it open to the fresh air they both needed.

"Alisa." Warren's heavy hand landed on her shoulder, turning her around to face him. God, he was stealthy.

"I can't let you break me," she said.

With one flick, he slammed the door shut. "Sometimes, we need to break things—so we can rebuild."

Squirming underneath his heated gaze, she found herself backing up against the wall in the foyer, playing with the edge of her scrubs nervously. That's when she realized that he wasn't going to let her leave—not without a fight. She should have known. She was screwed. It wasn't like it was easy to run from a Navy SEAL.

I'm not that athletic.

Warren's hardened eyes locked with hers. "For a minute, you got me thinking that maybe this was all a man needs. Maybe I could have a life outside the endless tours. Maybe I could be someone aside from being…a SEAL."

He slid his hand down her neck, pressing into her delicate throat. His move was both dominant and possessive, showing just how he felt. He slipped his hand down her arm and picked up her left hand where no ring sat, seeing that she'd taken it off after he'd left her the night prior. He kissed the back of her hand, kissing down to the finger where the engagement ring had once been.

"I broke us," he said. "And I'm sorry I did."

"You left me. You made it clear it was over. Are you going to leave again?"

"No." He dropped his head closer to hers. "Will you ever forgive me?"

The story he'd told her, about how he got his scar, was thrown silently between them. His confession at the hospital wasn't easy to forget.

"Will you ever forgive yourself?" she countered.

"If you do."

He hovered his mouth over hers, mere inches apart, and their eyes locked, never leaving each other.

"A wise man once told me that only God can judge you," she said. "What happened out there is between you and God." With her words, something in his demeanor shifted, more intent.

His eyelids grew heavier, his breathing intensified. He tightened his hand on her throat, as if sending a clear message. He wasn't there to play games anymore, like he'd once reminded her. A low growl came from him as he traced the throbbing artery on her neck, as if he could bend over and bite it.

God, she wanted him to.

His mouth still just inches from hers, he grazed his bottom lip with his teeth as he narrowed his eyes. His undivided attention continued pumping adrenaline through her body, reinforced and doubled as he ignored his cell, vibrating on his solid walnut dining room table.

Is he going to kiss me?

Testing him, she tried turning to leave but he immobilized her before him.

"Don't even fucking think about it," he said.

"Then ask me to stay."

"Stay."

"That's not asking," she said.

"You're right. I'm not asking. I'm telling you."

But he didn't close the gap. He kept hovering, making her wait, driving her insane. He didn't even flinch when she ran her hands up his core, feeling the hard muscle of his abdomen. Arousal was clear in his face, and his muscles snapped to her touch. As he held back, it only turned her on even more, making her need him in a way she couldn't process. Massaging up his chest, that damn mouth-watering core was her undoing.

Maybe she was just a submissive, hoping and praying he would be her dominant. Maybe he just did things to her. Whatever it was, she found herself cocking her throat at an angle that showed him she was completely giving herself to him. All he had to do was lean forward and take her. That was the moment she realized she needed him to break her once again.

Under his heated gaze, she slipped her fingers down the front of her scrubs, into her panties, teasing her clit. Fuck, she was wet. The rawness of her emotion surprised her more than anything and a warmth rose up her cheeks. The groan that escaped his mouth told her everything.

He's ready to explode.

"I need you to feel how wet I am for you," she breathed, her voice cracking in pure unadulterated honesty.

He immediately yanked her up into his body, carrying her. With a handful of giant steps, he found his dining room. He threw her down on his heavy walnut table like a rabid beast, holding her down like he was never going to let her get away. He ran his hand down her chest, over her breasts and down her stomach. Excitement and thrill shot through her as he found his way down to her scrubs, grazing her panties.

Looking deep into her eyes, she nearly choked as she realized he was finally touching her, tearing her scrubs down her thighs. He dropped his mouth, kissing her hard and angrily, as he dove his fingers into her panties, feeling her wet clit. He didn't wait to push his tongue into her mouth, passionately tasting every inch, just like he'd done once before. His fingers likewise moved fast toward the opening of her pussy, lathering her wetness, twisting and swirling. She moaned as he teased her, his focus as furious as his desire.

"Is this what you wanted?" he snarled.

"Yes," she cried back, breathless.

With his hands at that angle, he couldn't fuck her pussy fast enough, and quickly was pushing her back on his table. Trying to get a better angle, he ripped her panties down. He grunted in frustration as they rolled on her thigh, sticking. In one violent motion he shredded the lacy pair right off her legs, burning her skin. The pain only heightened her arousal, and her clit and pussy throbbed for him.

As he moved to kiss her deeper, he grabbed the back of her head. Desperately, she fumbled at his pants, needing his cock. She'd never needed a cock inside her as much as she did just then. Somehow knowing it, he dropped his pants and let his thickness pulse out. His purple head was shiny and ready, adorned with that pre-cum she loved so much. He pumped his cock with his spare hand as he fingered her harder and harder. She was nearing climax just with his skilled finger movement alone. The man made fast work of her, hitting every spot that felt damn good, like he'd been fucking her for years.

"Fuck, you are a beast," she said. She bit her lip just watching that familiar dark desire crossing his face. He was everything she wanted.

"Want me to go easy on you?"

"Please don't."

"Want me to break you?"

"*Shatter* me."

With his fingers, he caught a wicked spot inside her pussy, driving her to climax. She tightened and came on his fingers, and he lifted them to his lips to taste her orgasm. Obviously pleased, he moved his fingers to her mouth so she could taste herself.

In one motion, he picked her up and turned her around, bending her body over his table. He hauled her ass up, meeting his hard cock, teasing her with his head. Her toes barely grazed the floor as he gripped her body.

"You deserve it rough," he groaned, "for everything you've done to me."

"What did I do?"

"Made me fall in love."

Before she could think of what that meant, he thrust his cock up her throbbing pussy. Aggressive, he grasped at her hips like they were nothing more than handles for his fucking. Deep pain and bruising commenced as he held on tight, occasionally slapping her ass as hard as he could. She moaned in pleasure at every touch, every slap. She had never been so turned on.

She moaned louder and louder as he fucked her, hard and fast. Rough wasn't enough to describe it. Her man didn't ask permission. He just did what he wanted. God, she loved that. She enjoyed the reminder of how perfectly they fit together in bed.

"Warren," she cried out, savoring his length inside. "Fuck, Warren."

Between thrusts, he grabbed her hair, tilting her head back to him.

"You will call me 'Sir'."

"Sir." She gasped, a deeply electrifying wave of sensation flowing through her. If that were an orgasm, she had never felt anything like it before.

Before she could catch her breath, he took either ass cheek and opened them. Removing his cock from her pussy, he teased her with his pulsing head.

"Tell me how much you want this cock," he demanded.

He apparently wanted to hear her say she wanted him.

And she fucking did.

"For you — I want whatever you want," she said in her most submissive tone.

"Play with yourself," he ordered.

"Yes, Sir."

That seemed to hit him hard because not only did he groan in response, but he slid the head of his throbbing cock back into her pussy, gliding his length up. She found her clit with her fingers, off the edge of the table, and found a motion that worked with his pumping. He was right. He was rough.

In that moment, she knew she had to fully submit to him, to trust him. So that's what she did. She let her whole body relax as the length of his cock stretched her all the way to the end, filling her in ways she'd never been filled by any other man. What amazed her was how quickly he'd broken her again, making her whimper in pleasure. Her body soft and supple, she enjoyed the sensation of getting thoroughly fucked by him. Relaxing around his cock, she felt him climaxing. It was clear that not only was he her sexual kryptonite, but she was his.

"Fuck." He groaned as he came hard, clutching her hips and rib cage for balance.

Grinning in delight, she realized that she wasn't the only one having a mind-blowing orgasm. Like a good sub, she got off knowing just how pleased he was.

She turned around slowly in his grasp, panting. Lying back on the table in front of him, his body crippled over as he collected himself, regaining lucidity. She enjoyed the wild yet dreamy look in his eyes as he brushed hair from her face. He grasped his satisfied cock in one hand as he then looked her up and down, shaking his head.

"Now I know we have a problem," he said.

"What?" She propped up on her elbows.

"I might get addicted to you."

He let out a full smile, happier and rawer than she'd ever seen him.

As her mouth dropped, hearing his confession, he dropped his head between her legs and licked her clit, savoring the taste of their delicious sex. He fingered her sore pussy gently, using that come-hither motion that she loved. Every motion sent shivers up her spine. That grin never left his lips as he sent further shocks of pleasure through her body.

She had never had a man like him — and she never would.

"I think it's time I take you out for dinner," he concluded.

She bit her swollen mouth as she watched his sexy auburn head move to her breasts and nipples, tasting, sucking, teasing — then to her mouth, pausing. He hovered, watching.

"So, you'll stay?" he asked.

"Why should I?"

"Because..." he started, licking his lip.

She waited.

Finally, he said, "Because I'm in love with you."

The words cascading over her, she felt like she was falling off the table. Reflexively, she threw her arms around him like he was her last lifeline. She was unwilling to ever let go.

"I love you, too," she said.

He heaved her up to his chest, and something changed in his eye. He kissed her again and again, like he'd truly never get enough of her — like they'd never get enough of each other.

And, as it happened, they never would.

Chapter Thirty-Three

Warren
The next morning

Warren sat stiffly, alone on his couch. The sun's early rays danced through the window. His steaming mug of coffee in hand, he glanced around his living room. With Alisa still fast asleep in his bed, he drank in the peace of the morning. Everything was silent.

Mindful, he felt his body still.

As if for the first time, he took in a breath. There was no pain in his back or in his chest. He felt the air smoothly diving down to the very bottom of his lungs and back out again.

It was fucking weird.

Suddenly, he felt unmanageable stress creeping in. Just sitting there, doing absolutely fucking nothing. But that was it, wasn't it? He was doing fucking nothing. The plane had left yesterday. The op was going ahead...without him. He'd stayed behind. All the guys were on the ground, in the battlefield, guns out, ready to fight, as he sat there drinking a fucking coffee like a goddamn clown.

Like a coward.

What the fuck am I doing here?

The hot mug seemed to burn his hand. He flinched, ready to whip it against the damn wall. *I've got to get out of here. I've got to get over there.*

He jumped up and slammed his coffee on the table in front of him. His whole body flexed and snapped to attention. He couldn't just stay on the couch. He couldn't just be there, doing nothing. Being home. He had to go. Happiness didn't come for men like him. He had shit to do.

Get the keys, and let's go.

Twisting, plotting, he glanced around his house — a place he hadn't spent a lot of time. A picture of Katy in the distance smiled back at him, warming him. The nearby edge of his walnut dining table poked out, reminding him of how things had changed. *Alisa, a kid, maybe more.* He had more to live for than he'd ever appreciated.

So did Geoff. The memory of his former lead never left Warren's mind. Every time he looked at Katy he saw her father...his best friend. The picture of Katy smiling across the room tempered him. For so damn long, he had to pretend her dad was still around.

"He's gone," Warren grunted to himself. "He's never coming back."

Warren tightened where he stood as his stress response flooded his senses. He felt that same physical impulse to get on a fucking plane and get back to work, to get back to being a goddamn war fighter. That's what he'd been bred and trained for. If he left all the guys out there alone, fighting without him, how many more of them would die? How many more funerals would he get invitations to? How many more guys would he have to pretend were still alive.

It was never your fault. He heard Alisa saying something at the back of his mind, like her own voice had grown to be part of his conscience.

He exhaled slowly, deeply. He welcomed the morning air back into his lungs once again. He felt it go all the way down to the bottom and back out through his mouth, less smooth than before. He closed his eyes, recognizing his physiological responses. It was going to take a while to reintegrate. He'd been gone for a long time. He hadn't stopped for a long time. And whenever he had been back, he'd never really been back.

He reached down, picked up his mug and took a swig of the hot coffee. Damn, it felt good — much better than field coffee.

It was in that moment that he realized — both he and Geoff hadn't stopped but had kept going. The difference between them was that he could still come back, live. Geoff couldn't. Warren nodded, making the pact with himself, then and there. He wasn't over there. He was home. He sat his ass back down on his couch. He'd done his time. He'd given everything he had to a life of service. The best thing he could do then was what Geoff never could — come back and be present for the people he loved.

His cell buzzed. He reached for it, seeing an email coming in from the master chief.

These guys are singing your praises out here. You trained them damn well. Everyone's rooting for your fast recovery...so you can get back at it. I hate to say I told you so, but morale's way, way up. It's buzzing. You did something right.

Warren read the message five times, thinking about those work parties he hated going to and never showed up at. Alisa had made it all different—the engagement party, the wedding. Alisa had made him a little more human. And it looked like a little tequila between men had gone a long way to repair his bond with his guys, to boost morale.

He laughed to himself, sipping his coffee. Strange, the things a man could realize. Sometimes a good leader knew when to set an example—and take a knee to heal.

It's time to heal.

"Okay." Warren exhaled, slowing the stress reaction. "I got this."

He crossed his legs, settling in. He just had to learn how to stop. He just had to reintegrate.

As fucking hard as it was going to be, it got a little easier when he saw Alisa's adorable face poking around the corner from his bedroom, looking down the stairs at him. She beamed, tugged on his T-shirt that hung over her frame and slipped down the stairs toward him. There was no better sight in life. Apart from the fact that he could fuck her all day long, he enjoyed her company immensely.

If ever he had a chance at a life outside of work, it was going to be with her.

She got to the bottom of the stairs, holding the rail. It only took her two seconds before she seemed to realized what was going on.

Empathetic, she asked, "What are you going to do now?"

Warren laughed, taking in another gulp of his coffee, pondering the question.

"Train, get ready to get back to work—eventually."

Alisa stepped forward, grinning. "No, I mean—what are you going to do with your spare time?"

He shot her a conspiratorial look. "Guess I'm the boss of the Deadeye MC now."

Her mouth dropped, realizing the implications. She edged toward him, like a moth to a flame.

Savoring the view of her slinking to him, he continued, "I guess it's high time someone cleaned up that club."

"How are you going to do that?" She stopped inches from him.

He reached out and pulled her in, landing her square in his lap. Smoothing a stray hair back from her face, he grinned.

"I've got a couple of friends who can help."

Minne-sorta Falling in Love:
Semper Fitz
Aurora Russell

Excerpt

Clara Olafson hummed a little to herself as she walked heavily down the overgrown trail. This far out into the forest, the trails weren't maintained as regularly as the ones closer to the visitor center. The morning air was crisp—northern Minnesota in late August could feel like October or November in the rest of the country—but she liked it that way. The cool air buffeting her felt like a familiar, albeit chilly, blanket. Like *home*. Plus, it quickened her steps, which was good for her and the baby. A couple of times lately, she'd had the oddest sensation, almost like a trickle of ice-water down her spine, that she was being watched or followed, but she blamed the crazy pregnancy hormonal imbalance. This morning, though, she felt nothing but the fresh breeze behind her.

She'd started the habit of an early-morning walk when she'd moved out to the cabin two months earlier, and she intended to keep it up until the day she went into labor—which actually could be pretty soon. The OB she'd been seeing in St. Paul—*before*—had said to stay active, and she wanted to do everything she could to make sure that the little life she carried had the best possible start. She'd read several books, along with what felt like a couple of thousand websites, and she was avoiding lunchmeat, green tea, fake sweeteners, caffeine—even chocolate. Goodness, chocolate had been the hardest to give up, with coffee a close second. She now had a recurring dream where she walked into a dimly lit coffee house and ordered a massive frozen-mocha-latte-smoothie with curls of dark chocolate and mounds of whipped cream on top, but she always woke up before she could take a sip. Her mouth watered just thinking about it.

"No," she chided, half speaking to herself and also to the baby. "No chocolate for the baby, no matter how much Mama wants it." She reached down to rub her swollen belly, as she did so often these days, and smiled at the firm kick she got in response, right under her palm. A rush of affection and protectiveness so intense that it almost frightened her swept through, taking her by surprise. It was amazing to hold a tiny, growing human inside her, but also terrifying to be so totally and solely responsible for someone else.

Even in the midst of her awe, the craving persisted, so intense that she could almost taste the chocolate melting on her tongue. *Maybe I'm just longing for something sweet?* She wasn't supposed to have too much sugar, but fruit was definitely still okay. The berries on the blackberry and raspberry bushes a little farther down the path were just starting to ripen again. They would be tart and juicy. She licked her lips at the thought and smiled at her own eagerness. *Anyone who gets between a pregnant woman and her desired food deserves whatever happens to him.* She quickened her pace, thankful she'd worn long pants and sleeves to avoid the prickly bushes. If there were enough berries, maybe she'd even come back later with a pail and pick enough for a pie. *Oh, good Lord*, the idea of a piece of pie, even just a tiny sliver, warm from the oven with a flaky crust, was so wonderful that she almost groaned aloud.

Practically trotting and out of breath by the time she reached the bushes, she was thrilled to see a few ripe berries straight away, which she snapped off their thin branches and popped into her mouth. Cold juice exploded on her tongue, and she sighed with pleasure. The ripe berries were few and far between, though. Most of them were still hard and green. Even so, there were enough on each bush to take her deep into the thicket as she sought out every last berry that was ready to eat, crunching them with gusto. It could have been some crazy sensory thing, but she didn't know if she'd ever tasted anything more delicious.

At first, she thought the moaning might be coming from her stomach. Heaven knew it made all sorts of noises these days — gurgles, churns and growls so loud they woke her up at night. But this sound was too loud and too deep. She froze and tilted her head, listening. When the low moan came again, her heart seemed to jump right up into her throat. *What the heck?* Taking a slow, calming breath and narrowing her eyes, she scanned the thicket. *Probably a deer in distress*, she reassured herself. At least she hoped it was a deer, because if it were a moose or a bear, she could be in real trouble. She couldn't make out much of anything through the thick leaf-cover at first, but finally a slight shaking in the bushes ahead and to her right signaled the location of whatever injured creature was there.

She hesitated. A prudent woman would go back to the cabin and call for help. She knew this. She *should* be careful and not her usual impulsive self. But then the noise came again, so sad and filled with pain that it made her throat tighten and her eyes fill with tears. Pure, uncontrollable sympathy made her step one foot forward, and her distinctly *un*-prudent decision was made. *If the animal can make a noise like that*, she reasoned, *it's unlikely to be able to move enough to hurt me if I stay back. And I won't get too close.*

The stand of bushes was situated in a small valley with steep inclines that were blanketed with pine trees rising high on either side. As she got nearer to the wounded creature, she could see a faint trail of crushed and broken foliage leading to it from the opposite direction, and she guessed that the poor animal had probably fallen from the higher ground. Her heart squeezed with compassion. *It must be in so much pain.* She slowed her steps, carefully placing her weight on the balls of her feet instead of the heels and trying to breathe silently to avoid startling the mystery animal.

She braced herself for a very ugly scene, but what she found instead made her suck in a surprised breath. Two huge, black boots stood out dark against the green undergrowth, and her eyes followed their forms to two blue-jeans-clad legs, one of which looked somewhat twisted. Her gaze trailed up farther, to where the form was more obscured by leaves, but she could still make out an enormous hand and the weave of a thick green sweater, shifting slightly with the man's breathing. She hurried forward.

"Oh, my goodness, you poor man! Where's the worst pain?" she asked, trying to keep her voice quiet so as not to startle him. There was no answer, apart from another piteous groan, and when his face finally came into full view, she saw why. His eyes were closed, and an ugly lump had formed at his temple, already dark with a hint of the bad bruising to come. The blow must have also knocked him unconscious.

She lowered herself to the ground awkwardly, her movements hampered by the clumsiness of late-pregnancy and the ever-present swelling that made her fingers and toes feel like little sausages stuffed into casings that were too small. She wanted to assess where his injuries might be, though, and to do that, she needed to get closer. She'd taken several first-aid classes as a young teenager, practically a requirement as a doctor's daughter in a rural area, so she felt reasonably optimistic she could stabilize the worst of whatever his injuries were before she ran back to the cabin to call 9-1-1. *Why in the world did I choose today of all days not to bring my cell phone?* She cursed under her breath, immediately murmuring an apology to her baby.

As her movements brought her closer to him, she couldn't help but notice that, apart from his injuries, the man appeared to be in extremely good shape. His leg muscles bulged, even through the thick denim of his jeans, and his broad shoulders and chest looked solid and strong. She glanced at his face, noticing that his hair was cropped close to his skull — *the length a lot of military and ex-military men keep it*, she thought absently. Even if she couldn't see his eyes, he was undeniably handsome with high cheekbones, dark brows and eyelashes, a strong chin and nose, and soft-looking lips. He was younger than she'd initially thought, too. *Maybe in his early thirties.*

Running carefully light hands over his legs, she felt the spot where one of his knees was twisted and swollen, but she was relieved that she didn't feel anything else that seemed out of place on his lower extremities. There were a few areas that were uneven, but she guessed it could be fabric bunching or debris from the fall. She skimmed her fingers over his hips to his chest, which were just as hard and muscular as she'd guessed, to his bulky arms. To her dismay, one of his wrists also felt slightly enlarged. Finally, she moved a tentative hand to his head. She rose onto her knees, leaning over for a better view to see how large and swollen the area was, which should be pretty visible through his ultra-short hair. Head wounds could be tricky, bleeding internally as well as externally. The swelling there was almost certainly what was causing his unconsciousness.

Just as the tips of her fingers made contact with the most swollen spot, without a breath of warning one of the man's mammoth hands clamped around her wrist, stopping her from moving. She squeaked and tried to take her arm away, but his grip held her firm. When her gaze flashed to his face, he was staring back at her with bright blue eyes that were filled with a mix of suspicion and confusion.

About the Author

I'm a mom with three sweet young daughters. I have three jobs - mom, author, and analyst. Years ago, I grew up in a military family, went to a military university, worked alongside the military as an intel analyst, and my husband is (surprise!) a veteran. I've tried to write for anyone who wants to feel what it's like to be with someone from that world - with all the good and the bad.

My heroes are grounded in reality, and are inspired by guys I know in the special forces. Guys who've been in combat, tasted war, and fought for what they believed in. They are really heroes, but raw and rough and broken in their own ways.

My heroines similarly come from the best parts of the women I know, and the challenges we all face. The relationships that they fall into have familiar characteristics for many, myself included. These heroines represent all of us, with our good and our bad laid bare.

In my stories, I illustrate, romanticize, and celebrate the harsh realities of duty, service, and sacrifice.

Zoe loves to hear from readers. You can find her contact information, website details and author profile page at https://www.totallybound.com

Home of Erotic Romance

Sign up for our newsletter and find out about all our romance book releases, eBook sales and promotions, sneak peeks and FREE romance books!